EVERY TIME WE SAY GOODBYE

Every Time We Say Goodbye

Rosetta Livingston

FITHIAN PRESS
SANTA BARBARA
1997

Published by Fithian Press
A division of Daniel and Daniel, Publishers, Inc.
Post Office Box 1525
Santa Barbara, CA 93102

LIBRARY OF CONGRESS CATALOGING-IN-PUBLICATION DATA
Livingston, Rosetta (date)
Every time we say goodbye : a novel / by Rosetta Livingston
p. cm.
ISBN 1-56474-200-8 (alk. paper)
I. Title.
PS3562.I96E905 1997
813'.54—dc20 96-9787
CIP

To my family

The world is a beautiful place
to be born into
if you don't mind happiness
not always being
so very much fun
if you don't mind a touch of hell
now and then
just when everything is fine
because even in heaven
they don't sing all the time

FROM

A CONEY ISLAND OF THE MIND

BY

LAWRENCE FERLINGHETTI

EVERY TIME WE SAY
GOODBYE

1

Happenstance, not mystical predestination, formed the contours of my life; yet from early girlhood, a mindless passion seized me, refusing to be diverted, like a primeval force in nature, and I was drawn to the source of my desire and coveted it. Setting the stage for the role I was to play was the very manner in which I was conceived.

The story I was to be told about that and my earliest years came in bits and pieces and vaguely hinted references. It began when Ana Morgan, a young Jamaican woman, became an assistant to David Shaw, a prominent architect, in the studio-office he maintained in Monterey, California. Conscientious, she occasionally stayed late to finish some work. She had been there about a year when early one evening, just as she was leaving, an itinerant construction worker, a white man, seized and raped her and then vanished.

Subsequently, she gave birth and I was that child. My mother continued to work, bringing me to the studio and caring for me there. I was a cheerful baby and the architect became attached to me, bringing me little toys and pausing in his work to play with me. It also became plain to those who knew him and my mother that there was more than an employer-employee relationship between them. In fact, it was said he had named me Caroline after a beloved grandmother.

A veneer of normalcy concealed the illicit situation. David dwelled at home but did not truly live there, for he and his wife led separate lives, in contrast to the harmony that existed between him and Ana. They worked together in his studio and often, at the end of the day, they would leave together and he would remain at her apartment for the night.

That continued until I was three, when Ana received an urgent call from Jamaica where her only remaining relative, an aunt, was dying. Despite his wife's objection, David offered to take me until my mother's return in what she thought would be a week, and a nanny was hired to care for me in his home.

The following day my mother left, never to return. When her plane crashed in the sea, there were no survivors, and I became an orphan. Unwilling to give me up, David applied for my adoption. His wife had never wanted children, and especially not this child, so she was opposed to it. He insisted and it was done.

I was too young to perceive the chaos my small presence brought to that household, only years later becoming aware of all that must have gone on. My adoptive mother never overcame her resentment for the disruption in her life, and she made it clear that I was to address her as Martha, her given name, never Mother. But David was always "Father."

I was dependent on him for everything, and he never wavered in his affection. The nanny remained to care for me daytimes, and when he had to be away on work projects for long periods, she lived at our house. On entering middle school I told my father I was a "big girl" and didn't need her. He agreed, but reluctantly, always wary of leaving me alone with Martha.

We lived in a house he had built long before my birth. A half-hour's drive from the city, it was a site so secluded he had almost missed it as he drove along the coast. Stopping to look around, he had walked down a narrow incline to find a swath of white sand that followed the graceful curves of the bay and a sheltered space he had immediately visualized for our home.

Constructed of wood, with a flat roof and many broad windows that looked out on the sea, it was modest in most ways, but it had everything we wanted and was sturdy and comfortable. Over the years it has melded with its setting, weathered to the color of the scrubby terrain that now all but engulfs it. Only a sharp-eyed traveler moving at an unlikely slow speed would view it as human habitation. But it is still a wonderful house.

Although the beach was not intended for our private use, it might as well have been. An embankment, layered with shale, walled it off from the highway above, making it almost inaccessible to strangers. Besides, around the next bend in the road lay a grander beach, by far, with a proper entry.

All of us loved the sea. My father had taught me to swim and we swam together for the sheer pleasure of it now and then. Martha was a strong swimmer and swam every day no matter what the weather. Hers were Spartan qualities, she said to me, and chided me for not following her example. I had none of her toughness.

"If I had been a member of that ancient society," I told my father, "I would have been put out to die early in life."

"You please me just as you are, Caroline," he said.

As I grew into adolescence, Martha observed our attachment to each other with apprehension, expecting it to lead eventually to adultery and, if her suspicion was correct, to incest, as well. Whether the latter was true or not, she was insightful in her discernment of my fixation. Unaware of its hidden meaning, all I knew was that I loved him. Nor did my obsession end with maturity. Father was warmly paternal, nothing more, but that did not calm her fears.

Her containment, smoldering as it must have been, was perfect, except for one time—one time only. After one of my "amorous displays," as she termed it, when I was thirteen, she exploded in anger. Father had just returned after a long absence and I greeted him with joy, kissing him again and again. She called me to her room and berated me unmercifully. In hoarse whispers, she denounced my behavior as evil.

"You're a sinner and doomed, just like your mother," she said.

At first, I couldn't believe what I was hearing. Having been placed in a parochial school when she was already a teenager, religious instruction had an ambivalent effect on her. Occasionally, she would simply go off to church on Sunday, but usually, she appeared detached from her faith.

Recalling her education as one dreary memorization lesson after another, she recited for me the various sins and their categories: the original ones and the actual ones—those with subdivisions that included the venial and mortal and further subdivisions into the material and the formal. The most regulated of all were the sexual ones, and those could be not only of word or deed, but thought, as well.

That I found puzzling. How could something elemental in nature be wicked? I once saw a male dog so metastasized with cancer that before the day was out, he died, yet that morning he had pursued a bitch in heat and mounted her. His was a response to blind instinct, but humanity, with all its rationality, finds itself in a constant battle with its primitive forcefulness. Imbued with pleasure, sex can play havoc with our lives. Yet the concept of sin eluded me.

Listening to Martha's tirade, I knew her indoctrination had "taken" and in this emotional situation she reverted to her religiosity. I tried to make sense of what she was saying. How did love for my father constitute a sin? Which category of sin did it fit into? Which part of hell would I everlastingly burn in? It was not a serious reverie, since I had had a hedonistic upbringing by my father and knew that no matter what my thoughts might be, unless I did something hurtful, I was not guilty of anything.

Instead of biblical texts he had given me books of an entirely different kind. One that made a lasting impression on me was by Thoreau. "Do what you love. Do not be too moral," he had warned in it. "You may cheat yourself out of much of life so. Aim above morality. Be not simply good—be good for something."

Observing my distraction, Martha lost all her self-restraint and, lapsing into phrases she had learned as a girl, called on celestial help to reform me.

"Lamb of God, have mercy on this sinner!" she rasped. "Holy Spirit, take away her sin. Grant her peace."

Unnerved by her hysteria and afraid she might hurt me, I walked slowly to the door. She didn't stop me and I left. What I believed were her "weird" religious allusions didn't affect me, but her rage did. In an odd way, she accomplished what she had intended in her searing indictment. She had brought to the surface my sensuality, which until then had been unconscious, but now had been given criminal status. I was deeply disturbed.

The next day, everything appeared as normal as if the episode had not occurred, and Father was unaware of any of it, or that he was an innocent victim of it.

Before Martha's outburst, we were often together when he was not working. Only a few miles from our home was Point Lobos, a favorite destination for us. My father quoted Ansel Adams to me: "This is the greatest meeting of land and water in the world." To me it was pleasure in its purest form. We always went there during the off-season when the wildlife, less wary with few people in the preserve, appeared on the very cliffside trails we walked along.

The waters around the Point teemed with animal life, too—sea lions and seals and otters—and once we were lucky to arrive as the gray whales were on their migration to the Arctic. There must have been a hundred of them. What a sight for a small child, watching those behemoths cavorting, diving, then leaping high out of the water for a fresh supply of air before descending again. Some swam right in the shallow surf, so I could see them close up.

Big Sur was not far either, and there we went any time of the year. It was always fun to walk in the woods and then have lunch on the patio of the lodge and feed the raucous jays lined up on the rail. Our trips to the "city"—San Francisco—were less frequent, but I looked forward to them.

Once while we were there, being curious about Martha's early musical career, I asked my father to take me to an opera. *Carmen* was being performed just then, and it was a good choice.

"That was very exciting," I told my father. "And the music was wonderful! Don't you think Martha misses it?"

He nodded in agreement but said nothing further.

After Martha's outburst, all the good times we had together ended. I refused his invitations, pretending I had other things to do. To my father, the sudden change from my usual eagerness was perplexing. I could see he was disappointed and my heart ached with longing to be with him.

On one of his longer stays at home, he had begun to tutor me in Greek and Latin, languages he believed were important for a well-rounded education, and wanting to please him, I had worked hard to do well. That, too, ended. When he could not cajole me into continuing, he suggested I read the classics in translation. There I came upon the myth of the daughter of Agamemnon, and the lust I had become aware of became more disquieting. Was I tinged with Electra's tragic malady? I thought of pouring out my misery in a diary, but fear of discovery prevented it.

I made no attempt to conceal from myself the likely truth in Martha's angry words. My own abrupt awareness of my sensual feelings had made denial impossible. Being a precocious schoolgirl, I sought answers in textbooks, spending after-school hours in the library, going from one book to another until I arrived at one that contained the writings of Freud.

Emotional as the situation was for me, I had a strangely objective curiosity. Understanding myself became important. I drew out the book and twice renewed it, studying the scholarly text for hours each night.

My situation, I decided, had some of the classical Freudian analysis of incest, although my earliest years gave no hint of abnormality. It was true my father had lavished affection on me, but that was normal for all loving fathers toward their little girls. When my mother died, he cared for me physically, too, but again, innocently, with no erotic intent. That the touching and handling stimulated such sensations was part of my natural development.

So far I was no different from all other children. Had my mother lived, my life would have continued in its proper progression. Both she and my father would have acted in the sensitive roles parents know instinctively, putting in place the societal restraints that would have led me to a transition to adult behavior, repressing those sexual feelings before they could become fixated on my father.

But she did not live, and Martha, who hated me for what I represented, replaced my mother at that sensitive point in my early childhood. I responded with equal hostility, becoming deeply and forever attached to my father. Was my love indeed incestuous? Though no sexual relationship had existed between us, I knew my feelings were unquestionably directed toward it.

Years later, in mulling over that time in my life, I did forgive Martha's lack of compassion. It was not just my damnation she was concerned about. I recalled her words that awful night: "Pursue your unnatural love and you will cause great unhappiness." Her own, of course, because it revived an old fear, the threat to her proud position, which despite everything that had happened, she refused to relinquish.

Ana's death ended a poignant chapter in my father's life, but there was no turning back to a former time for my adoptive parents. Their alienation was complete. They remained together, "getting along" in a civil way, yet never exhibiting any affection and always sleeping in separate bedrooms.

Martha's embitterment was justified. How could it have been otherwise: to be rejected for another, to suspect that her husband had fathered his lover's child and then to have to bear that child's daily presence and witness their love for each other? The pain he had subjected her to troubled my father, but he could do nothing about it.

Only one thing cut through Martha's estrangement from me. Her religiosity intensified, her infrequent church attendance becoming a regular Sunday practice. She had found a source of support that made her life tolerable, perhaps even preventing a break-down. Along with it, however, was her aggressive attempt to provide me with what she believed was an essential religious upbringing. Once I had heard my parents arguing about that. Martha's voice had an urgency about it. She was intent on saving my soul, and soon, she said, it would be too late. My father's self control left him.

"Caroline is my child, not yours," he blurted. "I don't want her subjected to mythical beliefs. All we know for certain is the present. That's enough. She must be free to enjoy her life and live it fully. Let her alone, Martha!"

She could not stop. Her immersion in religion held the hope of salvation, a fresh start in a heavenly life that had to be better than her earthly one. But why she wanted to take me with her was puzzling.

My father began taking me to his office when I was very young, and it became my second home. That was the one place I could associate directly with my mother, and I visualized her presence there. Also, Martha never went there, so it was a sanctuary for me.

The studio was my introduction to architecture, and I loved it from the start. I was still a child when I learned to sketch, and my father would pull up a chair to the drafting table so I could stand on it and try my hand at drawing simple plans. He appeared surprised and pleased at my efforts and encouraged me.

That was the summer I was eight—the most carefree and happy of my early years. Father had gone to France the previous fall on a commission to do the architecture for a private library in Marseilles. When a building firm was contracted to do the construction, he felt free to leave and by May he returned home and didn't go away again until the following fall, when a new project began for him.

Years before, he started bringing me dolls from all the foreign places where he worked and this time he gave me a French ballerina doll. Though my "mama" doll, dark-complexioned with tight black curls, remained my favorite throughout my childhood, this one inspired me to make a detailed sketch of a doll-house, which I showed my father. He was impressed.

"*C'est bon!*" he said.

"*C'est bon?*"

"*Oui,*" he said, laughing. "That means 'very good.'"

He called Hal Turner, a carpenter who had worked with him on constructions, and asked him to come by. They studied my specifications and Hal built it—a beautiful little house for my dolls, with room for me to play with them, too.

I was delighted. "*C'est bon!*" I said.

"*Merci,* Caroline," Hal said, and gave me a big hug.

I never did learn to speak French, but *c'est bon* stuck and my friends knew it was my highest accolade.

My father's work was in some ways different from that of his contemporaries. With all his intellectualism, he was a romantic, and his buildings reflected that. They had modernity without the flashiness that had become fashionable in the seventies and eighties and yet were so distinctive in their elegance of design as to be immediately recognizable as his. Perfectionism was his one overwhelming problem, and he was lucky to have people working with him who were touched by some of that, too, especially his chief engineer, Walt Jackson, who had worked with him for many years, always accompanying him wherever a project might be. Sometimes Walt would act as supervisor on a construction, which gave my father the ease of mind to return home for an occasional month's holiday. Having known Walt since childhood, I knew he had me in mind, too, when he urged him to take more time off. I loved Walt for that.

As the years passed, I saw less and less of my father. He attained worldwide fame and was in constant demand. Honored with awards for the beauty of his work and the innovations he brought to architecture, he was, nonetheless, unaffected by the praise, never flamboyant, always generously extending himself to others.

My own life continued to have a quality of unrelenting inner turmoil. In high school, I dated boys and was briefly involved with one of them, but the relationship started off badly and did not improve. His immaturity should have foretold an unhappy conclusion. I will always remember that first sexual experience with sadness, for it is an event in a young woman's life that should be pleasant, if not perfect. I was disregarded and not allowed to maintain my dignity, being harshly and painfully penetrated, but he could not restrain his youthful fervor and had no patience with me so that I did not reach orgasm as he did, even in the few future times we were together.

Considered a student with "promise," I was thrilled to be accepted by Langdon University in northern California, for it was my father's alma mater. But there was a hitch. I was only sixteen, and my father was concerned about my lack of maturity.

"Too young!" he had said, and tried to convince me to hold off for a year before going on to college. I could hardly wait to spring the trap on life with Martha, and I knew that wherever I would be my father would see me as often as his work allowed it. The excitement of an independent life would, I secretly hoped, be a distraction from my deeply emotional frustration. I pleaded and he gave in.

I shall never forget the poignancy of our parting the day he left me at the dormitory. Both of us were pretty quiet. I loved him so much I never really wanted to part from him, and he was saying goodbye forever to the little girl he had raised. The next time he would see me I was bound to be different, a young woman, reaching for maturity. He gave me no instructions or warnings. I would be learning life's lessons as they appeared, and I think he had some confidence in my ability to handle them. Finally, he took me in his arms and held me a long time. His eyes were moist, and I, too, was on the verge of tears as we said goodbye.

During the midwinter holiday we had a heartwarming reunion at Langdon. I was proving I could handle college life and he was accepting of it, especially when I told him I had decided on a career in architecture. He bemoaned the paucity of woman architects and would have been happy if I became one.

My interest was academic, with a goal of obtaining a doctorate and teaching in a university. I was a diligent student, and in five years I earned a master's degree. When I told my father, he took me in his arms and kissed me and said how happy it made him, and that moment made all the years of getting educated worthwhile. But now I needed some time out from academia, and he agreed.

During my final spring quarter Father took a turn among other distinguished alumni in the arts and became a guest lecturer, giving a number of talks to students interested in architecture. He had arranged his time to coincide with my last weeks in school so that we could be together.

With his help, I worked up a series of lectures of my own that I called "Genius in Contemporary American Architecture." He and his architect-friends provided me with renderings and descriptive material relating to their work as well as photographs that could be projected on a screen and a film of one famous construction as it progressed to completion. I was elated with the response, but then I should have expected it from those unusual men. They were outgoing and uncompetitive, openly discussing their ideas without fear of having them stolen.

I directed my proposal to European colleges, indicating that I spoke only English. Several showed interest, assuring me that the students in their schools of architecture had a good command of the language. I knew being David Shaw's daughter influenced their receptivity, but I was determined to succeed on my own merits. I set up lecture dates to begin in the fall, and then, after graduation, prepared to leave for home.

As I packed, I realized I had few regrets about leaving. Those had been quiet years at Langdon. A few of us rebels tried to stir things up on campus to remind people that there was plenty to be disturbed about in the world, but we were ignored. None of the fire of my father's day remained. That was the Vietnam era, when crowds of activists gathered in the streets of the small university town to protest the war. Then, you could be a radical and still be accepted as a normal human being. My school had become an elitist institution and uninspiring.

My personal experiences were different in some ways from those of other students. Because of my celebrated parent I had status and was known as "the Shaw girl." On the other hand, I had inherited the skin color of my mother, not identifiable as white or black, which baffled some people, making them unsure "what" I was, and sometimes what I was was unacceptable.

My relationships with men had improved since my high school years, becoming more enjoyable, but never long lasting. No sentimental remembrances went with me, for they were loveless and easily dismissed. I had remained obsessive in my yearning for my father, sometimes even in classes, drifting off in love-sick musings, and lying in bed at night, fantasizing sexual relations with him that brought only lonely self-gratification.

If there was a moment's fleeting reluctance to leave, it was in the knowledge that now I was putting behind me my youthful preoccupations. "Life is real; life is earnest" kept running through my head.

I could almost feel the wrenching changes that were about to take place in my life and, like many young people going "out into the world," I was both eager and fearful.

While my father went off to have lunch with a retired professor he'd studied under years before, I got together with my best friend, Janie Myers, an exchange student from England. She, too, was leaving school, having earned her Ph.D. in botany and succeeded in getting a position as an assistant professor in a London university, starting in September. I planned to live in her newly acquired flat in London during the summer after school, although she would not be there, having made travel plans with her boyfriend, Matthew Darby.

We reminisced, already feeling nostalgic about our good times together, for we knew without saying so, that there would be no more of that kind ever again. Except for one summer when Janie's parents, who lived in New Delhi (her father being in the diplomatic corps), insisted that she visit them there, we traveled together on the Continent. I met her parents only once, when they visited her at Langdon. They could have been brother and sister, they looked so much alike: tall and aristocratic with perfectly modulated British accents and manners straight out of an etiquette manual.

Janie must have been an offshoot of another branch of her family. She looked totally different, and in another way, totally different from me. She was short like me, but I had curves and she was stocky and muscular. The first time we met I fell in love with her face. It was disarming in its liveliness. At first glance she had the sweet look of a child, even to the tiny freckles that dotted her nose. Her eyes—the clearest blue—innocent as a babe's, sparkled with animation as she talked. But her hair, deep bronze, was a giveaway that there was more to Janie than sweetness.

In the years that followed that first meeting I saw other moods reflected in Janie's expressive face. Sadness, sometimes, but never depression, as I was prone to, but there were bouts of anger, sudden and fierce, when her face would flush a deep pink as she spewed forth a stream of feculent expletives worthy of a seasoned whore, some I'm sure she had composed herself.

Janie took to me, too, and our affection and directness with each other created a friendship without end. The span between our ages, five years, made her bossy, but I accepted it. At sixteen I probably needed someone like Janie to take me under her wing. She had been living in the dormitory for a few years when I got there, not wanting to join a sorority. Neither did I, finding the dorm comfortable and convenient, being right on campus. In my second year we became roommates. Neither of us smoked, except pot, and that not on a daily basis; and we drank, but not to excess, either. We both had repertoires of dirty stories, but actually our conversations were quite literate.

Every one of our trips together was memorable. At the end of each summer's sojourn our travel maps were in shreds, but our friendship remained intact, despite the fact that sometimes her avid interest in mushrooming tried my patience. Her search for fungi took us to far-off places, once to Finland, where she found a rare specimen above the Arctic Circle.

I learned on that trip that I could not let her go off by herself because her keen interest led her astray. On our way to the Helsinki airport to return home, we stopped late in the day to rest in a village an hour's drive away. While I sat in its only hotel cafe having coffee, Janie went out "to make a quick survey," she said, of the nearby woods.

After some time I became alarmed and informed the cafe owner, who sent a couple of villagers to look for her. They found her deep in the forest digging around a tree trunk and filling plastic bags with new-found treasures. I told her we would have to reschedule our departure, and might as well stay overnight in the hotel. She agreed at once, ready to go back out to the woods.

"Don't you dare!" I told her. "There are bears and boars and who knows what else out there."

"Stop giving me orders, Caroline. I'm older than you."

Dumber, too, I muttered to myself. Janie took her mushrooms to the hotel kitchen that night and the chef let her prepare them. He was impressed by her expertise. What he didn't know was that mushrooms were her one and only specialty. She hated cooking.

•

During the summer Janie went to Delhi, I decided to go to San Francisco and get a job. Well aware of my advantaged life, I wanted to learn how less-fortunate young women lived. I did, indeed, learn. First of all, I had a hard time finding work, having no skills. At last, I did find a job: I became a taxi dancer in a cheap dance hall and rented a room in a building where some of the other dancers lived.

I didn't tell my father what I was doing, knowing he would worry about me. Although he was usually off somewhere in the world on architectural projects, he made sure we kept in touch. He wanted to know where I was at all times, and I was obedient about that, provoked at the inconvenience, but happy he cared so much. That summer I lied continuously to keep him from finding out.

Janie and I always communicated with each other, but only one other person in my life knew what I was doing that summer. His name was Andrew Pachat, a psychiatrist, who lived a short way down the road from us and with whom my father had a warm friendship. The more talkative of the two, Andy had a stock of stories gleaned from his practice that revealed the bizarre convolutions of human behavior. He was witty, too, and often I would hear them in the study laughing. He was many years younger than my father, but sensitive and wise, and able to distract him from the seriousness with which he took his work. With me he was playful and teasing but always loving, and I felt like his young sister.

I was fifteen, beginning my senior year in high school at the time Andy moved from Los Angeles to open an office in Monterey and buy his house near ours. At the age of thirty, he had already become well known due to a book he had written and which was on a non-fiction best-seller list for many weeks. Called *They Can't Tell You What It Means,* it was an analysis of the subconscious element that operates in the work of great artists. Few of them are willing to discuss what impels them to paint as they do. When asked to give meaning to what they've produced they often sound arrogant or refuse, leaving viewers in a state of puzzlement. According to Andy, artists are innocent of their unconscious motives. His book was not pedantic and was enlivened by humor. I enjoyed it.

He kept in touch with my father, too, and early in the summer I was taxi dancing, he mentioned to him on the phone that he was going to be in San Francisco for meetings the next weekend. Father told him to look me up and gave him a phone number, which was for a hall phone that others used. Luckily, he spoke to someone who knew me and she gave him the name of the dance hall.

What a surprise when he showed up with a roll of dance tickets! I'd never seen him in anything but jeans and sneakers before, and there he was in a suit and tie and what he called his "hard" shoes.

"I know how to dress when I'm going to take my girl out," he said, laughing at my look of disbelief.

The other women watched enviously as we danced. Andy always attracted feminine attention. He was not very tall, which pleased me, being short myself and always having to look up to people. He was, I thought, very good-looking, though his hair style was a little unusual, shoulder-length and held together in the back with a hair band. His beard, on the other hand, was always neatly trimmed. His explanation was simple enough: He hated going to a barber but could easily trim his own beard.

Andy danced with a few of the other women, too, and then we went to the wharf for a late supper, a wonderful respite from my occupation. He promised to keep my secret and came to San Francisco a few more weekends that summer. I looked forward to them. We both liked the city and had good times together.

Life as a taxi dancer was utterly boring. I never had a problem with the men who frequented the place except for the ones who were terrible dancers and stepped on my feet. Some were just lonesome for a woman's company and would use their tickets to spend a little time with me, having a beer and talking. One time a shy boy bought dance tickets, but what he really wanted, he confessed, was to get laid. He confided that he was a virgin and didn't have the nerve to approach a girl until he had had some experience. I felt sorry for him, but as gently as possible, I told him he would have to look elsewhere.

Andy sounded relieved when I told him about that, and I was annoyed that he thought I might have done it.

"Caroline, you're sweet, and when your feelings are touched, I think you might do something impulsive," he said. "That's a dangerous favor."

"Oh, it wouldn't have been so bad to help the kid out," I said, just to be contrary. I didn't really mean it.

Andy laughed. I guess he knew that.

My feelings were touched considerably that summer by both the women and men connected with the dance hall. Many of them were at a dead-end, and it didn't matter if they were smart, dumb, handsome or homely, or whether their morals were rigid or loose. Poverty was the culprit, and that experience radicalized my thinking from then on.

A particular dancer caught my attention. She was a loner and appeared snooty, so the other women made no attempt to socialize with her. Maybe they were jealous because she was a terrific dancer and always had a line of men waiting for her. She was a big woman with flaming red hair and always dressed in green, even her shoes, which I thought were beautiful. She stood out among the rest of us on the dance floor. I cultivated her friendship, and one night after work, she invited me to her room. After that I spent some time with her every night.

I would get a soft drink at a machine in the hall and she would get out her bottle of vodka from the closet shelf. Then we would take off our shoes and while I lay propped up on her bed, she would sit in a chair soaking her feet in hot water. For a while we hardly talked. Both of us were tired. She smoked like a chimney, puffing away, the cigarette hanging from a corner of her mouth, and squinting frequently to keep the rising smoke from burning her eyes. Every now and then she'd take a swig from her bottle.

"You're doing real good here, Caroline," she said. "The boss likes you. He's noticed how the same guys keep coming back to dance with you."

"I don't know why," I said. "I'm not a great dancer."

"Wake up, honey!" she said. "You've got something special. Kind of exotic."

A few nights later she told me Glen, our "boss," wanted to date me. I didn't answer for a minute, trying to think of how to handle it. I had no interest in going out with him, but I didn't want to insult him, either. I realized some of the other women might feel pressured to please him, even if they didn't want to, just to keep their jobs. Finally, I asked my new friend to tell him I never mix business with pleasure.

"He'll understand how I feel," I told her.

"Yeah, sure, honey," she said, and that never came up again.

In the dance hall my friend was known as June, but she told me she was not sure that was her real name because her mother often called her Jasmine. She was not sure of her original last name, either, her mother having used different ones at different times. She thought she was about thirty. I suggested she get a copy of her birth certificate, but the lack of personal data didn't bother her.

She did have a social security card which her mother had obtained for her when she was a teenager so that she could get her first job as a stripper in a Miami joint. From then on she moved across the country stopping in one city after another until she arrived in San Francisco. June/Jasmine followed her mother's pattern of multiple marriages. By the time I met her she had lost track of how many had occurred. Five, she thought. She was faithful to her religion, which did not permit sex outside of marriage, but as time went on, one or another husband would leave her or she would leave them, and she would simply remarry without benefit of divorce, which was also taboo.

After a few drinks, my friend would become garrulous. Having known June/Jasmine, the most foul language will never again shock me. She had a flare for it, telling outrageous dirty jokes and describing sexual experiences in her life in lurid detail. One time her stories lost their humor as she recounted incidents of abusive treatment. Another night she confided something which had disturbed her greatly. At an early age she had lost all the hair on her body.

"Just like that!" she said, snapping her fingers and pulling off her wig to prove it.

"A famous Irish singer deliberately shaves her head," I told her.

"Oh, wigs are okay, Caroline. It's the other part I can't fake," she said, suddenly turning modest.

She meant pubic hair, of course, and I tried to minimize that, too.

"It hasn't hurt your sexuality. Besides, some of the world's greatest artists of the Middle Ages painted nudes with no pubic hair. It's no big deal. Someday it will grow back."

That conversation, probably coupled with the booze, upset her. She became hysterical, laughing and crying, and then she came over to the bed and hugged me.

"You're a good girl, Caroline," she said, sobbing.

I felt awful, wishing there were something I could do to lift her spirits. I felt guilty, too, not having told her anything about myself, so, being good at rationalizing my lies, I laced some truths with untruths, such as my illegitimacy and a rotten love affair. She did not respond and perhaps did not believe me anyway.

One night when she was in a more cheerful frame of mind, I asked if I could try on her shoes. June/Jasmine's feet were remarkably small for her large body size and height, and her shoes fit me. I had never worn such spiky heels and wobbled around the room for a few minutes before taking them off.

One night she failed to show up at the dance hall, and after work when I went to her room, the door was wide open and the room was empty of her things. There was no goodbye, not even a note, but in the center of the room were the green shoes, obviously a farewell gift for me.

I felt depressed, wondering what would happen to her. The accumulated scars of her wounded life were like barnacles on an old scow. What would she be like in another ten years of drifting? I missed June/Jasmine, and soon after she left, I left, too, returning to Langdon to spend the remainder of the summer working on my thesis.

My college years were over now, and flying home with my father, I knew that this, too, was a trip I might never take again. Usually, being at home, in itself, was insignificant. He was rarely there, and I had no desire to be alone with Martha. But this time was different. Within a few days he would be leaving for a very long period in Tokyo, where his architecture would be used for a building sponsored by a Japanese cultural organization, the plans having been approved on a previous trip. Frank Lloyd Wright's phenomenal success with his Imperial Hotel had peaked Japanese interest in the work of other American architects, and in this case, my father received some of the same attention Wright had at an earlier time. Combined with my own fledgling venture, this was an exciting time for both of us. Martha posed as the perfect mate, content with whatever reflected glory was in it for her. She had become accustomed to my father's extended absences and may even have preferred her solitary life.

On the evening before he was to leave, my father went to his study to put his portfolio in final order, and Martha, being an early riser, went off to sleep. I, too, had gone to my room but just as on all the other nights before his leave-taking, I was filled with a childlike fear of abandonment, repeated over and over throughout my life. An emptiness would "fill" the cavity that normally held my organs, and I would feel weak and sick.

Here was the dearest person in my life, the source of my strength and eroticism, but also the source of my distress and fear of loss. So on that night, like a helpless child, I lay in the dark seeking consoling images from the past to ease my passage through the next day, but sad ruminations had a way of creeping into my consciousness. I sought clues to what might have brought me to my disturbed state of mind.

When I was still a little girl, Martha had told me I ended her career in opera. She had been given her first major role with the San Francisco Opera Company, but had forfeited it, she said, to raise me. That was ludicrous, for she had done none of the "raising."

Memorabilia of her former accomplishments filled her room. Included were old recordings of performances in which she had played roles. My father had given her fresh tapes of all of them, but she preferred the crackling sounds of the records and played those when he was away. Sometimes I would hear her singing and wondered if she dreamed of returning to a musical career. How I had wished she would, as compensation for my very existence, and possibly a softening of her treatment of me.

My father, on the other hand, was made for parenthood. When I was very young, I dreamed often of my mother, and I would awaken, crying and calling for her. He would pick me up and soothe me, sometimes taking me to his study, where next morning, Martha would find me cuddled in his arms and both of us asleep in his armchair. How painful it must have been for him, perhaps dreaming of Ana, too, and wanting her.

Those who knew my family in those early years of my life have told me other stories of my father's devotion to me. The fathers of children I knew were shadowy figures in their lives; mine was very much involved with me. During my elementary school years, he would unexpectedly drop in on my classroom and sit near the back, observing what went on. Sometimes he would appear at lunch time with a treat, usually paper cups of ice cream for the children. He and the teacher would have theirs, too, and then he would find out more about what school was like for his little girl.

My happiest memories were of visits to his study. I already knew when I was very young that I could not rush in at will. This was the place where Father did special work, so I waited for an invitation or politely requested entry. It was always given. Then I would climb on his lap and we would talk. We always had things to talk about.

It was there that I first became aware of how I looked. My father called me his "dark little beauty," and I realized I did not look like him or Martha, who were blue-eyed and fair. I asked him why I looked different. That gave him an opportunity to start the explanation of our relationship. Not wanting to destroy my sense of belonging, he told me a story of a beautiful dark princess, my mother, who gave me to him for safe-keeping when she had to leave me, and how happy that made both of them. It was a fairy tale I readily accepted, assuring myself that one day soon she would return.

A few years later, knowing that I had been too young to understand the seriousness of it, he went into greater detail. It was then that many things became clear to me as I recalled my hurtful relations with Martha. I had been foisted on her, it is true, but in her bitterness and false self-sacrifice, she assured herself an unhappy life, heaping blame on me for her frustration.

Sometimes when we were alone together she would call me "darky," which, as a small child, I did not grasp. But once she used the word in my father's presence and he became furious. He took her by the arm and led her to her room where I could hear him talking loudly and angrily. She never used the word again.

Even the "facts of life" came from my father. I wonder how many fathers provide that for their young daughters? He was direct in his explanations and unembarrassed about answering my questions.

Such were my random thoughts the night before my father's departure, skipping from one remembered fragment to another of my life's collection, not solving anything, until at last I fell asleep. I awoke at three to find my pillow wet with tears shed in a nightmare. The bedcovers were in disarray from my tossing about as I dreamed I was trying to escape a coffin lying beneath the sea. From time to time I would exert all my strength to lift the top, but the pressure of the water was too great.

Relieved that my awakening had rescued me from a watery grave, I lay quietly for a moment, when I heard the faint sound of music coming from the study. I tiptoed to the door.

"Father?" I whispered.

"Caroline, come in!"

I must have had a look of despair as he beckoned to me to sit beside him, and putting his arm around me, we listened to what remained on a Thelonius Monk disc. When it stopped, he asked if I'd like to hear more jazz. I did, so he rummaged through a drawer and found an album I had never heard—a reissue of some Cole Porter ballads with Carmen McRae doing the vocals. My father stood up and pulled me to my feet, and we danced.

He had on one of the *yukatas* he had taken to wearing at night since his previous trip to Japan, and I felt the closeness of his body to mine. At once I was aroused. McRae sang a few improvisational numbers, some had a little scat, and then she began a sentimental version of "Every Time We Say Goodbye." The appropriateness of the music to my mood was more than I could bear. Tears streamed down my cheeks. He turned off the disc player and we sat down again.

"Caroline, dear, I love you. Our separations are hard for me, too. I've never become inured to them. Shakespeare had it wrong: There is no sweetness in the sorrow of parting, but what can we do? It's the path I took in life."

"Father, you say you love me. Do you really love me?"

Sitting close beside him, I began kissing him first on the cheeks, then the lips, and weeping, I clung to him. "I can no longer stop myself," I told him.

Then I confessed my lustful story, Martha's diatribe that frightened me into concealment and the torturous years of suppression. My father looked anguished. He stood up and walked to the window, staring out at the blackness of the night, the surf barely distinguishable from the shore.

"All those years...," he murmured, almost to himself.

"Father," I said, coming to his side. "Talk to me. Are you angry at me?"

"How can I be angry at you, Caroline? Martha was wrong to attack you as she did. She gave you a consciousness of guilt, a cause for feeling shame. You did what you thought was right. How well I remember your sudden separation from me all those years ago. I didn't know the cause, and I felt deprived and longed for your sweet companionship. Now you have confessed your love for me. If it's wrong, then mine is, too. For I feel as you do.

"For many years I succeeded in repressing my desire as I watched you become the beautiful woman you are now. Then I began visualizing Ana in you, and I fantasized making love to you. The transference has become so real. There are times when I look at you and I see her. I've told myself a thousand times I should not feel this way, but I can't help myself. Talking to Andy hasn't helped. He can't condone our having an affair. I know that. He suggested we have a paternity test, but until now you have hidden your feelings, so I had no way of knowing that you shared them with me. If you want to have the test, we will."

"Do you think you are my biological father?"

"I'm not able to give you the answer, Caroline. I don't know. I loved your mother with all my heart, and we were having an affair. During that period she was raped. The man fled and that would have been the end of it, except that Ana became pregnant. We didn't know if she had been impregnated by him or by me. All we knew was that we loved each other, and when you were born, we loved you, too.

"I begged Martha to release me from our marriage. We had been leading separate lives long before all of that occurred, but her fury was manic. She threatened a long, ugly legal battle, and in those days, the divorce laws were on her side and uncompromising. I retained an attorney who was no help in resolving the conflict. At that point, if Ana had lived, I would probably have taken her and you and left. I didn't know or care any longer what the result would be.

"I thought I would never recover from the pain of losing her, and in a way, I never have. When she died she was just your age. I don't have any pictures of her, but you can see her image by looking in a mirror. The resemblance is striking, but more than that, you are so like her in every way—your little mannerisms, your laughter...."

His voice trailed off, and we stood, our arms encircling each other, not speaking, and then, overwhelmed by desire, I knew but one thing: I would wait no longer and raised my face to his. As if I had been waiting all my life for that moment, as if I had never been kissed before, it was the simple act, that lover's kiss, as much as what followed, that made me his and he, mine, and that would never cease to be. When he went to the door to lock it, I looked around that room in which I had found happiness from my earliest years, destined now to become the place for us to consummate our love. Along a glass wall was a desk positioned so that my father could look out at the sea. Off to one side was the small sofa and facing it, the armchair where countless times in my childhood I had sat on his lap as he read to me. Along the walls were book-lined shelves and cabinets.

In one of them he kept a *futon* for use on nights when he was up until the morning hours, and I watched him as he put it down before the warmth of the fireplace. He turned off the lamp and by the light of the fire's glow, we lay down together.

True to his nature, my father's every gesture, every caress had a tenderness about it. He was the gentlest of men, yet there was an intensity of passion in his love-making, as well, and at last, the struggle to keep our love imprisoned in our hearts was over.

Later that morning, Andy took my father to the airport for his trip to Tokyo, and the next day he took me for my flight to London. We rode for a little while without speaking. The pleasurable spell cast by what had occurred continued to envelope me. The desire of my life had come to fruition and I basked in it.

I had found nothing shocking in my father's revelations and consequently, a naturalness in what had transpired between us. For me, the consummation of my love for him was a melding with my mother, assuming her place, and for him, a reuniting with his lost love through her offspring. Was there madness here? I knew the involvement we were entering into had a strangeness about it, but passion is not concerned with correctness or normalcy—only gratification, and that we had found in each other's arms.

Andy broke into my reverie. "You're happy, aren't you, Caroline?"

"How do you know?"

He laughed. "That's easy—you're smiling to yourself."

"My life changed yesterday, Andy."

"I know."

It was my turn to laugh. "How do you know that?"

"I'm not clairvoyant—just your friendly neighborhood analyst who's known you a long time. Dave was doing a lot of smiling yesterday, too. It adds up to maybe the two of you being happy together."

"What we did—is it wrong?"

"Do you think it's wrong?"

"No! I feel different, wonderful. All my life I've gone through a siege of terror every time my father left for one of his projects. I've become physically ill because of the fear of being abandoned by him, of being left without him. It started out that way this time, too, but in the middle of the night I went to him and we stayed together until morning. When I went back to my room I felt calm, yet exhilarated. Those symptoms I used to have—they were terrible. Do you think this has freed me from them?"

"I don't know, Caroline. Let's hope so."

Then he changed the subject. "You know this coming year will be a different adventure from your summers traveling with Janie. I have a suggestion. Keep a journal. I did years ago, and I learned a lot about myself. And remember, Caroline, if ever you need me, I'll be here for you."

We were approaching the airport and our conversation came to an end.

"Don't worry about me. I'll do fine," I said, as we embraced and said goodbye, and I was sure I would.

2

The rain that greeted me on my arrival in London was unceasing. After trudging about for a few days, I settled into Janie's comfortable flat in Belgravia. By the time she would be back from her vacation with Matt, I would be gone, but in the meantime I made myself at home among the odd collection of furniture she had assembled there. It would have struck horror in the heart of an interior designer to see the eclectic mix and mismatch of half a dozen styles and periods that Janie had put together.

I had helped her, as a matter of fact, so the place felt a little like my own, too. In December of that year she had already been informed that she was hired, and she asked me to accompany her to London during our winter break in order to lease a flat. We easily found one, near shops and good transportation. Furnishing it was more of a problem. We spent the first two weeks of our month's holiday going from one second-hand store to another. Janie loved the old stuff, "antiques," she said, although not one piece was.

It was on one of our forays in an area of furniture stores that Janie met Matt and began a love affair I believed would last a lifetime. We had been attracted to things we saw in the window of a small shop. When we went in we met a tall, rangy young man whose outstanding feature was his nose, which was not just big but askew. His smile was big, too, and ingratiating. We liked him at once. This was Matt, the owner of the shop and the craftsman, as well, who designed and built the beautiful furniture on display. Later we learned he had acquired the bend in his nose and a few other scars playing rugby, a sport he loved.

Matt's merchandise was expensive, so after Janie explained her situation, we were about to leave. But Matt fell for Janie right then and there and didn't want to lose her. He offered to drive his van around to the various stores where her furniture was being held, pick it up and deliver it. Of course, she was delighted, and that was how their romance began.

It was fun watching those two. They squabbled, mostly over trifles, but they made up quickly, hugging and kissing and, with no hesitation, leaving me, to go off to a bedroom, and then they would come out a little later looking pleased with themselves. I was happy for Janie, whose sex life had always been like mine, transient.

"I miss him, Caroline," she said, after we were back at school.

"You love him," I told her.

Didn't I know how that felt, loving someone and missing him? But unlike the unfettered openness of their love affair, mine remained locked in my heart. Though I knew Janie would never judge me or care less for me, it was not until much later that I confided any of it to her.

That summer Matt closed his shop and they went to Scandinavia for their holiday. He admired the simplicity of design and fine wood used to produce furniture there, and he was eager to visit the shops of famous woodworkers. Except for Finland, Janie and I had never been to those northern countries, so the sights were new to both of them. Now and then they called to relate good times and sunshine as I lamented the unending rain that poured from London skies.

I missed them. I missed my father and Andy. I was lonesome. Then one day I acquired a housemate, a drenched and forlorn kitten, who had come mewing at the door. Dried and fed some milk, she looked good to me. A patchwork of colors, deep yellow and white and black with indigo eyes, she was obviously not purebred. But then who was I to consider that? Cat, I named her, and probably never having had a name before, she responded, leaping into my lap whenever I sat down and curling into a little ball to take a nap. Even though confiding all my aggravations to her got me nowhere, she was a welcome presence during that long, lonely summer.

The lifelong correspondence I had had with my father was not resumed during the summer, nor would there be much during the year that followed. It was too difficult, what with my constant moving about from one country to another, but it was a loss to me.

I have a clear recollection of his very first letter, although I was not yet four. I begged my nanny to read it time after time until I could "read" it myself, and I carried it around for days, not wanting to put it down until, wrinkled from handling and stained, Nanny prevailed upon me to put it in my dresser drawer. That letter may have been the stimulus for learning to write, and by five I was sending off letters to him in childish block print. Always diligent in his replies, he related funny little stories and details of his work.

Those letters were a lifeline for me when I was young, making the lonely periods of his absences, sometimes two or three months, more tolerable. Later I came to appreciate the time he took, in the midst of whatever he was about, to write letters of unhurried, vivid description. But now we communicated by phone, most frequently during the early weeks of my stay in London.

"Are you all right?" he would ask each time, and urge me to call if I needed him. "I will come to London at once," he said.

I knew his concern, for there was an ingredient in our love affair that had a touch of folly. I had stopped taking birth control pills during my final months in school, and now I might have become pregnant. Yet there was a quirkiness in me, for during that brief time, awaiting my body's decision, I was not alarmed and was, in fact, excited by the possibility.

Was it preposterous? I gave some thought to having a child by my father. If we were willing to bear the brunt of society's suspicion, what was to prevent us from having a child from so loving a union? As the days passed, I romanticized a love-child within me. How wonderful for my father, in his later years, to have a child follow him about happily as I once did, but this time with the devotion of both parents. The idea grew more and more appealing and was completely compatible with my philosophy.

At birth the spark of life is ignited and when we die, it is extinguished. Nothing more. To listen more closely to the dictates of those around us than to ourselves is pitiful, for we will not have lived in the space between those points of beginning and end. We can never please all of society in what we do. My own experience in college taught me that lesson. Even indelible things about ourselves such as the color of our skin, can be enough to reject us from a whole segment of society.

A little more time passed and I was able to report that I was "all right," which ended my fantasy. Buffeted by my emotions and strong desires, I did, nevertheless, have a rational side to me which was well aware of how unlikely, even impossible, that occurrence might be. But I did not forget about it.

As the rain-soaked days of summer continued in dreary succession, I read and did some boning-up for my forthcoming lectures. I was prepared, yet I had some trepidation about expounding on the marvels of American architecture to European students. I considered what my approach should be. Surely my students would feel pride in their own great builders and would be well aware of the tremendous influence they continue to have on Americans.

Today, Walter Gropius and Ludwig Mies van der Rohe are still discussed in awesome terms. Bringing their "roots" with them, those two taught in the States. Richard Neutra and Rudolph Schindler, coming from the "old" country, too, became famous, and Le Corbusier was the grand master of them all. Of Swiss-French background, he traveled the world, his ingenious contributions an endless source of influence. In fact, his designs were copiously appropriated by Frank Lloyd Wright. Even today, the most radical architects acknowledge their indebtedness to Le Corbusier.

My notes grew as I pondered how to make the giant-sized leap from then to now. Every style of architecture had its origin in Europe. Most have come and gone, yet Art Deco is still recalled in nostalgic revivals. The Streamline Moderne was followed by the International Style, that one stemming from the austerity of Bauhaus.

Then came the various versions of the Modernist style: Neo-Modernist and Post-Modernist.

Each brought innovations. All-steel framework gave greater strength to construction, leading to more changes. Horizontal lines became more interesting than vertical ones, glass walls opened dark interiors and houses were no longer bundles of boxy little rooms. Old ideas, as well as walls between rooms, came tumbling down and freed movement, giving an open feeling to architecture from then on.

No dominant style remains, and except for the brilliance shown by Japanese architects, the United States leads the world in the art. The latest variation is not a variation, for it leaves behind all the old forms. "My" architecture included an extreme departure from all of those precedents. Called Deconstructivism, the American genius, Frank O. Gehry, is its leading exponent. He and his colleagues are admittedly experimenters, their minds fertile residences of totally new concepts that startle and excite the imagination.

I had only to think about that to know it was there I would begin, leaving the past for historians to study and record. I would introduce my students to what will be their turn in the years to come. My subject had an exclusivity, and to indulge in backward glances would be a waste of time and interest, mine and theirs. A month in each college was insufficient to cover the topic in depth, for the performers on the stage of American architecture have gone far afield from traditional ways, and it would be enough for me to concentrate on the dynamic changes being created and the geniuses who were accomplishing them.

Slowly the sky over London began to clear. Now and then a shy and pallid sun would venture an appearance, before slinking away beneath a cloud. Taking a cue from Londoners, who never trust the boldest display of sunshine, I, too, carried an umbrella no matter how short my stay outdoors might be.

Many days of those first weeks were spent in the Royal Institute of British Architecture, studying in its library and scanning books in its bookshop. I was given directions there for walking tours of recent new buildings, pleasant enough generally, but the pull to retain the old forms is strong in England. When traditional buildings must be demolished, the new ones often repeat the former styles. One example is the construction of the Savoy Theatre. When it burned to the ground it was restored exactly in its earlier pattern, still user-unfriendly with countless steps to climb to get to the performance, and inadequate toilet facilities, yet every level is fully equipped to instantly serve liquor to any size crowd of thirsty imbibers at every break in the action on the stage.

I did find one classy new building—a two-level restaurant. Originally designed by Eva Jiricna, with lots of glass and steel in its construction and a light and airy appearance, it seemed functional in every way. The food that was served was marvelous, completely unexpected in a place with its name: "Joe's Cafe." Every now and then I went there for lunch. It was always crowded and noisy, but I welcomed the distraction it provided, being among other people.

Trying to keep occupied, I wandered around museums, saw films and occasionally went to a concert, but being alone made everything less interesting. The memory of my romantic night with my father did not fade into the past. It remained as fresh as the night of its occurrence, and I yearned to be with him. Knowing that might be a long time into the future, I grew more and more restless as the weeks and months of summer droned on. I had taken Andy's suggestion and started a journal. It did reflect my feelings, but now my jottings became repetitive with expressions of my inner tension and frustration.

I began acting impulsively, sometimes taking off in the middle of a sleepless night for a stroll around Soho to observe the action, if there was any, or to a jazz club. Being a single woman frequently led to misunderstandings and I tired of having to explain I was there for the music.

Experimenting with drugs had never appealed to me, though I enjoyed marijuana and now smoked more than I normally would. I drank more, too. What a way to conduct a love affair, I grumbled to myself, with my father in Japan and me in England.

•

Andy and I had long phone conversations, and I told him things I would never tell my father for fear he would worry, but I could let it all out to Andy, and I always felt better after I had talked to him. Sometimes he sounded worried, too.

"Are you keeping out of trouble, Caroline?"

"Just barely," I told him. I was serious, too.

One time I told him about a chance meeting I had with a famous British actor.

"A pub called Brambles is near Janie's, and sometimes I go there in the evenings, you know, just to be around cheery people," I said. "Well, one night James Manning came in. I recognized him right away. Everybody did. He sat at the bar for a while drinking and then he got up and came over to my table.

" 'Let's have a drink together,' he said.

"That wasn't the most elegant way to put it, but I said 'sure.' I couldn't see anything wrong with it, although he'd already had enough to drink. His face was flushed and he'd opened his tie so it just hung loose from his neck.

"We talked, and I found out he was better at reading lines than making up his own.

" 'I like colored girls,' he said. 'What'll you do for this?'

"And he put a hundred-pound note on the table.

" 'Nothing,' I said, not too convincingly. I was furious, but I decided to play along.

" 'How about two hundred?' he said.

" 'Is that your best offer?' I asked.

" 'Who do you think you are?' he asked. 'Okay, three hundred, but I want something extra fancy for that.'

" 'Let me see the money.'

"He put it on the table. 'Half now and the rest afterward,' he said.

"I smiled and for a minute I let him think we'd made a deal. Then I stood up. 'No, I don't think so,' I said, slowly. 'I'm not in the mood tonight.'

"Manning watched me as I paid my bill and left. I thought it was all over, but I only got a few steps from the pub when he came out after me and grabbed my arm.

"'That was a bloody rotten trick,' he said. 'I'm going to teach you a lesson, girlie. Come with me. My car's around the corner.'

"'No! Let me go!' I said, and yelled for help.

"He paused, but not to let me go. He was drunk, but he's a big guy, Andy, and he was mad as hell. He had an iron grip on my arm and was dragging me down the street.

"'Quiet down, you little tart! Just come along and you'll be okay. Yell again and I'll put a gag in your mouth.'

"'Yeah? How are you going to do that?' I said, and did yell again.

"That time the barkeep heard me and stuck his head out the door, but immediately ducked back inside. My heart fell, but in a minute he came out again, followed by every single person who'd been in the pub. It was a funny sight as they encircled us. No one except the barkeep said a word.

"'Let her go, Manning!' he said. And he did. 'Now bug off.'

"I barely had a chance to thank my rescuers—they were already trooping back inside, and I set off for home."

"I've heard of that old goat, Caroline. He has a terrible reputation. He's been in trouble many times. But I'm worried about you—your restlessness and wandering about. Listen, how would you like a holiday in Paris?"

"When?"

"I'll be there for a conference September third to the eighth. When I talked to Dave the other day and told him about my plans, he said he'd like to meet us there for a little holiday. Will you come?"

"How can he consider such a long trip just now? Two of those days he'll be in the air—jet lag when he arrives and jet lag when he returns. What kind of holiday is that?"

"You can stay as long as you like, but I know Dave. Taking even a little time away from a new project is hard for him. Caroline, he just wants so much to see you. So do I. Okay?"

"Okay!"

•

"Be sensible, girl!"

How often I heard that admonition from Martha when I was growing up, and now I heard her voice in my head. It was a trait I never fully developed, but now I had enough sense to go to a physician who gave me a prescription for birth control pills. Then the days poked along until they finally arrived at the proper one and I took off for Paris.

All of us had been there before, but never together. How different this visit was to be from previous ones! Andy had reserved a suite for us at the conference hotel, but we saw little of him except for nightly stops in the sitting room we shared. There we had nightcaps, always warm *sake*, which my father had taken a liking to long before he left for Japan.

Andy showed us his agenda and on it, to our pleased surprise, was his name. He was to be the featured speaker. I visualized our laid-back, pony-tailed friend, looking handsome in his suit and hard shoes, addressing his fellow psychiatrists.

He was constantly occupied with the activities of the conference, so my father and I were left to ourselves, and we made the most of the few precious days we had together. Our guest-room faced out on a pretty little park and we could see the Eiffel Tower just a block away. It was a romantic setting, but we didn't linger over it, wasting not one moment to be in each other's arms.

After some weak starts earlier in life, I now had a happy sex life, although a difference continued to exist in our positions, for as eager as we both were to please each other in our new intimacy, he remained the indulgent parent and I took on a childlike persona when I was with him. Having acquired some sophistication in the independent life I had led in college, I knew the meshing of his indulgences with my naive facade was directly connected and I understood its significance. Our lives together from now on would be different from the past, but we would always remain unalterably father and daughter. It could not be otherwise.

I had idolized him all my life; now he was my lover and I accepted that as my good fortune. The years of unresolved conflict appeared over, and I found my new life just as I wanted it. What darkened our happiness was the need for concealment of our affair. It was more involved than adultery alone, and could be further distorted by those bent on sensationalism. Personal lives should remain separate from public ones, but that is not how society views it. How quickly self-righteousness comes to the fore when the humanity of famous people is laid bare. If we permit ourselves to taste the tantalizing flavors of our own imperfections, why do we demand a diet of insipid purity in our leaders?

Still, the lives of princes and presidents have been touched by scandal and they have lost none of their popularity. Would our affair have any bearing on my father's career? I thought not, but it made no sense to flaunt it, either. Here we felt safe and able to express our love freely, letting our bodies become better acquainted with each other, for after all, they had been together but once before.

Sometimes my sexual zestfulness overwhelmed my father, and he laughingly told me to be more respectful of his advancing years. He was forty-seven, hardly very advanced, but I did try to curb my liveliness. We went out every day, our hearts filled with the joy of being together in that beautiful city.

Autumn was the season I liked best in Paris. The crowds of summer were gone, leaving a quieter, less bustling atmosphere. As we walked along the boulevard and side-streets of the neighborhood of our hotel, a crisp, chilly breeze swirled and gathered the falling leaves of the ancient chestnut trees in heaps here and there. Once we dropped into a small bar where, to our amazement, a Japanese woman served us our drinks and my father had a chance to practice his new language. The wine warmed us and in a little while we set off again.

Another place we liked was a *bistro* that looked a hundred years old with its sepia-faded pictures and lace curtains.

"There's Madame La Farge," Father whispered, indicating a stocky old woman sitting at the back of the room, knitting.

We were served a tureen of onion soup and a loaf of bread, simple French food, but delicious, and I kept ladling one bowl after another for myself until my father told me I'd had enough. I didn't say anything as, in a feistier mood, I would to anyone else.

Wherever we went I noticed how much visual attention he received. Around Monterey that was to be expected—everyone knew him. Although he was famous in his field, his picture seldom appeared in the press, so I was curious. Women, especially, looked at him longer than the usual glance given strangers on the street. He was rugged-looking, probably from years spent in climates that varied from freezing to tropical, and he had a warm and open expression, softened still more by the gray that had begun to appear in his hair. Often preoccupied, he appeared unconscious of the attention he was being given.

There were two "sights" we both wanted to see. The first was located on the Right Bank, near the Gare de Lyon and across from the Bibliothèque de France. Known as the American Center, it replaces the old center for the arts which closed years ago. This building, seven stories high, is the spectacular work of one of my American geniuses, Frank O. Gehry. We had seen a few pictures of it, but now looking at that unsymmetrical, skewed facade and knowing how complicated its design and building had to be, our reactions were the same. It projected a heart-warming playfulness, dominating the area with its avant-garde appearance.

Once inside, the structure became, along with many other aspects of its purpose for being, a serious showplace for a rich mix of universal and experimental art. I was about to shoot some pictures to show my students when one of the people connected with the Center, recognizing my father, approached us. In our conversation I told him about my particular interest in the Center. He asked us to wait while he left and a few minutes later returned with numerous transparencies for my use. I was delighted.

One picture did get into my camera as, once outside again, on an impulse, I asked a passerby to do a touristy thing for me. She took a picture of my father and me, grinning, as we stood in front of that striking building.

An addiction to coffee was my father's one vice, though there are those who might have considered me another. He was seeking the perfect brew—black, flavorful and strong. In his search, he drank many cups in a day and sometimes wound up with a terrible bellyache. That happened at the other place we visited, the Pyramid in the grand forecourt of the Louvre.

It had been finished only a few years before, and neither of us had been there. My father knew I.M. Pei and was an admirer of his work, and I would now have another of Pei's imaginative constructions to tell my students about. François Mitterand had chosen Pei for the honor of renovating the museum, and now the ten-year project was completed with the magnificent sight of the Pyramid at its entrance.

What a concept Pei did have! An analogy can be made to the ancient edifices of Egypt with their hidden treasures. Shaped like its name and built of glass, it looms up dramatically, an enlivening addition to the gray environs of the Louvre. Surrounded by a moat of water, fountains bubble up on each side of it. Nearby are an escalator and a graceful spiraling staircase that descend into the underground space which, in turn, leads into the three major wings of the museum.

We watched as a continuous stream of visitors made their way down into the forecourt below, so vast it accommodates everyone with ease. Standing there, in the midst of it, looking upward, we marveled at the sheer immensity of that glass canopy. Natural light enters through its translucence, sometimes a little sunshine, too, casting beams here and there. No need to fear the claustrophobic sensation people sometimes have being in an underground space.

On all sides are art stores and bookshops, and tucked in among them, little cafes. Museum visitors are a hungry lot. We, too, went into one of the little eating places. With our sandwiches we drank coffee, which tasted fine to me, but then I'm no connoisseur. My father, on the other hand, suddenly became ill and I was alarmed. I suspected something far worse than too much coffee, but he kept reassuring me.

"Don't be worried, Caroline," he kept saying. "I'll be all right. It's nothing."

We returned at once to the hotel, not having gone into the museum at all, though we had planned to see some of the renovations, especially the Richelieu Wing, which had been described to us as entrancing in its beauty.

By the time we were back at the hotel he had recovered, and we decided to slip into the back of a meeting-room where Andy was leading a discussion. It dealt with the increasing use of new mood-altering medications to ease the pain of emotional distress. Two scientists whose chemical formulas were currently in use explained their successful experiments and "miracle" benefits. Andy knew about their effectiveness, but his personal voice was for caution.

His humanity shone through his remarks as he expressed the hope that such medication would be selectively administered and monitored. In his own work he was deeply involved with troubled people and he feared irresponsible and indiscriminate medication. We were touched by our friend's warm human connection and when we left the room, we did a funny thing. As if we were congratulating ourselves on having such a fine person for our friend, we embraced each other!

As the days sped by, I noticed how often my father appeared deep in thought, his eyes focused on a distant place from where we were and I knew he was visualizing an aspect of his work, but he exhibited none of his usual eagerness to talk about it, and even when I asked questions, he showed reluctance to respond.

Puzzled and concerned, I decided to distract him by suggesting we take a walk along the Champs-Élysées. The last time I had been in Paris I was saddened by what had happened to that world-famous avenue. It had become commonplace with fast-food eateries and movie houses, the street littered and dirty. Then I read that the mayor of the city, Jacques Chirac, had ordered a complete restoration to its former glory.

We took a taxi to the Place de la Concorde, then walked the mile-long street to the Arc de Triomphe. It was indeed a dazzling transformation with everything—street lamps, kiosks, bus shelters, all designed in turn-of-the-century style. Hundreds of trees had been planted on either side and benches placed along its length. Pedestrians no longer needed to pick their way on a narrow broken street, maneuvering precariously among haphazardly parked cars. Underground parking had replaced that. Even the sidewalks were new, constructed of granite and greatly widened. It was a lovely walk, refreshing our spirits, and an inspiring example of how architecture, even in that simple form, can perform magic, if the will is strong enough.

On the night before we left, Andy asked us to go with him to a nightclub near the hotel. He had seen a leaflet in the lobby giving the names of a trio of American jazz musicians doing a gig there, and Andy knew the bass player, Ray Grace, whose home was in San Francisco.

"I'd like to think about a design I'm working on. You two go," my father said.

So we did. The nightclub was dinky and smoky and jammed with aficionados. We found a single space at the back and jockeyed to squeeze into it.

"Listen, Caroline," Andy said finally, laughing. "Sit on my lap so we can get around to enjoying the music."

"Is that all right?"

"There isn't a *gendarme* in sight. Now sit down!"

The music was mellow and sweet, and I loved it. Observing my pleasure, Andy whispered, *"C'est bon,* Caroline?" *"Oui,"* I whispered back.

After the set, people began to leave and Andy went over to greet his old friend. I could see them having an animated conversation. Then they went over to the bar where Andy picked up some beer for us, and a minute later Ray appeared with a glass of milk and a bag of cookies for himself.

"Can't take the sauce any more," he said.

Then he looked at me. "Well, hello, sister!" he said.

"This is Caroline Shaw, Ray."

"Hey! You've got a pretty little gal."

"I wish," Andy said, smiling.

When we arrived back at the hotel Andy asked me to come to the lounge with him. We found a corner couch and then he just sat looking at me without saying anything.

"Is something wrong, Andy?"

"I have a question."

"You know all the answers."

"Let me ask, anyway. Why do you persist in calling Dave 'Father'?"

"Lifelong habit, I guess. It's hard to erase the image of him as my father. 'David' doesn't feel right."

"It will get to feel right after a while. Look, I'm not going to lay any psychojargon on you. You and Dave are having a love affair; you're happy. But think about it: Why isn't it comfortable to address him by his given name?"

"Maybe because in some ways he still acts parental."

"He can't help that, either. But if you call him by his given name, it may help equalize your relationship. You would be simply a woman and man in love. I think this is a good time for you and Dave to have a paternity test. If you are unrelated, you could indulge yourselves as much as you wish. If you are indeed father and daughter, you could face the hard question of what the future holds for you if you decide to remain together. What others may think or know about you is not the issue, though concealment is based on that. You and Dave must not avoid knowing the truth about yourselves."

I began to cry.

"What now, Caroline?"

"There's something else."

"What?"

"Do you know about my mother?"

"Yes."

"David is making love to her when he's with me."

"That's nonsense! Dave thought he might feel that way before he was with you. After the first time he knew differently. You can be no one but yourself, and he's crazy about you."

"How do you know that?"

"He told me."

"Does he tell you everything about us?"

"Don't you? I'm Dave's and your closest friend. You can tell me anything. Now I've given you some advice. Think seriously about it."

"I love you, Andy."

"I love you, too, Caroline, but you're dodging the issue."

Just as I had left him hours before, David sat at the desk, studying material laid out before him.

"I'm not satisfied with that building," he said. "It must be redesigned."

"But the plans have been approved."

"It doesn't matter."

"What do you want to change?"

"I'm not sure yet."

He stood up, stretching. "Oh, I'm stiff," he said. "I'm going to bed. How about you?"

It was very late, but I decided to take a bath first. The tub was wide and deep and the warmth of the water felt good.

"David," I called to him, "Why don't you come and get in the tub with me? The water's very relaxing."

There was no reply. Then he appeared, and taking off his robe, slipped into the water. For a little while we lay snugly enclosed in each other's arms.

"What a wonderful suggestion, darling," he said and closed his eyes.

Then he looked at me and laughed. "But how am I supposed to relax with your pretty body beside me?" And drawing me out of the water a little, he caressed my breasts.

"It's curious, isn't it, men's attraction to women's breasts?" I said.

"I don't think so. It's the earliest and most satisfying experience in an infant's life, lying close to his mother's warm body and suckling the milk she offers, a memory stored in his subconscious, recalled only as an attraction to that beautiful part of a woman's body. I know nursing a child is never thought of as sexual, but women often have pleasant, even orgasmic contractions while nursing."

"What about girl babies? What memories do they store?"

He laughed. "I'll have to think about that. But tell me, don't you enjoy the fondling?"

"Don't stop," I said and kissed him.

"Once when you were an infant, Caroline, it excited me watching you at your mother's breasts. I didn't say anything, but Ana understood. She put you down and placed my lips on her still moist nipples and I consumed a bit of her milk as you had. I loved the sensation, but it was more than that: We, the three of us, were making a deeply intimate connection with one another."

I visualized what had occurred so long ago, and knowing as my mother had, what he wanted, I reenacted the scene with him, putting his mouth to my breasts. My nipples extruded and hardened and I positioned myself beneath him, wrapping my legs tightly around him. We rocked gently at first, with the water like a soft warm cradle, rocking gently with us. As our desire for orgasm became more intense, the water, too, became agitated, sloshing out of the tub. Afterward we laughed at our splashing and thrashing about as we came together. Love and laughter. What more was there to life?

On our final day, with my father's flight scheduled for six in the evening, Andy joined us for the short walk to the Eiffel Tower. We took the elevator to the restaurant for lunch before going the rest of the way to the top for a last look at Paris spread out before us.

Oppressed by the sadness of parting from one another, we spoke little, and soon Andy took off for his own flight home. I could not hold back the tears when my father had to board his plane. If the riskiness of expressing affection in public concerned him, he did not show it. He held me close, repeating over and over that he loved me and that we would be together again as soon as it was possible. A few hours later I returned to London, but was left with a gnawing fear that something was amiss. I worried about his frequent distractions and silences. I worried about his excessive coffee-drinking and his health. I worried.

Nothing had been said about Martha. We knew Andy looked in on her occasionally to make sure that in her reclusive life she was all right, but in a real sense, she had faded from our thoughts to a faint remnant of the past.

3

One week later, I left London for my first assignments in Glasgow and Dublin. I need not have had any of my early uneasiness, for in both schools serious students made my work meaningful. In fact, some of them had an intellectual indoctrination that made theoretical aspects of architecture overshadow their interest in the tangible challenges of actual building.

I was determined, in the short time I had, to make them aware of that. Writing and teaching are gratifying, but doing the actual work is liberating, and I pointed out the problem of over-intellectualizing. The French theoreticians and the Russian Constructivists were pioneers who laid the groundwork for many of our famous builders, but through no fault of their own at that time, they did not have the opportunity to perform. Two American architects, Peter Eisenman and Richard Meier did not have that particular problem, yet for a long period they simply did not do the work they so eloquently described. Eventually they did, and they have become among the greatest architects of the century. Eisenman, particularly, has all but destroyed the old standards as his bold ideas take hold and the public becomes accustomed to a look of disorder and diversity in contrast to dull uniformity.

Meier's latest project, and one of the largest of its kind anywhere, is the Getty Center in Los Angeles. The complex includes a museum, a Center for the History of Art, an auditorium, an administration building, small and large eating places, as well as other essential facilities. Each is different in appearance, but all are in a softly hued travertine, a departure from his well-known preference for white.

Renderings brought a comment from a student that the complex, with its hillside location, can be compared to the Acropolis and indeed, it is a dramatic sight.

Thus my career began in Glasgow. Nothing untoward occurred and the time passed quickly. I then went on to Dublin where I had a personal experience I was unprepared for.

The guesthouse where I resided was only a few blocks from the college, but leaving school one day in a downpour I hailed a taxi. Realizing the driver might be annoyed at the short hop, I planned to tip him generously. He was congenial, and as we rode, I commented on Dublin's frequent rain.

"Worse than London," I said, "And that was bad enough."

"That's what makes Ireland green and our pubs popular," he said.

"The green part I know," I said, "But how does it make your pubs popular?"

"Haven't you noticed how few people carry umbrellas in Dublin? That makes it necessary to duck into a pub till the rain lets up," he explained, laughing.

When he heard I was from America and lecturing at the college where he was a student in the theater arts department, he was elated. He told me his name, Brian Cleary, and asked if I would join him for a few drinks and conversation at his favorite pub. I liked the idea. He parked his taxi and soon we were cozily seated before a fire, drinking a dark brew I could not identify.

"What kind of beer is this?" I asked him.

"We don't drink beer in Dublin," he said laughing. "This is Guinness, 'the wine of our country,' Joyce said. It will grow on you."

Brian was popular and everyone stopped at our table with hearty greetings of *slainte* and the clinking of glasses. His boyish good looks and jovial manner belied the fact that he was a serious graduate student and several years older than I. Brian was the most literate person I had ever known, educated in Gaelic, too, and that impressed me, as well. Before long, although it was not yet evening, the place became jolly with laughter and singing and drinking—lots of drinking. I became as much a part of that convivial crowd as if I had been going there for years.

In the next room was a dance floor, and a small band of musicians was livening things up. Brian told me all of them were students of the music department of the school. Like him and his taxi business, they were earning a living in order to continue their education. They had modern instruments as well as traditional Celtic ones—the *uilleann* pipes, the *bodhran* drum and a fiddle—with which they played a variety of music, including jigs.

Brian tried to teach me one, a springy dance in triple rhythm that required intricate, rapid foot motions, but the ale was affecting my coordination, and Brian laughed at my attempts. By that time he was holding me close and I didn't object.

Drinking is insidious. After the first few potions, continuing becomes easy, and that is what I did. It was a way of life for Brian, and I had foolishly fallen in step with him. I spent the night with him, some of it sleeping off the liquor, but more than that transpired, and I distinctly remembered enjoying it.

So much so that I was not prepared to stop. The next night Brian gave me a ticket to a play in which he had a role, and afterward we went to the pub. I drank little after that first night, enjoying what followed more.

His bedroom was excessively warm, so he would open a window, and though a blind prevented the rain from coming in, the room had the atmosphere of a sultry summer night. Our bodies were moist with sweat, which only increased our passion. In the mornings we showered and then Brian drove me to my class at school. The situation struck me as amusing, and I was glad he wasn't taking it seriously, either.

My Irish students were a delight. I didn't have to convince them that contemporary architecture was a dynamic art form, and they themselves made some astute observations that pleased me.

"I like the sensitivity of your American architects," one of them said. "Wherever in the world they go they leave their personal imprint, but they incorporate something of the particular culture, too."

He pointed out their architecture in Japan's urban areas, where inches of space are treasured as yards to us and must be utilized to the greatest advantage, yet a sense of spaciousness, "emptiness," often illusory, is created. Which, of course, led me to think about my father and his enchantment with the Japanese way of life. The students wanted to know about his ongoing project, but I had nothing to tell them about that. There appeared to be a discontinuance of activity that I did not understand and that worried me.

Nevertheless, the pleasure I found being among those sophisticated students could hardly be called "work." In the evenings, I continued the pattern I had begun early on, relishing the wit and charm of my companion, and later, the lovemaking. Besides Brian, I will always associate Dublin with rain. It didn't cease the remaining weeks I was there, greening the landscape and jam-packing the pubs.

In retrospect I was dismayed at what had happened. Being a realist, I could hardly feel remorseful, having had a wonderful time. My inhibitions had been trundled off to a slumber chamber at the back of my mind and the image of my beloved had been tucked in, too, out of the ken of my conscience. I had left them and him sleeping soundly as I went my merry way. I realized how fortunate I was that Brian was the one whom I had met. With someone else things might not have had as satisfactory a conclusion.

Would that somber thought strengthen my resolve to conduct myself less frivolously, I wondered, or would I keep stumbling along my route through Europe? Now, with my father restored to his proper place uppermost in my heart and mind, I returned to London for a few days' visit with Janie and then crossed the channel to the Continent.

Not having set up a well-organized itinerary, I spent some time rearranging my schedule at various schools and postponing others until the following fall. Publicity brought more requests, which meant I had to set up dates for another year in advance. I had mixed feelings about looking that far into the future and held off doing it. It was flattering to be wanted and I did bring enthusiasm to my work, having been exposed to the architecture of our time through my father's influence and knowing the famous people who made up my "geniuses."

The problem that bedeviled me was that it had been almost immediately after I had composed my lecture course that my father and I declared our love for each other. It changed everything. A career that separated me from him for long periods was the farthest thing from my heart, and I put my mind to exploring some other aspect of architecture that would interest me in a professional way and also permit me to be in Japan with him.

Brussels and Amsterdam were my destinations during the fall months. I had never been to Brussels, and when I left I still felt as if I had not been there. It had a business-like atmosphere to me, and that was how I conducted myself, too, giving my lectures and "keeping out of trouble," as Andy had hoped I would.

A revival of interest in Frank Lloyd Wright was in full swing in the early nineties, and my students in Brussels, whose parents might only vaguely remember his significance, were engrossed in curiosity. Through me they thought they would learn more about him. When I showed reluctance to discuss him, they insisted.

"Doesn't he represent the beginning of modern architecture?" one asked.

"Yes, probably, but your professors will fill you in on Wright's work and how he worked. It's in the past, despite its importance. My subject is contemporary and goes far beyond Wright."

"You've had an association with people who knew him personally," another persisted.

So that was it: the human element. I was provoked on another score. None of them was curious about Louis Kahn, who actually followed Wright by only a dozen years and whose buildings in many ways were superior to Wright's. Kahn used his keen knowledge of science to complement his architecture. Among others it can be seen in places as diverse as Ahmedabad, India; Dacca, Bangladesh; and Fort Worth, Texas. It is the Kimball Museum of Art in Fort Worth where Kahn achieved a remarkable new way of bringing soft natural light onto works of art by means of double vaulted galleries.

I was most familiar with another of Kahn's buildings: the Salk Center for Biological Research in La Jolla, California. Built in the sixties, it is situated in an area known as Torrey Pines Mesa, on a cliff overlooking the Pacific, and remains one of the finest examples of twentieth-century architecture.

Unfortunately, perhaps, as far as his historical remembrance goes, he had none of Wright's flamboyance and penchant for notoriety. It was what those young students wanted to hear about, not Wright's work, so I spent a little time talking about him.

Despite his talents and enormous energy, problems hung like a dark cloud over Taliesin in its early years. The monstrous events that took place there were common knowledge—arson that nearly destroyed the compound altogether, the killing of Wright's wife by a deranged axe-wielding murderer and love affairs that filled the gaps in his busy schedule of work. He attracted considerable attention in those days, and deservedly, but an overweening hubris turned many friends away from him.

My father came on the scene long after Wright, but a few of the older men who were his friends had been apprentices of Wright during that period, and they had colorful stories to tell about their experiences at Taliesin.

The complex was nestled in the low hills of Wisconsin countryside and became an attraction for University of Wisconsin students of architecture, who were excited by the new ideas Wright was boldly setting forth. When he presented musicales in the auditorium on Sunday afternoons, small crowds would appear, more curious to see him than to hear the program. He would stand at the entrance, attired in a long cape, sometimes a flowing scarf around his neck, greeting people. His large handsome head and longish white hair made him appear much taller than he was, a fact that never bothered him. Sometimes he even built rooms with low ceilings, fitting them to his own height and preference.

Wright had a strong personality, which was characterized in different ways, depending on one's relationship with him. Some thought him arrogant and egotistical; others said he was kind and good-humored. No one denied his genius and some of the apprentices were as worshipful as apostles. One of my father's friends said he was resentful from his first day there, observing Wright's posturings, his strolling about the grounds making demands. He could not remember exactly, but he thought he'd paid around a thousand dollars for his year in the Master's presence, a huge sum at that time.

To visitors, the atmosphere was sublime. Everyone was impressed by the drafting-room with its immense stone fireplace at one end and the view open on the other sides to the pastoral scene. What they were unaware of was that the apprentices maintained the complex, their days beginning at dawn, hours before they sat down at their drafting tables.

Classical music was continuously piped into the huge room, which caused a problem, too. Young students, lulled by it, would doze off in the midst of their work, while others complained that it was an intrusion on their creativity, distracting them and compelling them to listen to the complicated language of the music instead of their own thoughts. But they never won a round with Wright, Father's friend said, and the music played on.

One of the others who had been an apprentice humorously compared those days to the Cultural Revolution in China, when people in the arts were sent out to the fields to experience the joy of work as farm laborers.

"That's what *we* did," he said, laughing.

It was not funny then.

I told the students about the wife of one of the apprentices who had come to Taliesin to be with him. She was assigned a cook's duty and "worked like a slave," she said. She, too, rose early in order to have the bread baked and food ready for the apprentices when they came in from the fields. She thought of her occupation as mindless and begged for music in the kitchen, but the "tyrant," as she called Wright, refused. She developed an intense dislike of the man, and years later still spoke venomously of him.

A favorite story involved Wright's trips to a nearby small town, Richland Center, his birthplace. He went there to get replacement parts for the vehicles that were used at Taliesin. There Wright had found an automobile parts dealer, who, in awe of the man, allowed him to accumulate a large bill, but finally refused to give him any further credit.

At that, Wright drew a picture of a check on a scrap of paper, signed it and handed it to the man.

"Keep this," he said haughtily. "Some day it will be worth more than the amount I owe you."

But the man refused. "I need the money right now," he said, and Wright was hard put to find another gullible merchant to take his business and charge account.

Rumors and truths about Wright's amorous nature were rampant during his lifetime, but being acutely aware of my own father's intimate life, which involved me as well, I was not about to discuss that aspect of Wright's life, though I knew how titillating the subject always is.

Despite their disparaging remarks, my father and all his friends appreciated the contribution Wright had made to architecture, not based wholly on his work, but on his role as a visionary, leading other great architects to dream of modern castle-building.

When I left Brussels, I thought how exemplary my behavior had been, but I was not proud of my restraint. I just hadn't been tempted. Amsterdam was a different matter. The tolerance of young people's antics endears the city to them, and for the most part they try to enjoy themselves without causing problems. Janie and I had loved it when we were there, and I was happy to be back.

Within a short time I settled into a routine. I seldom had much breakfast, and finding the staff cafeteria a good place to eat, I had my big meal of the day there. It was a small room and lively. Everyone understood English and was friendly, so I became acquainted with people in the department quickly. All of us sat wherever we could find empty chairs, and that was how I met one of the professors, Jan de Groote.

A few times he brought his tray over to my table and sat down next to me. Jan was not old, yet he had the appearance of an old-world gentleman, gray-haired and, as if to match, he usually wore gray clothes. Only his wide, colorful bow-ties were inconsistent with his dress and demeanor. One day he asked if I would like a ride on the canals in his boat after our classes were over. That sounded nice, so later in the day we met again.

It was enjoyable floating along, looking at the pretty Dutch scenes at the water's edge. After a while Jan turned off from the major canal we were on and took one of the countless small ones that crisscross the city. He said the houses in that area were built during the seventeenth century and stood on wooden piles driven into the soggy ground. Then he pointed to a building a little way off. Typical of Amsterdam architecture, it was tall, three stories, and very narrow with a gabled tile roof.

"That's mine," he said. "Do you want to stop in for a drink?"

Jan's bland image made his invitation appear innocent enough. Yet I hesitated. When was it ever "a" drink? After a few, I might find myself bedded down with a man I'd known only days. But I went, anyway. Andy once said he liked my spontaneity, but I thought it was more of an impulsiveness which, on occasion, led to misadventure and bruised feelings.

Jan's personality turned out to be nothing like his appearance and he was fun to be with. Sometimes a few drinks reveal a person's singularity. He was smart and witty and had a repertoire of ribald jokes that surpassed even June/Jasmine's.

"Do you live alone here, Jan?" I asked.

"I have a wife somewhere," he said, laughing. "We've been married a long time, but last year she just took off. Anyway, it's a rare treat nowadays to have a beautiful young woman's company."

That was nicely put, and the liquor was having its usual effect on me. He was not a novice at expressing affection and soon we were wambling our way to the third-level bedroom. At the second floor landing, he stopped and opened a door.

"This is my library. Come in and look around for a minute. It's a little unusual. I hope you don't shock easily."

"Well, I'm always curious," I said and went in.

It was not especially shocking to me, although he certainly had an unusual collection of books—all pornographic, a few thousand, at least, neatly arranged on shelves around the room. I looked at a few. He had some beautiful Japanese pillow books and many trashy pulps. Then he opened a double-doored closet, and at that I *was* shocked. Built for the purpose, he had all manner of sadomasochistic devices, some of them dreadful medieval objects of torture.

"Choose what you'd like to take upstairs," he offered.

"No!" I said and started back down the steps.

He lunged toward me. "Wait!"

I stumbled but caught myself before falling and grabbing my coat downstairs, rushed out.

It was late and cold as I made my way along dark narrow streets to the guesthouse, but I welcomed the walk. By the time I arrived my head had cleared and I had calmed down. I was feeling anger at myself, not Jan. Anger at my immaturity, drinking to excess and ready to have sex with a stranger. For the rest, if Jan had partners who found inflicting pain and being inflicted with it an enhancement of the sexual act, it was their affair, not mine.

After that, Jan and I ran into each other at school now and then and even had lunch together a few times. I marveled at his disguise, visualizing that other fellow, the owner of a closet full of dangerous toys. There in the lunch room he wore his facade of blah grayness, and the subject of our aborted amorous intentions never came up during the rest of my stay in Amsterdam.

Early in November, while I was still in Amsterdam, I received a huge manila envelope filled with material relating to my father's work. It contained plans for a complete revision of his building. Here was the answer to his long silences and distracted look in Paris. The letter he enclosed described what had gone on:

At first, all was chaos for me. Four months and not a foot of dirt

> had been moved. I knew I had to make radical changes but was unsure how to go about it. On my original trip there I was aware of a Zen Buddhist temple that stands next to the site and shares a small woodland to the rear. Being completely occupied in designing my own building I had given it no thought, but this time I was struck at once by its proximity and the effect a contemporary-styled structure would have on it. To put that ancient place in its shadow and relegate it to the past was wrong.
>
> I decided to visit the abbot, Hasumi Kanno, and introduce myself. My Japanese was rudimentary, but his graciousness made up for our lack of communication. Tea was served and then he took me on a tour of the building. Founded in the eighteenth century, it burned to the ground twice, but was rebuilt in its original form. The craftsmanship is superb.
>
> I accepted Hasumi's invitation to return and still later he suggested I live in the temple during the construction. It's convenient and I'm enjoying it, too. The garden, especially, appeals to me. Its serene atmosphere is conducive to quiet thought, and there I conceived my new plans. Most of all, I wanted to create a harmony between that fine old building and my modern one, drawing from traditional Japanese architecture to do it. I now believe International Institute will be a beautiful place.

I was overjoyed by the tranquil tone of his letter. Comparing the two sets of plans demonstrated his versatility. The original building would have been imposing, but the simplicity of the new plans was an illusion. It appeared so because it was deliberately architectural, untouched by artful contrivances sometimes used by builders to maintain their reputations as "progressive" Modernists, a misuse of the word, my father once said. And he was right. A design may be unusual, but it is only when new and practical elements are added that it becomes progressive.

These plans represented a single-level building, divided into two parts around a huge quadrangle, which would become a garden.

The extensiveness of the site made the original multilevel structure pointless, and he liked the idea of a low, unpretentious look, "a good neighbor," he said, to the temple next door.

With a heavily tiled roof and built of Japanese cedar and glass, its overall appearance would be subdued, but the entrance, dramatic. The wide, double doors of glass would be reached by way of a wooden bridge over a stream that made a curving course through the property.

The lobby, smaller now, would be more intimate and comfortable—more like a lounge. Again, rooms for various uses would branch off from it: a theater, an art gallery with a cafe next to it and a library where scholars would be able to conduct research. The Institute planned to stock it with books duplicated in several languages. Conference rooms and an auditorium would occupy the secondary portion of the building with a coffee/*sake* bar installed nearby.

"A civilized addition, don't you think, Caroline?" he had written along a margin.

I could visualize the project and was as impatient as he for all that loveliness to be transferred from plans to reality.

Along with the material he sent me was a sketch of the garden and some remarks on its planned appearance:

> It will fill the quadrangle and portions of it will be visible from every room. With some of the aesthetics of a Japanese garden, it will also have a natural wildness about it. Most of the trees and plants will come from areas of wilderness. With only a little nurturing by caretakers, it will remain unhampered, allowed to be free, to act on its own, with a vitality of its own. I invited Maki Kisho, a famous gardenmaker, to assist me in creating that image. He will do all the landscaping for the project and I'm happy about that.

I was surprised that the garden had captured so much of his attention. But in time, it became as well known for its unusual beauty as International Institute itself. Visitors found that it generated a profound experience for them as they walked through it.

With approval of the new plans expected almost daily, all of the project's preliminary technical details had been accomplished. A geological survey was approved and an office, now filled with equipment, had been constructed at the edge of the site. A Shintoist ceremony was planned for the groundbreaking. Only the final, formal acceptance stood in the way of beginning work.

Architecture was an exciting adventure for my father, but as always he would be embarking on a hard journey. He was never able to simply perform the function he was paid to do and walk away, and this time he had envisioned something that touched him philosophically, as well. Dedicated to internationalism, this edifice, standing with dignity and elegance next to that revered old temple, would speak far more of humanity than technology.

As I reread his letter, I became aware of how I reverted continuously to parental terms in my thinking of David. In a reflective moment such as this, I felt as ever I always had—like a child, a lonely child, not a woman—and yearned to be with my loving father. This I put in my journal, just as in the months that followed I would do again and again.

Late in November I arrived in Luxembourg. The students were familiar with my father's work, having an example of it right there: a museum of art. It gave them more than the usual curiosity, I suppose, although everywhere I went students were inquisitive about him. Knowing I was his daughter, they would ask again and again: "What is David Shaw 'really' like?"

"I'll tell you what he's really like," I said, and described an event from my childhood. In looking through a book of pictures of M.C. Escher's graphics, my father came on one that caught his special attention. He stared at it a long time. Then he phoned Hal, his carpenter friend, and asked him to stop by.

They discussed the possibility of transferring the optical illusion in the picture into a real structure for children to climb around. He drew a simplified version of it with specifications and Hal went to work. When he finished, it was massive, requiring both of them and two more men to make the installation outside my kindergarten room.

The object was a maze of covered passages, stairs and walkways that wound about and ended abruptly here and there. At first, the children were intimidated by it, standing back and checking it out, but in time it became a favorite object of play. Escher had manipulated space and perspective; my father created a piece of whimsy that he hoped would stimulate the imagination of youngsters to think in different ways.

I told them a little about his unassuming lifestyle, hardly in keeping with his fame, it would seem. I described his study, with its view of the sea he loved so much, and walls of shelves filled with books on subjects far afield from architecture—just now, on the culture of Japan. From early childhood, I told them, I heard music emanate from that room. His collection of albums was mainly classical and Mozart was his favorite composer, although he liked jazz, too. But most of all, that was the room where his magnificent architecture originated.

"That is what you are most interested in, I know," I said mischievously. If my students expected me to reveal eccentricities in my father's character, they were wrong. There were none to tell—or rather, none I would tell.

Nearing the end of my stay in Luxembourg, students inquired about the progress of International Institute. I knew no more than they and could only conceal the concern I had about it.

4

The winter holiday for European students was about to begin and I decided to go to Trier in Germany, just across the border. Years earlier while roaming around Europe, Janie and I had stopped there, and though we left the next day, I remembered the medieval look of the city—untarnished as many old places are or as some, not much more than dolled-up Old Towns in the custody of ugly new cities.

I found lodging overlooking a busy market square, then set out to see the sights. Always drawn to architecture, I felt as if I had dropped into Architecture Heaven. Trier was a two-thousand-year-old city and by making a walking tour through it in a few days, I saw remnants of all the epochs of its existence, from Roman walls, bridges and an amphitheater to monuments of Gothic, Renaissance and Baroque designs.

Curious to see where architecture was being taught I asked for directions and found the college. There I met one of the professors, Karl Wegner, and ours was an immediate rapport. He spoke English well and right away we felt comfortable with each other, maybe for me because he reminded me of Andy. They were about the same age, in their late thirties, not very tall and both had beards. They had the same sharp intellect, but they were dissimilar in other ways. Andy was unconventional and amused by the absurdities of life. He found things to laugh about that others didn't see. Karl was formal in his demeanor. Now and then a fleeting smile brightened his expression, but he never laughed.

Our first conversation introduced us to our divergent views about architecture. Unlike my young students, who were becoming emancipated from Europe's history and traditional ways of life, Karl's background held him fast. While they looked forward with eagerness to creating a new world for themselves, Karl was content to remain within inflexible boundaries that included architecture.

"It shows us our place. We must not lose that," he said. "Only by knowing our place can we know who we are."

"But we live in the present, Karl, and that can be more exciting than clinging to the past."

I tried to understand, but my background was different. The history of my country is short, and my own history non-existent. Change is difficult when there are great historical precedents. I didn't have those hurdles to overcome, and I could see many aspects of modern life in different ways, architecture certainly so, even as abstract art. That was impossible for him.

There was nothing we could agree on. He dismissed every contemporary version of Modernism, equally disdainful of "your East Coast architects and your gimmicky California builders."

"Karl, they're trying out fresh new ideas that go beyond Modernism. They themselves are rejecting much of the Modernism that originally came from Bauhaus, your own German roots. They are not frivolous, but serious intellectuals using scientific knowledge and artistic talent to create their work. Look at Helmut Jahn. He started in Nuremberg with all your European principles and now he says each generation must build its own city. Isn't that a wonderful challenge to us?"

"That man has lost his way," he said.

I roared with laughter. "Jahn is one of America's leading builders of skyscrapers. There's one in Frankfurt—the tallest in Europe. It's extremely complicated. Let's go see it!"

"I hate skyscrapers," he said.

"Well, are you familiar with Meier's museum on the Main in

Frankfurt? I've read that it has many novel concepts."

"I won't go to Frankfurt, Caroline."

"Okay, how about Berlin? That's an exciting city for new architecture. Let's go!"

"No!"

But by now I was avid to go. I was already making plans for the trip when Karl interrupted me.

"Caroline, you don't understand. I don't dislike all American architects' work. Wright and Kahn didn't totally abandon history. Some others haven't, either. Your father's architecture is inspiring. But I don't want to travel. Please stay with me in Trier."

In my enthusiasm I had failed to see that our conversation was making Karl uneasy. I didn't understand why, but if I were going to go anywhere it would have to be by myself and at some other time. At last I had enough sense to stop, and I didn't bring up the subject again.

Besides, I was having too good a time to invest any of it in disagreements. Karl told me he had lived in Trier all his life and offered to be my guide around the city. He was on holiday now, too, and we quickly became close companions. He picked me up each morning and we were together all day. In the evenings we went to classical programs put on by the university music department and to films, which fortunately were American, so I didn't have to suffer through dialogue I couldn't understand.

Within a few days after my arrival I was sharing my bed with Karl and in a few more, he moved into the apartment. For me, it was an enjoyable transitory episode in my life, and to promote that understanding I tried to keep our conversations from becoming serious.

One that was very serious came about unexpectedly. Wherever we went people knew him. They would greet him and sometimes stop to talk.

"Everyone likes you, Karl."

"Yes, and I like them."

"There must be more to it than that."

"Yes. You see, I don't have any family of my own. Trier is my family."

"I don't understand."

"Well, my people, all of them except my mother, were murdered by the Nazis."

"Was your family Jewish?"

"No. Communists."

"What happened to your mother?"

"A terrible thing happened to her, Caroline. She was saved by a farmer and kept hidden until the war was over. Then she remained with him for several years after the war's end. She was a young girl, and people said he kept her like his prisoner, abusing and raping her. But nothing was done about it. When she became pregnant, though, he threw her out and she came to Trier for help. Here I was born, but she died in childbirth. I was placed in an orphanage until I was in high school, when I found work to pay for my keep and education."

I had read countless stories of the horrors of that era, but now I had heard a personal account that left me unable to respond. So I remained silent, embracing him to at least let him know how sad I felt. In order to go on with life, a victim of such events sometimes becomes aloof from them, and now I understood better Karl's shell of stoicism that protected him from feeling the depths of his sorrow.

"Look, Caroline," he said, as if to reassure me, "it's all right. I have a good life in Trier. The people here want me to forget the past and be happy."

"Can you forget, Karl?"

"No."

"Are you happy?"

"Yes," he said.

I wondered about that, but could say nothing more without feeling cruel. How could he be happy there? How could he even remain there, the site of such heinous crimes? But for Karl, there was a binding connection with his town that held him captive. Later, I learned how true that was. Though my intention had been not to reveal anything of my own background, I now felt I owed it to Karl to tell him something about myself.

"I was adopted," I said. "I have no family history. That's not as bad as your story, of course, but it's sad for me, too, having a blank space where my past should be. What must I do? I have no interest in tracing minutiae that may lie in my background. I live in the moment."

He looked solemn, so reaching up to him, I kissed him.

"This is one of those nice moments, Karl," I said.

One day he took me to see an old burgher's house where Karl Marx was born, not so much to see the house but the treasures it held. *Das Kapital*, with hand-written notes in the margins, was there, as well as the *Communist Manifesto*. I didn't know Marx had been a poet, but volumes of his poetry were on display, too. Karl told me that although he was not a communist, he went there now and then because it gave him a symbolic communion with his family.

He was sharing that with me as another way in which we might grow closer. I was affected by the tragedy that had been inflicted on him, but I tried hard not to deepen our relationship with personal recollections. It was not what I wanted. Soon he understood, and by silent agreement our interlude remained just that—without any hope for a future together. Or so I thought.

Just as I had sensed the pain concealed within him, so Karl was witness to occasions of strange behavior in me. Mine was a playful sexuality usually, but sometimes, lying beside him, I would slip into a deep, deep reverie. I would become still and non-functioning, lost to my nice friend who cared about me. As I would slowly come out of it, I would see him looking at me as from a great distance.

"Caroline!" he would call to me. "Where are you? Come back to me."

The episodes probably lasted only moments. Then I would break into tears and ask Karl's forgiveness for worrying him, but I gave him no explanation. In my heart I knew that I had been transported to the place where I most wanted to be—in David's arms.

I was nearing the end of my stay, and after New Year's I would have to leave. On the evening of the holiday, we wanted to celebrate, but we also wanted to be alone together, so finally we solved the dilemma by doing both.

We walked through the Roman gateway called Porta Nigra, which leads into a central square, and there we had dinner in a restaurant that had become my favorite. Then we joined the revelers on the street. But we were bored, so Karl bought a bottle of brandy and we returned to the apartment.

I turned on a jazz station, and once we were out of our clothes and snugly ensconced on the featherbed, we lay listening to the music and drinking.

"Let's do this properly, Caroline," he said. "Let's take a nap and then wake up a little later and come together as the bells toll the magic hour."

But how could things work out that way? By the dim glow of the night-light we kept passing the bottle between us, and becoming unsteady, I dribbled some down my chin and onto my chest. When I reached for a tissue, Karl stopped me, and leaning over, licked up the spilled liquor. That felt good, so I poured more over my breasts. He licked that up, too, and kissed me again and again.

From then on, the idea of napping was abandoned and our coming together came early. The bells probably tolled, but we slept soundly through them until morning.

Karl looked stricken with regret.

"Caroline," he said, "We didn't do it properly!"

I wanted to laugh, but I could see he was serious.

"I was going to propose to you," he said.

"Oh, no!"

"Caroline, I love you."

"Don't, Karl. Enjoy me but don't love me."

In the afternoon we went to a party given by the head of Karl's department. No one appeared giddy with celebration of the new year. We were moving closer to a new century, but the general agreement was that we were, in every possible way, destroying our world, as if we were hell-bent to get it over and done with.

"Doesn't anyone have a good word for this New Year's Day?" one of Karl's colleagues asked.

"I do," he said, putting his arm around me. "Look what the holiday brought me."

Along with pastries, mulled wine was served, and I almost broke down when I tasted the warm liquor. It tasted nothing like *sake*, but it reminded me of my father, and there I was again, the child-woman, longing intensely to be with him. Karl had become sensitive to my mood swings, and though he had no idea what caused them, he never asked, and we left the party early.

That evening, as if we had not finished our earlier conversation, he began again. "Caroline, it is said that love is infectious. Let me infect you."

I laughed. "Karl, I'm already infected. I have strong ties elsewhere."

"How can that be? You have been with me every day for two weeks. We are so close. What is different?"

"What is different? I'll try to tell you: When I sleep I sometimes dream of being with him. When I am awake and momentarily unoccupied, I long for him. I hear his voice in my head. My eyes tear in their desire to see him. My nostrils want to breathe his scent. My arms ache for wanting to embrace him, my hands to touch him, my face to place next to his. My vagina moistens with desire to feel his penis within me. Every part of me—my mind, my heart, my body—belong only to him."

"Then how can you give yourself so freely and lovingly to me?"

"Why not? What I feel for my beloved remains apart, inviolate, unchanging. Time and distance are my enemies. They prevent my being with him for long periods, and I crave warm, human relationships. Isn't that natural?"

He didn't answer, and then he began to cry. A few times in my life I had seen tears in men's eyes, but I'd never seen one weep before, and now my normally stony-faced friend was crying uncontrollably. I held him close to me and waited for him to stop.

"You know I do care for you, Karl, but not as you wish me to. I must leave. In time the memory will fade and you will resume your life."

"No, you have spoiled me for any other woman, Caroline. I will never forget you."

The next day both of us were depressed as I prepared to leave for Barcelona. I begged him to go as far as Frankfurt with me, where we could have another day together before I would have to board a plane for Spain. He may have wanted to, but could not, and our delightful holiday came to an unhappy end. It was not my doing, but I regretted the part I had played in it. Karl had been "abandoned" by his family, left motherless in infancy, and now I had appeared, giving myself, as he had said, freely and lovingly, and again committing the same cruel deed, abandoning him. Abandonment: Was that not the theme of my own life?

It was necessary to spend the night in Frankfurt before departing for Barcelona, and finding myself alone once again, I had more time than I wanted to think about my life. It was not going well, and I knew I would not continue long in the career I had created for myself. Like a wandering minstrel, I was singing the praises of great American architects, a weak adjunct to my father's monumental work. I could do better with my mind and time.

The activities of daily life made temporary escapes from loneliness, but sometimes those escapes were in the arms of strangers. I was no older than many of my students who, with rare exceptions, were men, and overtures were made to me in every college. I valiantly resisted, although they were often attractive and I was tempted. It was not that I was leaving a trail of sexual affairs, but I was troubled by the ease with which I had entered the liaisons to which I did succumb.

Afterward, I would be assailed by confusion. My father might forgive me, for he was my father, but as David, would he want me as his lover? Would I ever commingle my relationship with him? Sleeping in his warm embrace had forever destroyed any possible acceptance of a solitary, sexually deprived life. Yet my needs were being met by men other than him. Was that how it was destined to be? The thought repelled me.

My melancholy was transmitted to Andy in phone conversations. Without him to talk to throughout the months of my journey across Europe, I would not have done well, or even perhaps, have carried on until its end.

"I feel like a penitent believer," I told him, "confessing my transgression, seeking forgiveness from the Heavenly Father through his intermediary, and then with soul washed clean, committing the same sin all over again."

"You have nothing to confess, Caroline," Andy said. "You're an appealing woman. You have no hostility toward men; you like them. They sense that and feel good with you. You've told me you're careful in your choice of partners and you make sure you're protected from disease. I don't know if you'd be better off trying to curb your strong sexual drive. Why can't you accept your humanness?"

Our conversation appeared to end on a consoling note, yet my journal continued to search for a better answer than an easy acceptance of my "humanness."

5

Frigid weather gripped all of Europe that winter, and Barcelona, with its milder temperatures, would be a good place to be. Disappointment was in store for me there for another reason. A few days before my arrival, a fire had destroyed a section of the college that housed the school of architecture, and transferring instruction to another facility was going to take an uncertain number of weeks. A date was set for a single general lecture, but in the meantime I was out of a job.

I liked being in Barcelona. Janie and I had spent most of one of our summer vacations in Spain, enjoying everything about the country, particularly the Moorish quality that lent enchantment to every aspect of life: Its arts and architecture, its distinctive cuisine, and in Barcelona we "discovered" the work of Antoni Gaudi.

We had just come out of a restaurant when we glanced across the street and saw one of his buildings. Both of us stood rooted to the spot staring at what, at first, appeared bizarre; but it didn't take us long to adjust to the differentness of Gaudi's creations, and we toured the city seeking other of his constructions. Each had its strangely contorted lines and spaces, often with facades that undulated in sinuous cadence across walls tiled in brilliant abstract patterns. We gazed in wonderment at the Church of the Holy Family, over which the artist, sculptor and architect that he was had labored for the last forty-three years of his life to build. Stone, nothing but stone, yet that towering edifice took on a living vitality before our eyes.

When I was still very young, my father took me to Corona del Mar, a seaside town in Southern California, to see the curious architecture of a residence. I knew nothing then of world-famous buildings, but now I remembered his having told me the house was a replication of the style of a certain Spanish genius. He meant Gaudi, of course, and now having seen both his work and that of Bart Prince, who had built the house, I knew how true that was. Prince's talents were recognized when he was young, and now in middle age, he was producing art in his work. In that structure, built inside and out with finely crafted laminated wood, Prince produced a continuous movement in the swirling patterns of the wood, just as Gaudi had done in other materials. Many architects strive for that sense of motion. I would remember to tell my students about the influence of their architectural genius on my own distinguished American builder.

The arrangement that had been made for me was excellent. Held in a photography lecture hall, equipment was available to show my slides and excerpts from films. I chose my subject carefully, for it would be my only chance to expound on my favorite topic, Deconstructivism, and on an American group of architects known as Site, who had created an example of the new architecture in Spain.

Heading Site are James Wines and Alison Sky who, like Gehry and Meier, are at the forefront of this movement. They didn't start out as architects. Both were artists. As a result, their renderings are in themselves artistic work. Wines has also written on the topic. In fact, his *De-Architecture*, published in the mid-eighties, predated much of the radical changes that were to occur in modern construction. A major aspect impelled Wines: He saw parallels between the new architecture and the unusual art being performed—work such as Christo's—as an imaginative departure from the past.

Major projects of Site are in as dissimilar places as Kisokoma-Kogen in Japan and Chattanooga, Tennessee. In Spain the architecture was for Avenue 5, one of the five pedestrian corridors which lead to various pavilions of World Expo, 1992, in Seville. Because of the Guadalquivir River's presence there, water was used as the design's theme. A thousand-foot undulating wall of glass, covered by a flowing sheet of water, was constructed. Vine-covered trellises and a forest of trees give a lushness to the scene. With diagrams and photographs, the students could see the manner in which Site incorporated nature with architecture. A few had seen Avenue 5 when they attended Expo, and I urged the others to go.

My lecture went well and when I prepared to leave, offers were made to drive me to the guesthouse. But I didn't have a chance to choose. One of the students, not bothering to ask, just went ahead gathering my things, boxing the slides and even replacing papers in my portfolio. I watched him, amused at his boldness. When he finished he faced me and smiled. I was startled for a moment. It was as if I were looking at a masculine image of myself. Though his skin was several shades lighter than mine, his eyes, like mine, were large and brown with thick brows and his smile was broad and friendly.

He introduced himself—Luis Lorca Koolhaas; the last, he said, was his mother's family name.

"There's a famous Dutch architect, Rem Koolhaas. Are you related to him?"

"No. I wish so. *Avant-garde, si?*"

Picking up all my paraphernalia, he indicated that I proceed ahead of him. "*Por favor,*" he said.

The others had left. If I were to be taken home, this was it. I looked at my escort. I could see no reason not to accept his kind offer and went out to his car with him.

It was then that I hesitated. At the curb was a Rolls Royce. In the front seat sat two men, not dressed in uniforms, but Luis identified them as his chauffeur, Piero, and his bodyguard, Carlos. Piero jumped out and opened the door for us.

I didn't get in right away. "Why do you have these people?" I asked.

"*Protección.*"

"Protection from what?"

In a mélange of English and Spanish and what sounded like Dutch, Luis begged me to get in the car, promising to tell me. The poignancy of his story affected me greatly. Great wealth is seldom thought to be a misfortune, yet in Luis's life, it was. Born into riches through his maternal grandfather, who still lived in the Netherlands, the family fortune was made in the diamond business. While on vacation in Spain, when she was still a young woman, Luis's mother met his father, and they were married. Their lives were blissfully happy until Luis was sixteen, when he was kidnapped and held for ransom.

To reinforce their threat to kill Luis, his kidnappers cut off a portion of a finger each day that he was held. He showed me his right hand. The small finger was gone and the first joint portion of the next was missing. His abductors were never found, and the ransom, a fortune in itself, was never recovered. From then on, the concern of his parents made a prisoner of Luis. The effort was warranted, as attempts to seize him continued to occur from time to time.

Two years later, a greater tragedy befell him. His parents, traveling in the north between Altamira and Burgos, took a route through a perilous mountain pass and died.

"The road...," Luis began in English, then reverting to his native language, he continued, "*In España es el camino mas peligroso.*"

As the accident was reconstructed, it appeared that due to the dense fog, they had driven carefully behind a truck, using its red taillights as a guide to stay on the narrow, curving road. Suddenly the lights must have vanished, for just before their own car went over a cliff, the truck had overturned on the other side of the road.

By the time we reached the guesthouse, I knew Luis well. Younger than I, his earlier bravado was a sham. I listened to him as in his medley of languages he described his hopes and fears.

"I want to be a builder of beautiful places. I want to be a great architect!" he said, "But I have *muchas problemas*, Carolina. People are afraid with me. They see danger to themselves."

When we had deposited my things, he said we would go out to eat. "First, *tapas y vino.* A good place, *animado*," he said.

It was not exactly an invitation. Like his escorting me home, he simply stated what we would do next, but tapas and wine sounded nice, so off we went.

The tapas bar was *mucho animado*, and we sat in the warm, noisy atmosphere eating and drinking, his buddies on either side of us. At dinner they sat at an adjoining table. Then he said he would take me to his home, but I refused, and he finally gave up trying.

"I want to see you tomorrow, Carolina," he said.

Only momentarily did I weigh being sensible and safe by not seeing Luis again as against the possible excitement and pleasure of it. There was no real contest; there seldom was. Loneliness drove me—I knew it was that. I longed to fill the emptiness of my life, and the sexual part of it was only an aspect of that need.

"What do you suggest, Luis?"

"La Costa Brava. We will drive to the border, then return. Only a few days. Come with me, *querida*."

Luis made his appearance before I had even awakened. Dressing hurriedly, I packed a small bag and we left. The car, being equipped with all manner of conveniences, had a pull-out table, and we had juice and hot coffee and sugar-coated rolls. While we ate, Piero slowly traversed Barcelona's outskirts and drove northeast onto the coastal route.

Within an hour we were in a town called Blanes and we stopped to look around. Set on a bay, the brightly painted boats of the fishing fleet are moored there, creating a picture postcard sight. On a hilltop overlooking Blanes is a medieval castle, and Luis and I went up there to get a close look.

It was winter, not the season for tourists. The town was still, resting before the coming onslaught of visitors. All the better for us, Luis said, and he was right. It was at Blanes that the spectacular scenery of the Costa Brava really begins, and we felt as if we had it all to ourselves.

The Mediterranean, deep azure, so beautiful, was a sharp contrast to the reddish-brown of the land, the pine-wooded hills and rugged cliffs above it. Along the jagged shoreline were little coves and sandy beaches and a few times we stopped to take a walk. Piero and Carlos went with us—now not so much to guard their employer, but to enjoy a walk themselves.

The Costa Brava was inhabited thousands of years ago and each of the small towns we passed through, some mere villages, had remnants of those early people. The Romans had been there. Plenty of ruins testify to that. Where in Europe, even northern Africa, are there not Roman ruins? There are still a few thousand-year-old churches to be seen, too, and the remains of fortifications that long ago were attempts to protect, but usually failed.

In Tossa de Mar we climbed to Vila Vella, a well-preserved Old Town in the headlands above the sea. Now, in the off-season, the charm of the ancient town was visible, hardly how it would appear in summer, its streets filled with sightseers, beachcombers and snorkelers.

From Tossa it is only a dozen miles to San Felíu. However, the short distance became an adventure when the road narrowed and there were corkscrew curves all the way. The ride gave us some dramatic views, but also made us aware of Piero's skillful driving.

Luis knew a considerable amount about the area we were going through. San Felíu, he said, was founded by Charlemagne, but relics from a far more distant past, the Iron Age, have been found there. It is the biggest town on the coast and even has a bullring. The four of us had a late lunch, tasty *paella*, then we took a walk. I had become accustomed to being with my companions, and we chatted amiably, though humorously. Piero and Carlos spoke a little English, but mostly Spanish, and when I didn't understand, Luis made serious attempts to interpret, but his own forays in English often left me more confused. It didn't matter—I was having a fine time.

Farther along, just past a town called S'Agaró, a break in the cliffs opened to a breathtaking sight. Seeing the gorgeous expanse of the Bay of Palamós, it was hard to imagine that it has been the victim of horrifying events throughout its history. In the sixteenth century it was Barbarossa and a Turkish fleet that destroyed it.

Palamós recovered, but again in the seventeenth century the French sailed into the harbor and destroyed the town. Next came the British in the eighteenth century. Finally, in the Civil War of the twentieth century, General Franco bombed it unmercifully from the sea. Each time Palamós rose from its ashes and lived again. Its great natural beauty cannot be extinguished. Once again a thriving town, it rises high above the bay—a striking sight indeed.

As we journeyed still farther north the terrain changed. Part of the time Piero drove inland, parallel to the sea, through forests of cork and pine and oak, and we opened the windows to breathe the crisp, cool air scented with woodland fragrance. Then we passed through areas of vineyards, olive and almond groves, all dormant and waiting for spring. The view of the sea was cut off from time to time, and I grew sleepy and curled up beside Luis. As he took me in his arms and kissed me, I snuggled up and fell asleep.

Some time passed, I didn't know how long, when I felt Luis's lips on mine again as he gently woke me. We had reached a town called Cadaqués, and he wanted to show it to me. It was a pretty town with whitewashed houses and resorts, lush with landscaping, even now in winter. We walked out onto its small beach, but didn't go far. Unlike the soft white sandy shores of others, this one was covered with a coarse red-blue slate, interesting-looking but uncomfortable to walk on.

Cadaqués had a special significance to Luis, for his mother took him there during vacations when he was young. She was a good friend of Gala, Salvador Dali's adored wife, who spent a lot of time in Cadaqués. Luis wanted us to stay there for the night rather than going to the border town of Port Bou. I liked the idea. Riding was becoming tiresome. Besides, I hoped we could spend a little of the next day at Figueras, where Dali was born, where he had spent most of his life and where much of his surrealistic art was created.

"In Barcelona, you will come to my house, Carolina, and I will show you my Dali *colección*, many originals given to me by my mother. You can have any you want."

It was Carlos who recommended our hotel. He and his wife had their honeymoon there, he told me.

"You are on constant duty to Luis, Carlos. Don't you miss her?"

He laughed. "No, I see her every day. She is a maid at Luis's house."

He described the hotel's Basque cuisine and the nightclub within the hotel, where talented Gypsy dancers performed Flamenco every night, and where there was a group of good musicians who played for those who wished to dance.

It was just as he said. Located a little way out of town on a cliff overlooking the sea, its decor was traditionally Spanish. Ornately carved chandeliers hung from thick, dark beams on the ceilings and tapestries of historic events covered the walls. The furniture, too, had an old-world look—heavy and elaborately decorated.

Luis invited Piero and Carlos to join us for dinner, and they ordered an assortment of Catalan dishes for me to try. Fish dominated their selections, one of which I was familiar with. When Janie and I were in Spain, I ate it whenever it was on the menu. Called *zarzuela*, it was composed of fish, fried, then cooked in onions, tomatoes, wine and spices. It was still my favorite. My new friends ordered a special winter treat—*angulas*—eels, tiny and silvery, cooked in olive oil with lots of garlic and hot chili peppers. That I liked, too, and the hard-shelled clams, steamed in a sauce with still more garlic—*almejas marineras*, they said. The bread, freshly baked, was wonderful and we drank glass after glass of the unbottled light house wine.

After dinner we went to the nightclub where Luis ordered a sherry called *oloroso* that was rich-flavored, dark and sweet. We watched the dancers, and then, when they left, a small combo appeared. They played Spanish and American music and right away, Luis stood up. As usual, he didn't ask me to dance; he just motioned to me. He was a good dancer, at first sedate and formal. Then he held me close, his cheek on mine.

"Carolina," he whispered when the music stopped, "Now we go to our room, *si?*"

"*Si*," I said.

A fire burned in the fireplace. Flowers and a decanter of wine were on the table. The bed, with a headboard deeply carved in plump little cherubs, was not very big—small, in fact, but high from the floor. Then I noticed that on one side of our room was a door to an adjoining room, obviously for Piero and Carlos. I tried it. It was unlocked.

"They must be able to come in if there is an emergency," Luis said. "But they will not disturb us. Don't worry."

"How can you live like this?" I asked him.

"What can I do? My money is a curse."

Ironic as it was, he spoke the truth. I proposed an idea.

"Luis, give it away!"

He laughed. "How?"

"Easy! Give your property to a worthy cause. Set up a foundation to contribute your money to those in need. Leave an amount that will give you a sense of security, but not enough to make you vulnerable to criminals. You can pursue your career with peace of mind. Earn what your creative talent deserves. Freed from fear, you'll have a happy life."

I thought my idea an excellent one and would have expanded on it, but he interrupted me. "No more talk," he said.

By now, I understand Luis's way of speaking and was not annoyed at what appeared to be rudeness. He didn't want a serious discussion. He wanted to make love to me, and I let him know I was willing. I put my arms around him and kissed him.

When we were undressed, he lifted me up onto the bed and went around to the other side to get in with me. He looked at me.

"Ah," he whispered, "*muy hermosa.*"

From then on, he spoke only Spanish. I not only didn't mind—I liked it. The setting was romantic, the softly suggestive intonations of the language were romantic and I was anticipating an enjoyable night. We lay in each other's arms, kissing, touching and feeling good together. His erection was certainly impressive and I was aroused, too. Moving close to him, I pressed my body against him.

Then something happened. His erection faltered, and knowing I was aware of it, he had an expression of absolute misery. He turned away from me, and in so doing, fell out of bed! I couldn't help it—

the laughter just bubbled out of me. His curses, I assumed, were directed at the bed's narrow size. But he wasn't injured and got back in.

"Luis, put your arms around me," I said.

He did, but his originally proud display was virtually gone, and he was immobilized. Dismayed, I lay waiting and wondering how I could help him. I caressed him. I kissed his sadly diminished penis. To no avail. My gestures might have been wildly reassuring to another. Not to Luis. Then I raised my knees and taking his hand, placed it between my legs.

"Do you like it, Luis?" I whispered.

"*Si.*"

"Show me."

And he did recover, only to fail again. Nothing like that had ever happened to me. What was going on here? Luis had told me that he put women in two categories: those who would not go out with him, knowing his past and the fearful possibility of being abducted when with him, and those who appeared only too eager—the latter raising his suspicions that his great wealth was their motive.

Unlike either of those, did I intimidate him, being the person I was, uninhibited by nature and ready to share a loving relationship "with no strings attached"? I liked Luis for himself, for his sweetness, his earnest desire to make something of his life despite its melancholy and peculiar background. The situation baffled me until I realized this virile man might still be a virgin. It didn't dampen my desire. But what was I to do?

"Luis," I said finally, "Please let's not be in such a hurry. We have all night. I'd like a little wine. *Si?*" I added, smiling

He poured some for both of us, a good bit more for himself, I noticed, and we sat up in bed, the comforter draped around us. I was determined that we succeed. It was not just face-saving for Luis that I was concerned about, I was aroused by this man despite his inexperience. As we sipped the wine, I told him about a funny article I had read describing eccentric animal behavior.

"We think of species other than ourselves as acting instinctively in courtship and mating. Not true. Do you know rhinos can spend a month at foreplay and an hour copulating before they reach a climax? The article told about a pygmy hippo that in twenty years of captivity couldn't figure out sex. He didn't know where to put it. He'd try her ear or under her 'arm'—never the right place."

He laughed at my story. Maybe the wine helped, too. Anyway, he relaxed and at last made what was perhaps his first conquest. But that was the end of our night of love. At the height of his orgasm, he gave an agonizing shriek and fell onto the bed in great distress.

In an instant Piero and Carlos burst into the room. There they stood, loyal bodyguards that they were, both only in their shorts, brandishing pistols menacingly. The three spoke in Spanish. Then Carlos left.

I felt giggly but controlled myself. "What's wrong, Luis?" I asked.

"A back *problema*," he moaned. "I was injured playing tennis years ago. I have wrenched my back."

What a finale, I thought, feeling sorry for my inept lover.

After Carlos returned with a heating pad and aspirin, he and Piero left. In a little while Luis fell asleep. I sighed with relief and went to sleep, too. In the morning he was much improved, both in his back and morale. This time his love-making went off without a hitch.

Then he made a pronouncement. "Carolina, we will be married and you will live with me in Barcelona."

"Luis! We have just met. You barely know me."

"How long must I know you to know I love you."

It was a shocking moment. I had never thought of myself as a *femme fatale*, yet within days two men had insisted I remain with them. I said nothing more, wondering how I was to tell Luis that on the following day I would leave Spain and we would never see each other again?

Karl's romantic attachment had been traumatic for him and worrisome for me. Now I had Luis to deal with. I was nervous and wanted to return to Barcelona quickly to arrange my departure, but we were close to Figueras. He knew I was interested in surrealism and the Teatro Museo Dali. I decided not to raise an objection and we left early to go there.

Despite my anxiety, I enjoyed the museum. So did my companions. We walked about the main gallery, enchanted by the fantasy of Dali's art. Even in old age, he remained the *enfant terrible*, continuously jarring the art world as he produced one astounding example of his creativity after another. In his Teatro Museo, the vast collection included sculptures as well as paintings and the range was from bizarre, even revolting, depictions to the ethereally beautiful.

Gala, his lifelong model, was in picture after picture, usually nude, either alone or as part of more complex compositions. One of the latter fascinated all of us. At first it appeared to be an abstraction, merely a jumble of large colored blocks, although the nude figure of Gala was imposed on the foreground. It was a pretty picture in itself, but then as we stepped back, it was transformed into a sharply defined portrait of Abraham Lincoln!

When we left, Piero drove us to a cafe that served *sopa de pescado*, a soup filled with tiny clams and prawns, better than French *bouillabaisse*, I thought. From there, we started our trip back to Barcelona, arriving in the late afternoon. It was then that I told Luis I would be leaving the next day for Morocco.

"I will go with you, Carolina," he said.

"No, I am going alone."

"When will you come back to me?"

"You'll have my answer tomorrow," I said, and in my mind I was already penning a note that would try to make him more realistic about our relationship.

I said goodbye to Piero and Carlos, and at the door of the guesthouse, I kissed Luis, for I did feel affection for him.

"I am afraid," he said.

"Of what?"

"You will not come back to me."

I kissed him again, saying nothing, and ran into the guesthouse without looking back.

In the years that followed I made no attempt to see Luis again, fearful of tampering with his strong feelings for me. But I did think of him with tenderness and would have liked to know all was going well for him, but dreaded the possibility that it was not. Would he take my suggestion and divest himself of his fortune and free himself of its burden? It seemed unlikely.

6

After my Spanish trip with Janie, she had returned to school and I had continued alone, crossing the Straits of Gibraltar to Morocco, where I had settled into a culture I had never known. In Marrakesh I had become friendly with a woman my age who was a belly-dancer, so it was Marrakesh I remembered best. Now, with two weeks to go before my stint in Aix-en-Provence, I wondered if it would be the same.

Then, the heat had been excessive, a hundred degrees most days. Although the nearby Great Atlas Mountains were snow-covered much of the year, the city was inland from both the Atlantic and Mediterranean and enveloped by the heat. In winter, Marrakesh would be much warmer than Barcelona, but not hot, a good place to thaw after Europe's chill.

Besides, I wanted to distance myself from my recent experiences with Karl and Luis. I had tried carefully to be direct with them and impress on them that I didn't want a permanent attachment. Thus, the similarity of their responses to me was unsettling. It was not just the uninhibited nature of my sexuality. Reining in the naturalness of my behavior was impossible. I could only be the person I was. Sex is not love—they knew that. Why had they at once become serious? Weary of thinking about it, I decided it was simply the strange allure of the unattainable.

That evening I called David and asked him to join me in Morocco. Without giving the idea a moment's thought, he told me it would be impossible. Why impossible? I was well aware of the impasse that had occurred with his new Institute plans. The pleasure we had felt about his revisions evaporated as weeks turned into a month, two, now almost three, and the approval he had expected quickly did not come. The directors of the institution preferred the original, thoroughly contemporary design, even though drawings depicting both, with the temple included in them, clearly indicated the glaring disharmony the earlier one would impose. My father's integrity was involved here, and I knew he would not budge from the changes he had made. Sometimes, in exasperation, he spoke of requesting a termination of his contract and returning to California.

But he didn't do that. He continued to live in the temple despite the fact that construction had not begun. His increasing fluency in Japanese made for good communication between him and Hasumi. The abbot told him about his life: Never fully recovered from a crippling childhood disease and unable to have an active physical life, he found his niche in the priesthood. After years spent in a Zen Buddhist college learning to chant and handle the services, he became a prominent member of a sect that David liked. He said it was free of many religious austerities and asceticism.

"I know he is in pain the way he leans heavily on his cane, but his stoicism is admirable," he told me. The two became good friends.

As the stalemate continued, Hasumi tried to reassure him. "It's the Japanese way," he told him. "Be patient."

I worried about that long interim of inactivity. How was he filling his time? Once, in what had become our infrequent conversations, he told me a little of what his life was like. It sounded pitifully dull. I knew Hasumi was trying to distract him. Every afternoon they played *shogi*, a game similar to chess, and he read. By now he was able to read books in the original Japanese that dealt with the country's history and culture. I made suggestions: films, theater. He made no response. I asked if I could come to Tokyo.

He reminded me of my own responsibilities. "You have a schedule to keep and work of your own to do, Caroline."

"I'll gladly give it up if you want me to be with you."

"We'll talk about it again," he said, but we didn't.

David was deeply enamored of Japan, and I had consoled myself that some of his time was surely being spent becoming familiar with Tokyo and looking around at its stunning architecture. Now I believed differently—that he had sequestered himself in the temple, trapped in an endless waiting game. Was he not lonely with only Hasumi for company? Even Walt, tired of waiting for work to begin, had a month earlier returned to California.

I begged him now to give himself a holiday. "I miss you so much. Please come to Marrakesh."

His reply was tinged with irritation. "I told you, Caroline, that's impossible. I'm not leaving Japan."

The tone of his voice took me aback. I could think of nothing more to say and our conversation ended abruptly. Then I tried Andy, hoping he would want to share a holiday with me. His answer was the same as it had been previous times when I asked him to come to Europe—no.

"Andy, I miss you. Don't you miss me?"

"Yes, but I can't come right now."

"That's what David said, too. Maybe neither of you likes me anymore."

"Caroline! You know both of us love you. You and I...," he started, then stopped, and I asked him what he was about to say.

"We'll talk on the phone more often, darling. Go to Morocco. You'll have a nice vacation."

I didn't think that was what he was going to say, but the endearing sound of his voice did cheer me some. Halfheartedly, but not knowing what else to do, I took a boat to Morocco. In Marrakesh I stayed at the same hotel as I had before, and as soon as I was settled, I asked if Liza Baladi was still working there as a belly-dancer. She was, and a little later we got together.

Since last I'd seen her she had matured into a gorgeous woman with a voluptuous body. Also, she had become a prostitute. Men from

France and some from England came to Marrakesh on business—or pleasure—and were attracted to Liza. Along with her native Arabic, she spoke French well and enough English to get by nicely.

"Why do you do it, Liza?" I asked.

"They pay a high price for me," she said. "I'm saving my money. Some day I'll quit."

On days when she had no assignations, we went out together as we had before, and we did all the same interesting things. I liked walking along the ancient stone streets of the *medina*, but wouldn't attempt it alone again, having once so wound myself around that intricate maze it took me a frighteningly long time to find my way out. Liza had no family except cousins who lived in a quarter called the *mellah*, where we liked taking a respite. Her relatives were hospitable and always served us glasses of fresh mint tea.

Once a week a Berber *souk* near Marrakesh was the site of a camel sale and on other days at nearby *souks*, cattle and sheep sales were transacted. We hired a driver a few times to go to them. That was serious business, but for me it was pure entertainment.

Other things went on at the *souks* beside animal sales. At one of them a "dentist" was in attendance. I watched a man sit down and have a tooth pulled with an instrument that resembled a mechanic's pliers. Obviously it worked—the patient was smiling with relief when he left.

Sometimes handmade craft objects were for sale. At one of those Liza bought metal and coral forehead ornaments for herself and me. It was fun to watch the essential bargaining and then the satisfied expressions both had when it was over.

Because I chose to wear Arabic dress and because of my color, venders would often address me in Arabic and then Liza would have to come to my rescue, explaining that I was an American. That always brought pleased looks, Morocco being one of the rare places in the world where we are liked and made welcome.

The square of Djemaa El Fna was the place I liked best in Marrakesh and I went there every day for an hour before sunset. The colorful atmosphere intrigued me and I could enjoy it fully, mingling with the crowd, because my appearance led everyone to accept me as a native.

Among the first to arrive were craftspeople of every kind—leather and wood workers, basket weavers and pottery makers—who quickly put out their merchandise. A few "blue men" always appeared, displaying the colorful rugs that, in the dyeing, turned their skins a deep shade of blue, as well. Then there were the entertainers—musicians, dancers, jugglers, who strolled about the huge square. A snake charmer, with his basket of writhing serpents, was always there, too, putting on his act to earn a bit of money.

Along with the music and singing was the hum of voices with occasional guttural cries, that grew louder as the area filled with people. Then, at sunset, the crowd would disperse, and I, too, would go back to the hotel to have a drink with Liza at the bar, and later observe her performance in the clubroom. She was magnificent. No wonder she aroused men to want her for their own, even at her enormous prices.

One day as we sat at the bar, the three musicians who accompanied Liza in her dances began to play. One had a rounded goat-skin-covered instrument he called a *bendir* that produced an exciting pulsing resonance. The other two had simple stringed instruments.

"Do you remember any of the belly-dance lessons I gave you, Caroline?" Liza asked.

"Maybe."

As the musicians played, we danced together, and watching Liza undulate her body to the rhythm of the music, I imitated her.

"You haven't forgotten! Let's practice for a few days. I'll give you my most seductive costume and you can perform."

That sounded like fun, and by the end of the following week she decided I was ready. She introduced me to the audience as if I were a native dancer. Afterward, an Englishman suggested I go to his room with him. I looked at him for a moment. Burly and broad-chested, he had strange eyes, brown-green in color, known, I think, as "hazel." They were overshadowed by thick, unruly brows and, as if to match, he had a full, equally unruly mustache. I liked what I saw. But it was not for me, and I declined as graciously as I could, which led to a brief conversation when he realized I was an American.

"You really had me fooled," he said, laughing. "You're a good dancer."

"I had a good teacher: Liza Baladi."

"Ah, yes—Liza!" he said.

I went off to tell her my "success story," and got a look of relief from her.

"He seems to know you, Liza," I said.

She laughed. "Yes, Jim's very nice, but when I saw you talking to him I was afraid you'd do it just for the experience. You're crazy sometimes."

Not that crazy, I thought to myself. In truth, I felt sad that my friend was involved in selling that which should always be a gift. But the world over, prostitution has always existed and perhaps always will. Who is to say it is wrong? For Liza it represented a necessary evil. She had suffered a poverty-stricken childhood that left her fearful of an insecure future.

A few weeks passed and I became restless to finish my current assignments, and with or without David's permission, I was determined to go to Tokyo. Why, I wondered, did he permit this insulting impasse to continue? He had made tentative plans to build a museum in Virginia to begin in two years. It would now be impossible. What had he done about it? But more than that, my heart ached to be with him. Did he not feel so, too?

On my last night in Marrakesh, Liza's cousins prepared a farewell dinner for me. It was traditional in every way: We sat on cushions around a low table, and because Moroccan food is eaten entirely with the fingers, a special bowl, a *tass*, was filled with water and passed around for hand-washing.

We had roasted lamb and a *tajine* of chicken with olives, prunes and almonds flavored with lemon and spices. To eat the *couscous* we rolled it into small balls in our palms. Later, a plate of rich, honey-flavored pastries was served.

I derived a childlike pleasure eating with my fingers, and I told Liza such divine food was second only to the enjoyment of sex, a remark she laughingly translated to her relatives.

My departure for Aix-en-Provence the following day was a tearful one. "We will be friends forever," was the way Liza put it, and I agreed.

7

A wistful nostalgia accompanied me wherever I went in Aix. For both Janie and me it had been the high point of our first trip to Europe. She was twenty-three and I not yet eighteen. Everything was exciting then, especially that old city. Having escaped the rush to industrialize after the war, much of it remained a pictorial scene of the seventeenth century, romantic and pretty.

It was a place made for young people, and thousands, many from America, gravitated to Aix for summer fun and to its prestigious colleges in the winter. During our short stay, only a week, we walked countless times up and down the cors Mirabeau, and sat in little nightclubs listening intently as our contemporaries created unmemorable music for us.

Little changed in the intervening years, except as everywhere, Aix had become less affordable for those vagabonds, so they stayed in hostels and splurged one time at the glamorous Le Clos de la Violette before leaving. Quieter in winter, the atmosphere took on a serious tone, with exchange students filling the outdoor cafes, as warmed by heaters, they huddled over their texts, applying themselves to mastering French.

It was I who had changed, not Aix. I had just turned twenty-two, hardly a grand old age, yet that was how I felt. I was beset by dissatisfaction with the course my life was taking and bedeviled by sexual desires that I indulged in, but in measured amounts, for I had a dread of becoming promiscuous. And now I had a new and terrible concern about David that I felt helpless to do anything about.

Except for him and Andy, and occasionally Janie, I had little communication with other people in my life. But in Aix, Karl caught up with me. His call was alarming. It was not that he wanted to see me—he *needed* to see me, he said.

"You must come to Trier at once," he said.

His voice sounded unnatural. I felt threatened.

"Karl, I can't," I told him. "Almost as soon as I would arrive I'd have to return to begin my lectures in Aix. Come here. Aix is nice. You would like it."

He was insistent. "No excuses, Caroline."

The entanglement I had feared during my holiday with him was now a reality and I didn't know how to disengage myself. I told him I would have a little time before leaving for Rome, my next assignment, and would consider it then. That was a month away. By then, I hoped, if he wanted to see me enough, he would break through the invisible cords that held him prisoner in what he called "his place" and free himself from his unhappy past. Then, I reasoned, he might not need me so much, freeing me from him, as well.

Karl's immobility reminded me of a little sculpture Andy gave me long ago. We had gone to Carmel, a small town near Monterey, to see a Sunday matinee and afterward, we walked around its quaint shopping section. There he found the object in an art store. Made of black metal strips, it was shaped like a bird cage with its gate wide open. Inside, opposite the door, was a metal stick-figure of a human being with one foot on a rail, looking out, unable to escape through the open gate. As glued down as that figure was in its cage, so Karl was glued to his place in Trier.

Not one of my students had been to the Vasarely Foundation a few miles out of Aix. As an example of outstanding contemporary architecture I wanted them to see it, along with the showcase of art inside. The school had a bus and driver available, so off we went.

Aix had given Vasarely the grounds on which to build, but he himself paid for the entire construction, a unique aspect of the project. It also proved his creativity as an architect as well as an artist. His hope, he had said, was to influence others to do the same and by so doing, "satisfy one of the psychic needs of humanity, the pleasure of the eye, of which it is frustrated because of the withdrawal of nature."

The facade of the building is in itself worth going to see. Composed of a series of gigantic cubes at either side of the central portion, each anodized aluminum block is covered with alternating rounds of black on silver backgrounds and silver on black backgrounds. Inside, the artist designed a perfect habitation for his treasures. Every gallery is giant-sized. They have to be to contain the immense tapestries and canvases he created. Some are conventional rectangles, others, circular, cube and hexagonal-shaped pieces and all in glorious colors. After the students left, I remained to look again at particular tapestries, when suddenly I heard a voice behind me.

"Ah, a belly-dancer on holiday!"

I turned to face my admirer from Marrakesh. We both laughed and simultaneously asked, "What are you doing here?"

He introduced himself—Jim Crawford—and explained that he was an art acquisitions expert for London museums. The Vasarely Museum had nothing to do with his work, simply a place he liked to visit when he was on business in Marseilles, only a short drive from Aix. I told him what I was doing there, and we quickly found how similar our tastes were.

"Are you familiar with Vasarely, Caroline?"

"Only that his birthplace was in Hungary and that he lived in Paris for many years before coming to this area."

"I knew Victor and his wife when they lived in Paris. Claire was a marvelous painter, too, but very different from him. I acquired several of their works for London museums and each of them gave me a gift of one of their paintings. Victor's covers a wall. When both of us are back in London, will you come see them?" he asked.

"Yes, I'd like to."

When he offered to take me home, I accepted. There we were,

wanderers in foreign places and by coincidence having found each other again.

The following day we took a drive together. Not far from Aix was Gordes, the site of a sixteenth-century chateau where more of Vasarely's art is exhibited. Jim told me that from the day the Vasarelys first visited the feudal hillside village with its chateau they fell in love with it and spent their summers there from then on. They rented the chateau for a thirty-year period, at a symbolic annual amount—one franc, but for that they were required to completely restore it as a museum for his work. It was exactly what they wanted to do. Now we were enjoying it as countless others had over the years. In its unusual setting it is even more exciting than the original foundation in Aix.

A few miles from Gordes is what is called the Bories, reached by way of a narrow, one-way road to the top of a hill. Dug up out of the past, it has been restored—a neolithic period drystone-built town of round, beehive-style houses.

"How do you find these out-of-the-way places, Jim?"

"I seek diversions on my long trips on the road, but sharing them with you makes adventures of them, Caroline."

We had dinner together that night and by then we were chatting like old friends. I had no idea how old Jim was. It didn't matter, except that I was touched by a sadness that hovered about his face, and which I thought made him appear older than he probably was. When he took me home, he hesitated momentarily at the door, and I knew he was about to ask if he might spend the night with me. I embraced him affectionately and told him I hoped we'd meet again.

With that, he gave me his London card.

"I'm going home tomorrow, Caroline. I want to see you again, too. I'll always be available—anywhere you want to go or anything you decide you want to do."

Jim was nice, just as Liza had said, yet I had held back. What had stopped me? From the first, something about him reminded me of someone else, but of whom? It was almost as if a kinship existed between us. I scanned my men friends' images but no one fit. The feeling persisted, but the answer eluded me. At least, I thought, it was comforting to have one male friend in Europe with whom I had not slept.

During my last few days in Aix I had been devoting my lectures to the work of Frank Gehry. Perhaps it could be argued that not all of my architects were geniuses in the purest sense, but I was convinced that any definition of the term would put Gehry in that rare category. I am far from alone in such lavish praise. A few years ago he was awarded what amounts to a Nobel Prize—the Pritzker Prize in architecture. If Gehry receives no others, an unlikely possibility, he will have been given the crown of preeminence.

On previous days I had covered as much as I could of the work Gehry had done over a span of thirty years. From the beginning he challenged the very basis of the architecture of the past. Naturally, there are critics. Originality is always dogged by controversy, and right there in Paris was an early example: the Eiffel Tower, considered a monstrosity when it was built. Now it is a beloved symbol of that beautiful city. As to the American Center, "sheer madness" is the way Karl put it, and there are those who, like him, want to stick with the comfortable old geometry of balance and symmetry.

Gehry's buildings, they say, sometimes look as if they are about to fall in on themselves or are already piled in a chaotic jumble. They are wrong, for despite the differentness of their appearances, they have a solidity, a permanence that is reassuring. There's whimsy, but no capriciousness. This architect is dead-serious about making sure every aspect is properly accomplished. They will "stand their ground," his buildings, enduring the test of time, the abuse by the elements—and the critics.

On what I thought would be my last day in Aix, I lectured on the American Center. Having gone over the plans with my students, I was about to pass out specification sheets when there was a sudden commotion at the back of the room. Standing there was Karl!

I could hardly believe my eyes. He had made it!

"Karl, welcome! I'm happy to see you," I said. "Come up here. I'd like to introduce you to my students.

"We're in luck today," I told them. "Dr. Wegner is a professor of architecture in Germany. I hope he'll speak to you for a few minutes. His views are different from mine," I added, laughing.

"Caroline, I'm not here for a social visit or to talk to your class," he said. "I'm here to take you back to Trier with me. Are you coming?"

I was taken aback, but tried to cover my embarrassment.

"I'll dismiss my class in a few minutes, Karl, and we can talk about it."

"No, no more talk, Caroline. I'm not leaving without you." Despite what sounded like an ultimatum, Karl's voice was low and calm. I thought I could deal with him.

Then, like a character in a slow-motion film sequence, he began moving very slowly toward the rostrum, and as he approached closer, I saw the expression, or rather, the lack of expression in his eyes—wide open, unblinking, staring at me, and I became frightened. I didn't know what to do. I had lost control of the situation.

"Yes or no, Caroline?"

"Karl, let me talk to you!"

"It's 'no,' isn't it?" he said.

Suddenly, a student near the place where Karl now stood yelled a warning.

"Look out! He's got a gun!"

I saw him raise it and instinctively turned sideways and stepped back. As I did so, I tripped, lost my balance and fell with the papers I had been holding flying out of my hand and scattering about the floor. At the same time I felt a stinging sensation in my upper left arm.

I lay cowering on the floor, afraid to move, afraid to even look up. Students rushed to my side and helped me to my feet.

"Where is he? Where's Karl?" I asked.

"He's dead, Ms. Shaw. A shot to the head. It's all over. Are you all right?" one of them asked.

"Yes, I think so."

"Your arm. It's bleeding," he said, and pulled up my sleeve to look. "It may be serious."

Someone handed him a handkerchief, and making a bandage of

it, he placed it over my wound. "You're lucky. That shot was meant for your heart," he said.

Meanwhile, a tumult was occurring in the room as people from the next classroom, hearing the shots, joined my own students in a cacophony of excited voices. Milling around, they stared at me and craned to see the body on the floor. Their professor ordered them out and dismissed them for the day. Then he gave his attention to me.

"The police will want to talk to you later, Caroline. Is there anything I can do for you right now?"

I thanked him, and a few minutes later, an ambulance arrived to take Karl and me to the hospital. As the paramedics made their hopeless efforts to save Karl's life, I held his hand and waited. At last they stopped. I was overcome with grief and wept at this final dark moment in my dear, unhappy friend's life.

The gun, confiscated by the police, was a Nazi Walthers pistol. Where or when he had got it I would never know—nor how long he might have planned that horrible deed. His purpose was clear, but he had accomplished only half of what he'd set out to do: He had not taken me with him.

As I waited at the hospital for a surgeon to remove the bullet, a morose thought seized me. From Karl's distorted point of view it was logical to "take me with him." Indeed, had I not contributed to his desperate act? As each day of my Trier holiday had passed I knew Karl was falling in love with me—in my freedom from constraints, my adventurousness. Sensing that, I should have left quickly, but I remained, and in my immaturity tampered with the delicate membranes that held him together. My continuing presence forced him to confront everything he had blindly accepted all his life. In what must have been a heartless act to him, I had refused to stay and help him in his struggle to create a new way of life for himself. Alone, he could not cope with the conflicts I had brought to the surface. The challenge was too great, the fears, too overwhelming.

As soon as I returned to the college guest quarters, I called Andy. He wanted to take off for Aix to be with me, and I did want him, but I discouraged him from coming.

"I'm all right, Andy dear," I said. "I'm only feeling remorseful that I might have triggered Karl's act."

He tried to console me. "Think of it this way," he said. "You gave Karl the most satisfying experience of his life in those few weeks. The fact that you brought inner conflicts to the surface does not change the fact that they were already there and would not have lain dormant forever. You told me Karl was a highly intelligent person. Surely he visualized the exciting prospect of a fuller life. It isn't your fault that he could not or would not pursue it."

It didn't help. I longed for a future time when my distress would subside.

It was inevitable that the news story in the Aix paper would travel. Even when not sensationalized, the headlines were variations of "Spurned Professor Wounds Lover and Kills Self." I refused to give interviews. A few of the students did, describing the violent scene, and the media made a point of referring to me as "the daughter of the famous American architect David Shaw." That was sure to make the story more widespread in its distribution. What a twist! Notoriety had come from a source other than the one I had always feared.

My friends didn't let me down. Andy called every day, and Janie offered to come to Aix. She sounded agitated on the phone and I could visualize her pretty face, red with anger and concern.

"Caroline, be more careful with whom you go to bed," she warned me. "That loony bastard might have killed you!"

I didn't expect to hear from any of my former students, but I did. The mail bulged with cards and notes from them. It was what I needed just then: to know people cared about what happened to me.

The only one I didn't hear from was David.

Although I was due in Rome in less than two weeks, I remained in Aix at my doctor's request so that he could check on the healing of the wound. As the days passed, I became increasingly troubled by the lack of communication with my father. Something unpleasant, maybe serious, was happening to him. As I dwelled on the possibilities I was sometimes seized by panic, breaking into spasms of sweating and palpitations. I filled a prescription for tranquilizers that the physician had given me and took them.

Andy once told me that sometimes people manufacture crises in their lives. A crucial detail, he said, once revealed, can prevent disaster. I must not become hysterical, I told myself, but I had just gone through a terrible experience, and as my anxiety grew I took more of the pills to maintain a semblance of calm. I knew my fear was not based on an illusion.

I called Andy and told him my decision to go to Tokyo. "I must go. Something's wrong. I seldom get David on the phone anymore, and when I do, he doesn't sound good."

"I know."

"You know, you know! Damn it! If you know, why don't you tell me what you know?"

"You're mad at me. What have I done?"

"Andy, I'm sorry! It's just that I'm worried. I always lean so hard on you to help me."

"Listen, Caroline, I've been bringing my practice to a close over the last year. I want to do some research and teach. I've had some offers and I'll tell you about them at another time, but I'm free right now and I was thinking of going to a symposium in Tokyo coming up soon. I'll see Dave and call you from there."

"You're lying. You're not going to any meetings."

"Why do you say that?"

"I'm a more proficient liar than you, Andy. I can tell you're worried, too, aren't you?"

"Yes, but I don't want you to go there without me. I'll see if I can get a flight for tomorrow. You do the same. I'll call you in a couple of hours and we'll coordinate our arrival in Tokyo. All right?"

"Andy, what would I do without you?" I asked, feeling weepy and relieved.

"Hold the tears, Caroline. You'll never have to do without me."

8

Andy arrived at Narita Airport five hours before I did and went to a nearby capsule hotel to rest. He told me later it amazed him with everything within a few feet of crawl-in space: television, radio, an alarm clock, and he was able to get some sleep before returning to meet me. Despite my worry, and his, too, we were happy to be together after such a long time and just kept kissing and looking at each other. We took a train into Tokyo and found a hotel in the area of the temple. I wanted to go over there right away.

"I want to talk to you before you do that," Andy said. "Besides, it's six a.m. Tokyo time. Why don't you get a little rest first?"

I did, and then making a bolster of the pillows, I sat up in bed as Andy brought a chair to the bedside for himself. As articulate as he always was, he was having trouble getting started.

"I know something has happened, Andy. You know what it is. Why do you treat me so delicately?"

"I care about you and don't want to see you hurt."

"Will I be hurt now?"

"Yes, the crisis in Dave's life has been foisted on you, too. It's inescapable. The situation began a few months ago. He was in a turmoil over the state of his building plans. Nothing like this has ever happened to him. Dave's never known rejection—always acclaim, even in his youth. You know how unaggressive he is. Instead of pressuring the Institute to make a decision or going on to something else, he drifted, doing nothing.

"Dave yearned for you, too, Caroline, but his paternal feelings didn't permit him to worry you, so in addition to everything else, he suffered from unfulfilled desire. The days were long and without purpose, and Hasumi watched in sorrow as his friend sat for hours staring into space. As he saw Dave falling into despair his heart went out to him, and he decided to act. He did a very Japanese thing: He brought him a *geisha*.

"Her name is Mayumi Yamada. At first, she was a charming companion, nothing more. *Geisha* are not prostitutes; they're trained from girlhood for their profession. She's attractive and cultured and at once she began to distract Dave from himself. She pleases him and they spend a lot of time together every day. They go out, but more often stay in. Now they have become intimate and I think she may have fallen in love with him. She arrives late in the day and after dinner she entertains him and spends the night. In the morning they have breakfast; then she leaves.

"For a time Dave appeared happy and Hasumi was reassured that he had done the right thing. Now he is worried again. Mayumi has become indispensable. When she doesn't come one day, Dave is distraught, and Hasumi thinks she is doing it deliberately to keep him from becoming complacent about her and binding him more closely to her.

"We know this isn't a normal lifestyle for him, but it may continue. It's complicated by his feelings of kinship with the culture of Japan. He is becoming more and more Japanese and plans to remain here. But remember, his infatuation is not the problem, Caroline. Dave has lost his direction."

Andy looked at me intently. "Have you been listening to me?" he asked.

"Yes."

"Tell me what you're thinking."

"I'm filled with guilt, Andy. I should have disregarded his putting me off and come here long ago. He's done nothing wrong. He needed me and I failed him. I will stay now if he wants me. You love David. If you're free to remain for a while, will you stay, too, and try to help him?"

"I want to, Caroline."

I asked the taxi driver to stop at the construction site. The office was as David had described it, but now weeds grew all about and in patches here and there over the empty space. Desolate, lifeless, it deepened my already depressed thoughts, and we hurried along the path that led to the temple. When we reached the garden, Andy stopped. I was trembling.

"Come here, Caroline," he said, and took me in his arms. "This is one of those unforeseeable events in life. How hard it may be! But you have a store of strength you're unaware of. Whatever occurs and whatever you decide to do, don't sacrifice your own needs. That never works."

As he held me in his strong embrace, not saying any more, just holding me, the tension left me.

"Go on now. Dave is expecting you," he said. "Stay as long as you like. I'll take a walk and then sit here in the garden and wait for you."

Hasumi greeted me and took me to David's room, where he left me at the door. I knocked and went in. The room was not exactly a monastic cell, but little more. A small desk held some books, and a cabinet at one side was probably for clothes and a *futon*. In *yukata* and slippers he was kneeling on a cushion. Before him on a low table were papers and brushes and I could see the calligraphy he had been doing.

He stood up, arms outstretched, and I went to him. I felt faint with happiness. This was where I belonged and wanted never to leave.

"I've missed you, Caroline,"

"Then why didn't you let me come here to be with you?"

He didn't answer, and at once I began to feel uncomfortable. Perhaps it was physical, I thought, being unaccustomed to sitting on floor cushions. I looked around the room. There were no chairs.

"What have you heard from the Institute?" I asked.

"A letter came a few weeks ago requesting a meeting. I haven't answered. It's meaningless. I've gone to other of their meetings. One board member refuses to give his consent to build. It doesn't matter anymore. I've lost interest."

"Why?"

There was no answer.

"David, most architectural projects are slow to begin and then take ages to complete. You know that. One of your own buildings took six years."

"This is different."

"No, it isn't. You know James Ingo Freed. He almost gave up the idea of building the Holocaust Memorial in Washington because of uncertainty about how it should be built. Now, look at it—a masterwork. International Institute will be built, too, and it will be beautiful, David."

He mustered a wan smile, then looked away, detached, silent. We who had always had so much to tell each other, now had nothing to say. I searched his face for a remembrance of the past. Was this Japanese man my father, the love of my life? I could not find him in that face. I sought the warm responsiveness I had known since childhood. It was not there. Someone else, a stranger, sat beside me.

I tried to hold back the tears, but could not.

"I have always cried too easily," I once told Andy.

"You've had things to cry about, Caroline," he had said. "I'm glad you're able to."

This was one of them as I glanced around the barren room. Fear accompanied the tears. Would Andy be able to lead David out from these imprisoning temple walls, out of his malaise and restore his vigor? Or would it be impossible now that there was Mayumi who made the idleness a pleasure?

"Caroline, why are you crying? Aren't you happy to be with me?" Come, lie down," he said, taking out a *futon*.

A shyness I had never known before came over me.

"What's the matter with you?" he asked.

He was frowning, annoyed, impatient, and I quickly took off my clothes and got under the covers as he removed his *yukata* and lay beside me.

Then he saw the bandage on my arm.

"Is this where you were wounded?"

"Then you knew!"

"The whole world must know about my daughter by now."

"I heard from many people who were concerned about me."

"Former lovers?"

"That's unkind."

"You didn't hear from me. Do you think that means I've stopped loving you?"

"Have you?"

"Lie back and I'll show you."

"You're confusing love with sex."

"Tell me, Caroline, how many men have you slept with since the last time you were with me?"

"It doesn't matter. You are the one I love."

"It matters. You must stop the wildness. You belong to me."

Unwilling to continue our bitter conversation, I was silent. He became pensive.

"It's my fault," he said, almost to himself. "I loved you too much when you were young. You were a wild little thing and I indulged you in everything. I should have disciplined you, punished you when you misbehaved. Look at you now—just as untamed as when you were a child."

The tone of his voice was sentimental, not unpleasant, and I could not believe he meant what he had said, but I dared not belittle his remarks, either, or show amusement, which I did feel.

"David, I'm not wild—I'm free. That was what you taught me. You alone guided me through my difficult early years. It was you who produced my free spirit. You taught me that sexuality was an intrinsic and wonderful part of a person's life. It hasn't made me wild, only more loving, as I love you. When I was growing up you gave me direction. You made life seem full of exciting possibilities and I was eager to give them a try. Much of the time I feel good about myself, not wild. I wish you would find me so, too. I try to live by what you taught me. Do you remember? 'It's very simple,' you said. 'Live life fully and try never to be hurtful to others.'"

"You've done something very hurtful. You led a man to his death."

"Listen to me, David. That man said he loved me so much he could not live without me, yet he tried to kill me before he committed suicide. A bullet removed from my arm was meant for my heart. Who was the hurtful one? I don't know why you're so angry with me, but it's made you unreasonable. You don't know what you're saying."

My contradiction infuriated him. "Don't ever talk to me like that again, Caroline. I'm going to tell my *geisha* to teach you some manners when you're with me."

"You're going to do what? David, you're being ridiculous!"

Now I had gone too far. He reached across the *futon*, grabbed my arm and slapped me on the cheek. "You haven't learned when to stop, have you?"

A lifetime of gentleness ended with that blow. But it was not the pain in my cheek that hurt so much—it was the one in my heart, and I began to cry.

Totally exasperated, he shook me.

"There you go! Stop that! You always resort to tears to get what you want."

"What do you think I want?"

An appeal to reason was not solving anything and I tried to control myself. We were talking, but not listening, sending messages that weren't being received. I didn't hear—or feel—the pain beneath his emotionalism. Talking sense in the face of it was pointless. We could as well not have spoken at all. We weren't connecting. Finally, futilely, he had become physical—telling me in action—making me hurt, too. Suddenly I saw a comic element in it all, or perhaps I was hysterical. I began to laugh.

"Damn it, Caroline! Stop that! You cry, you laugh. I'm tired of this. Be still!"

He took me in his arms, and I closed my eyes, hoping desperately that I might recapture the passion I had always, with blissful abandon, shown him. It was not there. And now, the perfumed scent of another woman's body rose from the futon and I turned away from him.

"For Christ's sake, what now? Give yourself to me!"

"I'm not ready."

"Not ready? You're always ready."

"Not now."

"You've heard about Mayumi, haven't you? You doubt that I still love you, don't you?"

"No, but you're concealing it well."

"What do you want me to do?"

"Do you want to know?"

"Caroline!"

"Okay. Stop hurting me and try making love to me as you have in the past. Seduce me."

He looked incredulous. "Seduce you?"

"Isn't that what passion is? Giving yourself up totally to someone? Haven't you ever felt seduced by me?"

"That's nonsense! You do this all the time with other men. It's my turn."

Flushed and agitated, he brutishly pushed my legs apart and thrust his penis into me. In a flash of remembrance I saw the young lad of my adolescence, feverish with excitement, knowing nothing of the joy of a shared loving intimacy. But this was my beloved, a man of the world, acting as oafish as that boy.

Then, just as abruptly as he had begun, he withdrew. I was bewildered, knowing he was not through with me. Crouched on his knees, he stared down at my body beneath him, saying nothing. Then he moved to my side. Fearful of what I might have to endure, I wanted to escape and gingerly tried to slide to the edge of the futon.

"Come back here," he said, and pulled me roughly to him. "Turn over."

"No, I don't do that."

"Why? Many women like it."

"I don't want the experience."

"Are you saying you've never done it?"

"Never."

"Well, you'll feel like a virgin again."

"David, please don't!"

I struggled for a moment, then stopped. Jaws clenched, his look of determination frightened me, and I submitted to him. With no arousal, no lubricant and the large size of his penis, each forceful rapid thrust was an infliction of pain. In a few minutes it was over. I lay still, numb, overcome by his harshness.

When he returned from the bathroom, he lay back on the *futon* and put his arm around me. Smiling, his sexual desire now satisfied and his anger spent, he leaned over and kissed me. My punishment had been meted out. All was forgiven.

"That wasn't so bad, was it? Sex doesn't have to be the same every time."

"Has it been so for us?"

"You're too sensitive. Nothing has changed between us."

Nothing has changed, David? In tragic dimensions everything has changed. What have you proved? No one owns me. Not even you. Will I be able to forgive you? Will I be able to erase this scene from my memory? Or will I be fearful of your rage, inhibited in our love-making?

Cheerful and talkative now, his topic was his *geisha.* Although no physical evidence of Mayumi was in the room, I felt her presence everywhere, and now, one by one, he cataloged her talents and charms. From time to time I drifted off from the sound of his voice, listening to my own unhappy one, until a word, a phrase would reach me and I would listen again.

She was a paragon, indeed, and I was aware of my envy. He described her artistic talents, her musical accomplishments, especially her virtuosity on the *koto* with a repertoire of classical and modern compositions. Gifted in poetry as well, that was her true métier, he said, having had some of her own poems published. They read the *haiku* of Basho to each other, a favorite of both.

From time to time he paused, entranced by his vision of her. I waited, both outraged and fascinated, wanting to break away, but continuing to lie quietly. He smoothed the covers around us and held me close to him. It felt like affection, but was it? I had become his buddy, his pal, someone to whom he could recount delectable tidbits of his intimate life with his *geisha*, and this he did in rhapsodic details.

In a curious way, as distraught as I was, I saw the absurdity of the situation. Not that I had some kind of grand objectivity; obviously I did not. It was a simple insight into the perversity of human behavior, its incongruity and sheer funniness. All of David's wisdom and sophistication could not prevent him from being childlike and foolish.

"Like an Utamaro courtesan, the essence of her beauty is in her delicacy," he said, and described the translucence of her skin, her lips, puckered slightly as if waiting to be kissed; her mysterious hooded eyelids; her long silken hair that unpinned at night, fell gracefully down her back, down to the cleft in her buttocks, so pretty, so erotic. I reached up to touch my close-cropped head of black curls. Nothing to unpin here.

"She has the budding breasts of a young girl, with sweet little pink nipples," he said, pausing again, relishing all that comeliness.

Though aware of how insensitive his recital was, I sadly compared my differentness: my dark skin, my large eyes and full lips, my breasts that years ago had matured from "buds" to rounded fullness.

"After we have sex, she brings a bowl of warm water and washes my genitals. Then we go to sleep."

Was I mad? Why was I listening to such drivel?

"Is that some kind of ritual, David?"

"No, she just likes to do it."

I could not withhold my sarcasm. "Does she bring you a urinal or must you go to the bathroom to relieve yourself?" I asked.

He didn't respond and may not even have been listening, spellbound by his image of his paramour.

David, what has happened to you? Always before, I basked in your tender embrace, wanting nothing more from life. How we loved each other! Now you lie beside me salting my wounded heart. I want to hate you, but cannot. Then why am I seething with anger?

I stood up, my shyness gone, and ran into the bathroom and washed. Streaks of blood stained the towel and I wondered if I were injured internally. Hurriedly, I dressed. How I hated that cloistered room and wanted never to see it again. Would that I had never seen it, and now, would that I might destroy its memory.

"I'm leaving, David."

"Why?"

"I want to go before your next guest arrives."

"Will you remain in Tokyo?"

"How can I stay? Your enchantment with Mayumi doesn't seem strange to me. I can't give you any of those things that delight you about her. For me to stay, you would have to give her up. Will you do that?"

"Stop, Caroline! It's you I love. I don't know what I feel for Mayumi, but I don't want to give her up. You don't understand. It's acceptable here to have a *geisha*."

"I'm an American woman, David. I can't accept it."

"You'll become accustomed to it."

"What arrangement would you make for Mayumi and me? Would it be she or I who has visitation rights? Certain hours, certain days?"

Heartbroken and filled with anger, no longer able to control myself and wanting to lash out at him, I knew I must leave quickly before I hurt him as he had hurt me.

"Caroline, wait!"

"For what? You've given me your answer. I can't stay. In time you'll know how much Mayumi means to you. You may find contentment with her and I'll become a memory just as my mother has."

Before my resolve could weaken, I turned away from him and left, running to the garden and into Andy's arms, weeping, weeping, weeping.

"Caroline, you *are* a cry-baby," Andy said, as a taxi took us to the hotel. "Stop for a little while. You're drenching my shirt. Tell me, when did you eat last?"

"On the plane."

"Well, it's time to have some food. It's hard to eat and cry at the same time, but you probably can do it. Let's find out."

Afterward, we went to the lounge where a small ensemble was playing American ballads, and Andy ordered some drinks for us. I began to feel better—enough, anyway, so I could tell him what happened.

"Dave's in bad shape. Now look what he's done to you. I shouldn't have let you come here," he said.

"You couldn't stop me. Andy?"

"What?"

"I have a premonition. I know how irrational it sounds, but I've lived with it all my life. Some day David will leave me and not return. He'll abandon me. For a while I deluded myself into thinking I was free of the fear."

"Look what you've done. You just left Dave. Now you've reversed it in your mind."

"Andy, if you had heard him—it was strange, that outpouring of praise for his *geisha* and the pleasure she gives him. All the while he was holding me in his arms, but I could have been halfway 'round the world from him in his detachment from me. I asked him to give her up, but he refused. He set the terms. What could I do?"

"Mayumi provides him with something he needs right now, or thinks he does."

"Can't I give it to him?"

"No, Caroline, listen: Mayumi is not your rival. What she and Dave have is nice but superficial. *Geisha* have their limits, too, but within those limits, Mayumi will do whatever Dave wants. His stalled building project has been a blow to his confidence. I suppose Mayumi accepts without question his domination and that gives him some kind of emotional satisfaction. You demand equality. That's very different. But abandonment of you? Never."

"If that's true, why—why do I have this obsession?"

"Reach back into your childhood and you'll find it. Think about what happened. Recall when you were little your father told you your mother left you in his good care, but you didn't understand why your mother had to leave at all. And why didn't she return? You didn't analyze it or put it into words. You felt it. Didn't she want you?

"Then your father had to leave you from time to time to do his work, sometimes for long periods. You didn't know why he left you. Where was his good care then? Maybe he didn't love you, either. Now both your parents were gone and you were left with the wicked witch. Right?"

I began to laugh.

"Tell me what's funny."

"Well, I really thought of Martha as a wicked witch. I hated her so much when I was little, but once I gave *her* something to worry about. It was very satisfying. I don't know how old I was—probably four. My father had just come home from a long stay overseas, and I begged him to buy me a doll that looked like Martha. Knowing how much I disliked her, it was an odd request, but it must have seemed harmless, and he did. It had Martha's pink and white complexion, her long blond hair and dainty little mouth.

"I was delighted and immediately took it to my room and went to work on it. My zestful attack on that doll knew no bounds. Using finger-paints I smeared black color on its lips and perfect little white teeth, and red on the rest of its face. I pulled out its hair. I ripped off its fancy ruffled gown and shredded it with my scissors and tore off its cute little black patent-leather slippers. Then, not knowing how to spell her name, I painted a big red 'M' on the doll's denuded body.

"Pleased with my handiwork, I placed it on the floor outside Martha's room and went back to my room, the mess in the middle of it untouched, and sat down in the window seat, hugging my "mama" doll. After a while I heard loud and angry sounds in the corridor.

"Martha was hysterical. 'Vicious!' she kept saying over and over. 'She's a vicious little monster! Get rid of her, David.'

"I heard my father trying to calm her. 'She's a lonely little child, Martha. You're the adult. Try to understand her. Feel for her. You know I won't let her go. If she goes, I go.'

"There was quiet then and in a few minutes my father knocked on the door and came in. He took me by the hand and we went to his study. He put me on his lap and for a long time we sat together not saying anything. He must have been trying to think of just how to talk to me about the incident, but once in a while he seemed to be smiling to himself. Maybe he secretly enjoyed my mischievousness, although, of course, he didn't say so.

"'Caroline, you have made your feelings very clear to Martha,' he said finally. 'She can't help the way she is, but you know she will never hurt you. You must not frighten her or hurt her, either. Do you know what a truce is? Make a truce with Martha. I can't take you on my long trips—you're too little—but I'll try to come home more often to be with you. All right?'"

"Dave was right, wasn't he?" Andy said. "You're still good at making your feelings clear, Caroline. But back then, even if he did come home more often, he still had to leave again, and your fears were repeatedly reinforced and no amount of reassurance changed the situation for that frightened little girl.

"You grew up and you understood what happened, but the symptoms had long been in place. Every time Dave left it triggered their return and they plagued you until that night before Dave left for Tokyo.

"Your love for each other was enhanced by the sexual intimacy. You were mesmerized, delirious with happiness. Dave could leave you now. You knew he was not abandoning you. You knew it deep inside yourself. It was wonderful.

"Now after a long separation from him, a traumatic event has made you fearful again. But not like before. Today for the first time, I think Dave saw you as the mature young woman you are. More adult than he, as you put aside his foolishness and got to the heart of your relationship. Overwhelmed by grief and still unable to shed your fears, you made no compromises and bravely said goodbye. Your decision was the right one and now you must accept it. Let a little time pass. Let's see what will happen. Remember, I will be here."

He put his arm around me then. "I haven't seen you in a long time, Caroline. You've changed."

"How?"

"You're prettier than ever."

"What would my life be like without you, Andy dear?"

"What would mine be without you?"

"If I can get a flight to Rome, I'll leave tomorrow."

It was still early in the evening, but both of us were tired, so we kissed goodnight and Andy went to his room, which adjoined mine. For a little while I lay pondering the day, unable to sleep. Scrounging around my mind I sought any bit of cheer but found only snatches of bitter conversation, David's callous treatment of me and a dreamy picture of a lovely *geisha*.

I got up. Unbuttoning my nightgown and pulling it down to my waist, I stood in front of a mirror examining my breasts.

I called to Andy.

"What?"

"Please come in here."

"Omigod! Now what?"

"What do you think, Andy?"

"What do you mean—what do I think?"

"Your opinion. My breasts, do you like them?"

He looked stunned. Then he began to laugh and couldn't stop.

"I'm serious!"

"Do I like your breasts? Yes, I do."

"Not too big?"

"Caroline, I think this situation has made you a little crazy, too. I suppose Dave gave you some bullshit about Mayumi's breasts. The size of a woman's breasts has nothing to do with love. People don't do an inventory and take measurements when they fall in love."

I was on the verge of tears again. "I'm so mixed up, Andy. I may never see David again, but I can't help loving him and wanting to please him."

"Believe me, your breasts are very pleasing. All of you is, darling. Now, before you get me nuts, too, and I do something I'll regret, please go to sleep. I don't know if I'll be able to now, but I'd like to try."

And he left the room, still laughing.

The next day he wanted to take the train to the airport with me, but it was a long trip and made no sense.

"You don't look well. Are you all right?" he asked.

"Sure, I'm fine."

But I lied. Along with my unhealed wound, I felt feverish and ill, very ill. The sore throat I had when I arrived in Tokyo had become severe and I could barely speak. Andy had heard it all, the pain of my broken heart, my shattered dreams. I dared not add to his concern, and holding back a gathering deluge of tears, I left, promising to call when I arrived in Rome.

My sense of separation from David was real now. It was not just time and space that kept us apart, as I had told Karl, but the breaking of a bond that had always held us together. Andy might succeed in bringing David back to his former vital self, but would it restore our attachment to each other? As the plane ascended into the sky I peered down through eyes blurred with tears at the rapidly vanishing scene below. Would I ever return?

9

As soon as I arrived, I went to a physician. Diagnosed as having a throat infection that had spread to my lungs, I was placed in a hospital for a week. Gradually I took up my lectures, going to class a few days a week.

My students in Rome were a distraction from my illness and the despair I was feeling, and they provided me with a fulfilling finale to my travels around European colleges. Lively and vocal, they turned my talks into enjoyable conversations with them. The class time sped by.

Humanity has often lagged behind what is new and different, unable to adjust to change easily, fearful of unknown consequences. But I could foretell the new wave of twenty-first-century architecture, at least in Italy, by the enthusiasm of those young people for the most unusual of present-day builders. They were familiar with my own heroes, who were theirs, as well.

One of my last lectures was on Arquitectonica, a firm based in Miami, Florida, and headed by a wife and husband team: Laurinda Hope Spear and Bernardo Fort-Brescia. Not as challenging as the Deconstructivists, Arquitectonica has stayed well within the mainstream of Neo-Modernism, yet their work has a youthfulness and futurist element that flavors everything they do. Their large-scale projects have originality in style and are bright with cheerful colors.

One of them is the Banco de Crédito of Lima, Peru, which is set against the Andes, high above the city. The lobby is a spectacle—a gigantic elliptical glass space.

That building holds a precious memory for me. My father knew Spear's and Brescia's work and wanted to see it when completed. He took me with him—a graduation present, he said, my having just finished high school. We were in Lima for a week and had a wonderful holiday, father and daughter, happy together, yet often for me, emotionally disturbing as I rigidly controlled the erotic feelings he stirred in me.

On my final day in class I chose the late Charles Moore for my subject. Moore's versatility was awesome. His architecture changed with every project he was commissioned to do, making it hard to classify him, but in that way, more interesting, too.

I had a special reason for choosing Moore. I wanted to tell them about his Piazza d'Italia in New Orleans, Louisiana. Built of steel, marble, brick and painted wood, it has a little of everything—simplicity on the one hand and ornate complexity, on the other, straight lines and curved ones, and replete with pillars, arches, raised and lowered levels, a water fountain—a bit of Italy in the south of my own country, and delightfully so.

At the end of the lecture, my students appeared reluctant to let me go. I liked them, too, and promised we would have a reunion at some future time if it were possible. But that was not to be. I didn't know then that was not only my final lecture, but the end of my career.

As I left the classroom I looked back, thinking that many of my students would become exceptional architects, though genius is rare. If there was one who might achieve that exalted place, I knew who he was. He watched me leave now, too, but neither of us spoke.

His name was Jomo Ngala; his home, Kenya; and he was in Rome on a student visa. His work sparkled with originality, but for me there was more to him than architecture. No one would describe Jomo as handsome, yet I caught my breath that first day he walked into the classroom. Every part of the man was as rough-hewn as a sculptor's unfinished figure: very tall, every feature outsize—enormous eyes, large nose, thick lips. Some say no pure race exists, that centuries of blending cultures and peoples makes it impossible. That may be, yet here was a member of a long-gone noble race, black to the depths of his soul. I knew he was attracted to me, too. Perhaps finding his lecturer to be a young racially mixed woman surprised him, and more than a casual glance passed between us that first day.

He continued to distract me on those days when I was able to come to school, and right there on the podium I fantasized having sex with him. I wanted to see all of that black body, lie close to it, caress it, be enveloped by it. He knew that, smiling, as I looked furtively in his direction. He knew he could have me whenever he wished.

My desire for sex knew no respite and frequently welled up in me. Its satisfaction lightened the oppressiveness of my life and now, consuming an increasing amount of liquor, I craved it, well aware of what was happening to me, but simply not caring. My recuperation was slow and the days I spent at school exhausting. At least when I was there I was not thinking about the disaster my life had become. Even though the notoriety of my recent experience in Aix had followed me to Rome, it came up only once when a student inquired if my wound had healed. No one asked questions or made comments, and I appreciated that.

During the days when I didn't go to class I spent most of my time in bed. Feeling lonely and ill in a foreign place, I longed for friends and familiar surroundings. I no longer had a home, a place, "my place" in the world, as Karl had said, and now I heard the wisdom of his words.

The one thing I looked forward to in my dull routine was talking to Andy. He hadn't known my first calls from Rome came from a hospital, and for some time afterward I lied convincingly about my illness. Then one day I slipped and he wanted to come to Rome.

"You can't drop whatever you're doing every time I get myself in trouble, Andy."

"Caroline, I worry about you. I want to be with you."

"Stay with David. He needs you more."

In my heart I did want him very much—his comforting ways, his humor, his affection. He had put his life on hold as he tried to patch up the life of a friend who'd messed up his. Once I asked him if it was a financial strain living in Tokyo, hardly a cheap place in which to live.

"I did all right in my practice and that book was successful, Caroline. You know how I live," he said, laughing. "You've seen my one good-for-all-occasions suit, and just think of the money I've saved not going to a barber. I never expect to be rich and that's okay. This is the way I want to spend my money. Don't worry about me."

But I did, along with an unprocessed backlog of other items. My mind was as disorganized as my life, which was not going as I had planned, and I could resolve nothing. No wonder Karl had slavishly sought order. How satisfying it must be, I thought, to know exactly what one was about! So different from him, I likened myself to a tiny teddy bear my father had given me in my early childhood.

Attached to it as little ones are to special toys, I was never without it. My nanny was forever sewing one leg or another back onto its body, and with one glass eye lost, she used a button to replace it, but there was no way to keep the ever-loosening strands of stuffing from poking out.

My teddy's life ended when Martha, "disgusted with the foul thing," tossed it in the trash. I was inconsolable despite all Nanny's efforts to draw my attention away from it. She even tried to retrieve it, but by then it was, indeed, a foul thing. For days I would run outside and set up a terrible wailing, calling for my father. Martha, fearing his anger when he returned from his current European project, gave me another. In a rage, I dragged a chair out to the trash can and climbing on it, I threw the new teddy bear in. Then I stopped my lament.

The unraveled strands of my life dangled as helplessly as my teddy bear's. Was I ready for the trash heap, too? In response to my complaint that I was not sleeping well, my physician prescribed a sedative. I liked its effect and took more than was indicated and slept more hours than I was awake.

•

Late in the afternoon of my last lecture I came back to the guesthouse feeling feverish and weary. I had not eaten since breakfast, but wasn't hungry. I changed into a nightgown after taking a couple of pills and went to bed.

I was awakened not much later, it seemed, by a knock on my door. It was Jomo. Bearing sweet-smelling roses of deepest crimson and a bottle of wine, with glasses and a bottle-opener he'd picked up in the guesthouse kitchen, he had prepared for a pleasant visit. I was drowsy with sedation but happy to see him.

Handing me a glass of wine, he pulled a chair up to the bed.

"Ms. Shaw?" he said, smiling.

"No. 'Caroline.'"

"I'm leaving for Kenya tomorrow. A firm in Mombasa is taking me on as an apprentice and it's too good an opportunity to refuse."

"You'll succeed, Jomo. Some day I'll be looking at a journal of architecture and I'll see pictures of your work."

"This afternoon may have to last us a lifetime, Caroline."

"Then we must seize the moment," I said.

He closed the blinds enough to partially shut out the strong light. Passion knows no certain hour, but neither light nor dark has the mysterious appeal of semi-darkness. I watched him undress and lie down beside me.

All my previous sexual relations had been with white men. Now, lying in Jomo's arms, his beautiful black body next to mine, I sensed a difference from other times with other men. I belonged here, belonged with him, and when he made love to me, I responded not only with my body, but with my heart. There was a strangeness about it I couldn't decipher, and he said it was true for him, too.

"My color attracted you to me. I know that, Caroline. But I think there's something more between us. When I read about what happened in Aix, I couldn't conceive of a man choosing death rather than life without a particular woman's love. Now we have made this loving connection, and I understand."

"That's a frightening thing to say to me. I have no special powers. Other men who have known me don't feel as Karl did, and this is only the first time we've been together."

"What is it then, that makes me feel as I do? I may never know."

"Jomo, I don't know anything about you. Tell me what your life has been like."

"There's not much to tell," he said. "I'm older than you. I was born in a propitious year, 1963, the year my country won its independence, and my father named me after his hero, Jomo Kenyatta, who was a member of our tribe, the Kikuya. When I was a small boy he took me to meet him. Father told me to remember that and live up to my illustrious name.

"When I finished high school I became a construction worker. That's why I arrived in college so much later than most people do. I didn't want to leave my country, but going to this school in Rome could mean a career in architecture, and that was what I wanted.

"Every time I go home I see more changes in my country, especially in Nairobi. I remember it from my childhood, a mile-high, beautiful, countrified place. Now a Western way of life is taking over. Most people speak Swahili, but English is common. Mombasa is different. It's an island city still clinging to the past. What I like to do is travel around the country, stopping in old villages where people live as they did long ago and speak dialects unfamiliar to me. When I do that I remember who I am and where I come from."

A nostalgic sound came into his voice, and I knew that was where he longed to be. I was happy for him that his career would begin there.

"Do you think you might want to go to Kenya some day and see my country with me, Caroline?"

I didn't answer at once as I reflected on the sorry state of my love life and the closeness I felt to Jomo.

"Yes, maybe."

The rapport I was experiencing with this man didn't exist with any of the others in my transitory relationships. Was it the echo of an ancient racial call? I didn't want him to leave.

"It's hard for me to leave you, too, Caroline," he said. "But you're not well. You look very tried."

He gently turned me to one side and tucked the covers around me. Then he bent down and we kissed goodbye. In a few moments I was asleep. When I awoke the room was dark and I was alone. What had transpired was like a vivid erotic dream, but there were the flowers and a half-empty bottle of wine and I was feeling better than I had in a long time.

"Go to hell, David! I don't need you," I said to myself, and immediately broke into a spasm of weeping.

April and still cold. Would spring never come? Changes in medication didn't improve my condition or my outlook. I continued on antibiotics and now my physician added mood-elevating pills to lift my spirits. I saw her once a week, but she had little to say to me.

"I don't know why you're not responding, Ms. Shaw. I sense an underlying sadness in you," she said. "Do you want to regain your health?"

"Of course I do."

"I suggest a few sessions with a psychiatrist."

I laughed. "My dearest friend is one but he's far away."

"You have terminated your work here. Go to him."

I was not about to tell her that Andy had a more serious commitment to another friend who had lost his way. She referred me to a specialist in pulmonary diseases, who continued my treatment. Nothing changed.

I canceled my final appointment of the season in Athens, where I was due in May. Instead, I remained in Rome, continuing to live at the guesthouse. By now I was hooked on drugs. With little energy and no motivation, I drifted in a lethargy of indecision. Jomo's invitation was appealing to me, but I was well aware of my ill health and drug addiction. He was just starting his career. I could not inflict myself on him in my present state.

I was too listless to wander about Rome as I had in the days of my youthful travels. Even then I had been dissatisfied and hadn't stayed long. Transforming rubble and stone into a vision of grand amphitheaters and villas was beyond me. They represented something other than greatness, as I pictured legions of Roman soldiers roaming the world in conquest of other lands and peoples.

The grandiosity of the Vatican had not affected me, either, and I had fumed with anger as I'd marched through miles of its museum corridors, viewing the priceless art that had been wantonly stolen to fill those sealed cases. Lauded as unequaled in its scope and majesty, even the Sistine Chapel had disappointed me as I stood far below the vault, craning my neck. Only by looking at photographs of sections and details of the fresco had I been able to see the genius of Michelangelo's art. In those I found the tragedy of his theme, the despair he put into his characters and the pessimism he himself must have felt.

I conjured other Italian cities I had enjoyed far more: the fantasy that is Venice, romantic Verona. My inward eye saw Florence from its hills and Padua with frescoes I liked better than those of Michelangelo. Two hundred years before him, Giotto had covered the walls of the little chapel of Arena with the drama of human experience. With stunning realism, he had revealed humanity in the richness of life.

Always Andy's first question was whether I was off medication and always I gave him the answer I thought he'd like. This time he was more persistent.

"I still take some antibiotics, but I'm off the cortisone for the lung infection," I said.

"Nothing else, Caroline?"

I lied. It was easy to lie.

Sometimes he told me about David.

"Don't be dispirited," he said. "I'll turn him around and you'll have him back if you still want him."

More weeks passed and his news became more than hopeful. Andy had persuaded him to send the board of the Institute an ultimatum, requesting an immediate answer, and it worked. The director came to the temple, expressing his regret for the delay and offering a signed contract to begin construction.

Everything began to happen at once. The groundbreaking ceremony took place followed by an enormous crew of workers. It was not just David who had been waiting for this event. Craftspeople, engineers, including Walt, appeared on the scene, and the office was crowded with people waiting to consult with him, now made easy by his fluent Japanese. Andy said he loved the atmosphere of excitement and especially, seeing David back in stride.

"It was a risk worth taking, and a stroke of good luck. Meanwhile," he added, chuckling, "I'm stealing him away from Mayumi. I think he likes me better."

They went to theaters and they ate Japanese food. They went to nightclubs and listened to American jazz and ate in American-style restaurants. They went to a *sumo* match. They got together socially with people involved in the construction of International Institute. On weekends they visited famous buildings and marveled at the dazzling array of architecture that covers the city.

"We're having a wonderful time, and I'm keeping him very busy." he said, laughing. "In fact, most of the time, he's going to bed alone, too tired to want Mayumi.

"She's not important in his life, Caroline. I think you know that, and I can't do anything more about it, anyway. Dave has a strong sexual drive that you should understand—you're just like him. You wouldn't want him to stop. That would be a greater concern—believe me. He's had brief affairs over the years. He likes women just as you like men, and he's no more promiscuous than you are.

"Feel nice about Mayumi. She's been good to him and good for him, but he won't see her much anymore. He's too occupied doing the work he enjoys. Dave loves you as much as ever. A long time ago he tried to explain to me how he felt. It's complicated for him, just as it is for you—the loving parental closeness as well as the erotic attraction you have for each other.

"A few years ago you stopped in at his office to see him. He told me that when you entered he saw Ana, not you. Your striking resemblance to her was disturbing and sexually arousing. You're the age she was when she died, so you were a reincarnation of his beloved. We talked about it a number of times. I urged him to have a paternity test. Maybe he wanted you so much he didn't want to face the possibility that he was your true father. That's how you feel, too, isn't it?"

"Yes, but Andy, a terrible thing happened when I was with him in Tokyo. I can't forget the hurt, the humiliation. I feel as if I've awakened from a dream and found a harsh reality. From childhood I've lived that dream about David. He was my noble knight who could do no wrong. The spell's been broken. The sheen on my knight's armor is tarnished, and it will never regain its luster. I will always love him, but differently now."

"So he's human, as complex and flawed as the rest of us. Isn't that better than a phony dream of perfection? Forgive him, Caroline. He was subjected to enormous stress with his architecture. Then he read a tabloid with lurid details about you and Karl that made him crazy with jealousy. Now he feels his behavior was despicable. He's ashamed and wants to go to Rome to ask your forgiveness, but he's afraid to even call you. What should I tell him?"

"He's back at work. He shouldn't come here."

"Then you go to Tokyo."

"Tell him I will."

"I'll be gone when you get here. I'm going home. But I have a question that worries me. What medications are you taking now?"

"Not much. An antibiotic is all."

"Why do you suppose I think you're on drugs?"

"Because I lie sometimes. I guess you know that."

"Do you know why you lie?"

"It's become 'second-nature' with me."

"Why?"

I didn't answer.

"Say it, Caroline! Why?"

"I think I'm concealing—covering up—one particular secret that way."

"You know that, don't you?"

"Yes."

"Then stop! Nobody's asking you about your personal life. You say you don't feel guilty. You don't have to feel guilty, but you act like it."

"I don't live on another planet, Andy. Could David and I withstand a scandal?"

"Those who love you won't stop. The others don't count. But now listen to me. I have given you this advice before. I'm doing it again. When you're in Tokyo tell Dave you want a paternity test. He'll do it. Be brave. Face the truth, darling."

"Andy, I've told you before—I know the truth. The test would change nothing."

"What if you become pregnant?"

"I would welcome it."

10

The flight to Tokyo was a nightmare. Delayed for hours even before take-off by a malfunction in an electrical system, the plane was at last airborne only to have the same problem recur several hours later, requiring an emergency landing in Hong Kong. I had not slept throughout the flight and as the plane took off again, I ached to reach into my handbag for pills from the small arsenal I had in a zipper compartment. Others were stashed away in my belongings.

I pictured them. It wasn't even necessary to see what I was taking. I could do it by touch: the cute little yellow ones with heart-shaped openings in their middles to put me to sleep, and the plain round ones for a lift any time of the day. I resisted, wanting to free myself of the compulsion, but it was hopeless, and I gave in.

Insomnia since the horror in Aix, made worse by my severed relations with David, had started me on drugs. When I slept without them, I had bad dreams; with them, my nights were devoid of dreams. That was what I wanted and I took to the pills easily, my illness being a perfect excuse to continue, filling one prescription and renewal after another given me by both doctors who were treating me. More than an "underlying sadness," I felt bereft of hope for good things in my life. Nothing was worth staying alert about, and I doped on them, sleeping endless hours, eating little and not feeling much of anything.

As the plane made its way to Narita, I fell into a deep sleep. Turbulence, sudden and violent, awakened me. I was disoriented for no more than a moment, but in that moment I knew only that I was on a plane and going somewhere, but where and the circumstances of it eluded me.

Think, I told myself, think! And then in a rush of awareness, everything returned—all that I was about and what my destination was and a remembrance of a time past when just such a jolt had occurred. I was a child, around six. Then it had been an earthquake in the night, and my father had walked rapidly, not running, into my room and without a word, scooped me up in his arms and carried me to the doorway. He stood there, holding me tight, his cheek on mine, until the last tremors ceased. Without turning on a light, he put me back in bed, covered me and kissed me.

"Go back to sleep now, Caroline," he had said.

That was all, but it was enough. Not knowing to be fearful, I did as he told me. Here now, so many years later, moving swiftly through an uneven stretch of sky, I was on my way to that loving embrace again. And now, just as then, I did as he had told me and went back to sleep. But this time my sleep was drugged. When the plane landed, a flight attendant woke me. Groggy, I was unsteady as I got to my feet. She gathered my things together and helped me off the plane.

David was grinning as he watched me make my way to where he and his driver waited. I must have looked like a bedraggled waif, wearing an old college backpack and under my arm the enormous portfolio I went nowhere without. I had let my hair grow long and now the curls hung in ringlets around my face. I wondered if he would like it or even notice. It was still too short to reach the cleft of anything.

My bouts of crying were well known, but why do some of us "cry for joy"? Seeing David sent me into a shower of tears. He laughed, and in a more reasonable show of pleasure, took me in his arms and kissed me. For a few moments no one else was in that crowded airport. Then he introduced me to Toshi Ichikawa, and we went to the car and Tokyo.

Snuggling up to him, I slept all the way. The first light of day was appearing when we arrived at the Okura Hotel, where he had stayed before moving to the temple. Toshi left us and we went in. It was a beautiful place and our suite of rooms as luxurious as any I'd ever seen, but the necessity of subterfuge disturbed me. We would be using only one of those rooms.

As soon as we walked in, I dropped my handbag on the floor by the bed and lay down, falling asleep again. David woke me, helped me undress and opening the covers, picked me up and put me in bed.

Leaving a bedside light on, he lay down beside me. "Caroline, don't make me wait," he said. "I want to make love to you."

"Please let me sleep."

As he lay facing me, his body touching mine, he propped himself up on an elbow and remained so, looking into my face. "Open your eyes," he said.

When I did, he put his face close to mine, and for a moment we looked into each other's eyes as I became more and more pleasantly aware of the pressure of his warm body on mine.

"Do I have your full attention, Caroline?"

"Yes."

"Are you ready?" he added, smiling.

"Yes."

Oblivious to time, I awoke hours later in the darkened room. Where was I? Shouldn't my father be here? But he was not. I felt like a child again, alone and frightened. I sensed the onset of panic. Remembering that I had dropped my handbag on the floor when I came into the room, I adjusted to the dim light and fumbled about on my knees until I found it. I took out a couple of tranquilizers and swallowed them. Then I lay back again, my arms tightly folded over my chest in an attempt to control my trembling.

Maybe ten minutes passed. The door opened and David came in. He opened the drapery and came over to sit beside me at the edge of the bed.

"Caroline, what is it? Were you worried that I wasn't here? I went down for a newspaper."

"I'll be all right in a few minutes."

"Have you recovered from your illness?"

"Yes, sure."

"Do you take any medication?"

"No."

"Why is your handbag next to you on the bed?"

"David, stop interrogating me."

"Then tell me the truth."

"About what?"

"Andy thinks you're on drugs."

"Andy bugs me."

"Caroline, show me what you're taking."

"No!"

"Okay, we'll talk about it later. Move over and I'll read the Japanese paper to you," he said.

"What time is it?"

"Ten. Whenever you're ready, I'll order breakfast. Toshi will be here at one to take us for a ride through some of Tokyo. You'll like it."

Gradually I calmed down. David was eager to please me, to reassure me that what had happened would never recur. The past would not be forgotten, but love persists, residing in a deeper place than hurt feelings and angry words. I didn't want anything to spoil it. The drugs? I would taper off. I could do it. He and Andy could stop worrying.

I wanted to go to the construction site first. David introduced me to his supervisor, Yoichi Saito, and the three of us toured the building, maneuvering around scaffolds and saw-horses. It was now well past the framing stage, and I could easily visualize its eventual beauty.

As we stood talking, Walt came out of the office. Years had passed since we'd seen each other, and I was shocked by the changes time had wrought in him, paunchy and balding and his face deeply lined. His look of surprise showed, too; he had last seen me before I went away to college.

We were always fond of each other and now we made our own tour together. He wanted to show me the "shake table," a table-like device constructed in various sizes to test the amount of disturbance a model of a planned building can withstand during an earthquake.

Serious as he had always been, like David, the two were good friends. "This is the most enjoyable place I've ever worked," he said. "I've never seen your father happier about the way things are going, but he should get away more. See if you can persuade him."

"It's hard to take a person away from something he loves to do, Walt."

David came over to us just then. He was on his way to pick up some papers at the temple. My angry vow never to go back there was meaningless now, and we went together, taking the path through the meadow. Midway I pulled him down in the tall grass, and we lay kissing and hugging and laughing.

"You make me feel like a kid again, Caroline. I love it."

Although we had been out only a few hours, I felt exhausted. Jet-lag, I told myself, and we went back to the hotel where I went to sleep again. Early in the evening Toshi took us for a ride through two major areas of the city, Shinjuku and Roppongi.

People fill the streets of European cities at all hours, but I was unprepared for Tokyo. A mass of humanity was on the move everywhere. The streets and buildings were illuminated as brightly as Las Vegas. That was one time I didn't mind heavy traffic, being able to see everything while riding slowly through it.

We passed Roppongi Corner, a popular rendezvous for the young crowd, and crowd it was, with hundreds milling about. Many were on their way to a multi-storied, bright pink coffee shop called Almond. David said Andy and he had been there and gave the coffee only a passing grade.

We made one stop. Toshi dropped us off at a jazz club, the Pit Inn, and David told him we'd take a taxi back to the hotel. When we came in, a singer was doing a rendition in perfect English of "Make Yourself Comfortable," which Sarah Vaughan had popularized. It was an impeccable imitation of Vaughan's style, and at the break I went over to congratulate her. But she couldn't understand a word of English! David explained to her that I wanted to compliment her on her performance. Of course, that amazed *her*: an American speaking excellent Japanese.

By the time we returned to the hotel late in the evening, I was drained of energy and had no desire for dinner when David suggested it. Instead I lay down.

"You're ill, Caroline. I'll call the hotel doctor."

"No, no! I'm fine, just tired. It's jet-lag, that's all."

While he ordered dinner served in our room, I took a few of my pep-up pills. Combined with wine while we ate, I felt less fatigued, and afterward, we went down to the lounge.

"Let's have coffee and cake," David suggested.

The thought nauseated me and I couldn't answer.

"Caroline, are you all right?" he asked.

"I'm fine," I said. "I'll be right back."

Sweaty and sick, I started for the women's room, but became dizzy. David caught me as I fell. He picked me up and ran to the elevator and our room. I vomited repeatedly, then feeling weak and shaky, I almost fell again. He helped me into bed.

"It was something in the food. I'm fine now." I said.

But it wasn't the food and I knew it. In a little while I felt better. We talked about plans for the summer.

"Walt says you should take a vacation, David."

"I will—soon. There are so many places I'd like to show you, Caroline. Maybe we'll take a cruise around the Inland Sea."

With happy thoughts for the future, I cuddled up beside him and went to sleep. It was not to last. In the middle of the night I awoke. Once again tremulous and covered with perspiration, I could hear my heart pounding in my ears and I ran to the bathroom. I didn't understand the anxiety that produced my symptoms, but I had found the answer in tiny yellow pills. I must sleep, I told myself, and gulped down four or five, having long before stopped counting, and went back to bed.

It was not until early the next afternoon that I awoke. David was sitting next to the bed. He looked overwrought and kept calling my name.

"Yes, I'm fine," I said, not fully awake and not focusing well.

He looked angry. "Stop saying that! You're not fine. You're sick. Why do you lie to me? Tell me where you keep your pills. Tell me, Caroline!"

"They're mine."

"Tell me or Dr. Yoshida will put you in the hospital."

I pointed to my backpack and he brought it to me. I handed him the packets of pills. It was then I became aware of a Japanese man standing near the foot of the bed. David handed him the packets and he opened a few, scanning the contents.

I felt embarrassed. I was a bad child being reprimanded, my secret wicked treasure confiscated. Now they were speaking in Japanese.

"That's rude," I said, irritably. "If you want to talk about me, go outside."

They apologized and David sat down on the bed and put his arm around me.

"I don't like doing this, Caroline. I don't know what to do! I'm very worried about you. I'm responsible. You started on this stuff right after you were here in Tokyo."

"Physicians prescribed them when I was ill, David. It's not your fault if I'm an addict."

"I don't blame your father for being concerned," Dr. Yoshida said. "I am, too. Your lungs sound clear, but you may still have the infection your father mentioned to me. Also I think you overdosed. That can be extremely dangerous. Try to taper off. You may lose your life if you don't. Get up when you feel like it, but stay around the hotel for a few days until we see the test results."

The analysis had no surprises, no different from when I was in Rome: a higher than normal white blood count and now, chemical evidence of the drugs I'd been taking. Dr. Yoshida dropped by a few more times. My temperature remained elevated and he prescribed another antibiotic for the infection. David kept a close watch on me, knowing I had more pills, but he was too honorable to search through my things. He became my keeper and I hated it.

"Let me be free, David," I told him. "If I'm going to kill myself, you won't be able to stop me no matter how hard you try. I've developed a dependence on drugs and when I don't take them I feel awful."

"You're not free. You're a slave to pills," he said.

No more was said about it. I made feeble attempts to stick to a regimen of fewer amounts but failed. By now, the serenity I had sought and found in them became more and more transitory and the insatiable craving itself became the symptom. I worried about the reduced stock of my pills, compulsively counting them from time to time and wondering how long I had before they would be gone. I thought of little else, and plotted picking up street drugs. Surely there were places in the dark alleys of Tokyo where that was possible. Just to tide me over, I told myself. Until when? That wasn't a question I asked.

But seeking to boost my reserve was impossible. David's vigilance was continuous, never letting me out of his sight. Probably Andy had told him what might happen if he did. When he went to his office or to check on work that was being done, he insisted I go with him. One time he chanced leaving me for a few hours and I seized the opportunity to escape. I remembered a neighborhood we had ridden through that looked like a possible source, and I went there. But my inability to speak the language made communication too difficult and I rushed back to the hotel, empty-handed.

Now and then for a few days I would gather the strength to forego the drugs. The symptoms were excruciating. My muscles cramped with pain. Sometimes I became dizzy, bumping into things or falling. Often I felt as if my skin was on fire and I stood shivering in cold showers to temporarily relieve it. If those were mild signs of withdrawal I knew a total withdrawal would kill me, and I went back to a comfortable dosage again.

On days when I was more fit, David took me on excursions around the city. Spring is a pretty season in Tokyo. Temperatures are mild and early flowers appear everywhere in massed beds. Cherry trees, coming into bloom, look like giant pink cotton candy. Soft and fluffy, they have no resistance to the slightest breeze that scatters great bouquets of the delicate blossoms into the air.

One time we took a local train to the Wisteria Garden of the Kameido Tenjin Shrine. I had remembered seeing a picture of a wood-block print of that garden made by the eighteenth-century artist Hiroshigi, and I wanted to see it.

Tucked away in an unpretentious neighborhood, the garden is a retreat from Tokyo's hyper-modernism, with the sights and sounds of areas like Ginza left far behind. We were lucky to be there when *fuji*, as wisteria is called, was in bloom.

Entering was like stepping into a picture, a remnant of a former place and time. Everywhere we looked were the pale lavender blossoms, completely dominating the scene. They hung in long pendants from great trellises, swaying gently in the breeze, surrounding the pond with its inner fountain and around the red-lacquered, arched bridge just as they appear in Hiroshigi's image of them, memorialized hundreds of years ago.

Unlike extensive Japanese gardens, this one is intimate, easy to stroll around, with walkways traversing the area around the pool. Thick, gnarled roots and twisted vines leave no doubt about the wisteria's hoary age, yet nature annually disregards that manifestation and brings forth fresh young blossoms to take their turn performing the spring rite.

We brushed some of the fallen flowers from a bench and sat down. One by one blossoms sifted down into the water, their soft purple hues contrasting with the dappled *koi* floating just beneath the surface. It was a sight I will never forget.

When we left, we walked around the neighborhood. Known as the *shitamachi* district, one of the oldest and most traditional still lingering in the city, it is a working-class area of shops and residences that has not yet caught up to the glitter of other parts of Tokyo. Then, not willing to brave a crowded rush-hour train, we took a taxi back to the hotel.

Another day David said he would show me his favorite place in the city. I wasn't surprised that it was a coffeehouse. "It's easy to get to," he said. "Only one stop north of Tokyo Station."

"You've been there a few times, haven't you?" I said, laughing.

Rihaku is located in Jimbocho, the largest used-book section in the world—mostly Japanese books, naturally, but some foreign publications as well. The first time David went there, he said he was in search of a particular book. He had wandered around, going from shop to shop when he came onto Rihaku. It is in an old two-story building, and the atmosphere is old, classical in style and reserved, for there you find serious coffee drinkers, not cappuccino sippers such as I.

David chose a coffee from the list and then we watched the procedure. Only the finest coffee beans, aged for many years, are used and they are treated like tiny treasures. Having been weighed, ground, brewed and filtered by an expert, the coffee was served to us in beautiful antique cups that had been scalded first.

No wonder Japan pleased David so much—even its coffee tasted best to him.

11

One evening a reservation was made for us to stay at a *ryokan*, an inn, in Hakone National Park, a two-hour drive from Tokyo. David told me about it—how thousands of years of volcanic eruptions had formed a colossal-sized crater that was now the park. Spas called *onsen* are everywhere, places where thermal springs bubble up from their underground cauldron.

Centuries ago, when the West was still wallowing in abjectly foul conditions of life, Shinto priests were extolling the virtue of bathing, and it had become culturally imbued in the Japanese. In Hakone, surrounded by idyllic natural beauty, people soak away their cares in the hot mineral waters of the *onsen*.

Early the following day Toshi took us to our destination. Along the road were great masses of azaleas and on all sides a landscape of tranquil mountain scenes. The *ryokan* was a single-story wooden building of traditional architecture. On entering, we were greeted by a kimono-clad woman who took us to our guest room.

Gaijin, as foreigners are called, are seldom seen in places like that, and we were an unusual pair of *gaijin*: a tall, fair one who spoke Japanese and his small dark companion. The attendants carefully avoided staring at us and we felt almost invisible—just what we wanted—although we knew that secretively we were being looked over and wondered about.

The atmosphere of our room was that of another era. On a low lacquered table were fresh flowers and a thermos of warm *sake*. There were *tatami* mats on the floor and legless chairs covered in silk cushions and a closet that held *yukatas* and slippers. A small sofa was a concession to modernity as were the concealed contents of a cabinet: a television set, radio and telephone. Breakfast was a simple meal, but dinner by candlelight was elegant and delicious. We slept on a *futon* with covers of silk.

A sliding *shoji* screen opened to our private little garden where late every evening I stepped out to the steaming spa and lay soaking up its intense heat until David came out to get me. He wrapped me in a big towel and dried me, just as in my childhood he had given me my evening bath and dried me and put me to bed.

But now the act was sexual as the warmth of my body and handling me became the source of arousal for both of us and we had sex quickly, passionately. We could not have enough of each other and night after night we awakened and made love.

One time was different. I asked him if I could stop taking birth-control pills. "David, I want to have a baby."

"Caroline! That's impossible!"

"Why?"

"You know why. Besides, you're addicted to drugs. You don't dare have a baby."

"If I become pregnant I'll quit."

He didn't answer and just looked at me.

"Well?" I said.

"All right. Quit first."

"Believe me. Trust me. I'll stop."

"Caroline, do you remember all the times in your childhood when you made one promise after another you didn't keep? You didn't intend to and I'd let you get away with it. Without your mother, and with me gone so much, you had a troubled young life and I wanted to ease it as much as I could.

"But now you're a woman—the woman I love so dearly. This is different and very important. Promising won't do. You have to bear the misery and overcome this addiction. Then we'll consider having a baby. All right?" he said, smiling.

I went to my portfolio and gave him the last remaining cache of drugs.

"You'll cut down a little every few days and see how it goes. Tapering off gradually will prevent withdrawal symptoms. You can do it, Caroline."

We stayed at the *ryokan* two more weeks, going for short jaunts within the park. A few times we took a boat out on Lake Ashi to visit fishing villages around the lake. Often we sat in our sunny little garden, enjoying the beauty of our surroundings and the view of Mt. Fuji in the distance. Then it would be night again, and David was as romantic as a young lover, "seducing" me. My desire to have his child became a powerful force in my battle with drugs, and as time went on I knew I was winning it.

Yoichi had told us to be sure while in the Hakone area to go to an outdoor museum called the Woods of Sculpture. Although other quicker ways would have brought us there, he suggested we take a taxi to a town called Odawara and take the single-gauge, two-car train that plied a zigzagging course up and down the mountain. We were glad we took his advice.

The train was crowded with local people and we couldn't find seats, but the trip was to be short, so we stood at the very front of the train where we could watch the motorman in his immaculate uniform, cap and white gloves, performing his duties. Occasionally, he would stop to let passengers off or on, or for a momentary switchback. Sometimes he stopped for what appeared to be no reason at all, though there must have been one. He made graceful but imponderable arm gestures, too, which must also have had meanings, at least to him.

Most of the trip is through a gorge profuse with wild vegetation. A stream runs parallel to the track and here and there waterfalls descend from the side of the mountain. The ride was so thoroughly enjoyable we were a little disappointed when the diminutive train made its final ascent to the top of the mountain and stopped at a station called Chokoku-no-mori, which leads directly to the museum.

•

What we found was a wondrous sight, a meshing of physical and aesthetic atmospheres and the remoteness of another world. Misty clouds hung low and moved rapidly over the area, their shadows casting mysterious effects on the sculptures. We, too, were engulfed in the mist and an enchanting unreality prevailed over everything.

Each masterpiece has its uncrowded space. Many, monumental in size, challenge the mountains that surround them. Yet true to the Japanese aesthetic, no contest exists between nature and artifact. The beauty in both are harmoniously bonded. Even though the setting appears limitless, the great heights provide walls, and as the ranges dip low, windows open onto grand vistas. Through one of these Mt. Fuji is visible. Thus the museum, in its grandeur, maintains a sheltered, human, dimension.

Now I understood why Yoichi had urged us to go there. Along with its natural beauty, the museum is a showcase for architects, demonstrating the use of outdoor sculptures in the planning of huge urban buildings. Placed in open green spaces they enhance the environment and refresh the human spirit.

What a showcase this is! In bronze, brass, wood, stone, foam, marble, steel and more—the whole of mankind's condition is explored: our victories and defeats, the comedic in our nature and the grotesque, the tender moments and the bitter anguish. It is all there. Many are created by Japanese artists, but the world is richly represented. Familiar masterpieces have their rightful places: Calder, Moore, Rodin, Maillol, de Kooning, de Chirico and Lipchitz are some of them. Others, less well-known are Gargallo from Spain; Ju Ming from China; Kim Soo Hyun, Korea; Nikolaides, Greece; Cárdenas, Cuba.

It is fitting that the work of the late American genius of sculptural art, Isamu Noguchi, should be in this place. Noguchi regarded nature as the grandest work of art and he created designs that follow the dictates of nature. His own gardens, incorporating its elements—rock, water, gravel—are as awesome in the modern sense as the stone and raked sand of the Zen gardens of the past and equally as symbolic in their fusion with nature. On the grounds of the museum are two of his masterworks.

The magnificence of the area and the worldliness of the art would have been sufficient. But as we traversed the walks leading from one point of interest to another we were by gentle degrees reminded that we were in a specific place—a Japanese place. Amid groves of trees and masses of flowers we became aware of the symbols of the country itself.

A stream, crossed by either of two bridges, is home to exotically patterned *koi*, along with a vivid floating sculpture. Just beyond, by ascending a few steps, we came upon a parasol-covered pavilion where we stopped to have tea.

Off in another direction we followed a path of stepping stones to the very heart of traditional Japan: the tea ceremony house. It is hidden from direct view, as it always must be, by dense foliage and a bend in the path. Amid heavy banks of moss we arrived at our destination. Near the house are the essential well, with its well-head and pulley, a wooden bucket and a dipper. Every minute detail is exactly as prescribed hundreds of years ago, a replication of the first tea-hut of the distant past, with its atmosphere of solitude and serenity, tucked away among these sculptures of the modern age.

Mindful of the deep feelings such symbols engender, I forgave the designers for what appeared to be an intrusion on the internationalism of the museum. The Japanese compulsively incorporate some of these symbols in every garden scene. The garden's classical beauty, three-dimensional art in itself, is undeniable, but it is also true that we of the West feel a vague uneasiness at not being privy to its underlying philosophical principles. Our gardens have a sweet innocence: "What you see is what you get." The Woods of Sculpture does not dispel its mystery. But the sculptures speak for themselves, accentuating the beautiful terrain with their universal modernity.

We made a stop at the gift shop before leaving, and David saw a necklace he wanted me to have. On a simple chain was a small disc of bronze, molded into the shape of one of Picasso's female heads, a memento of that wonderful day. Then we went to the little coffee shop next door where we had bowls of creamy corn soup. I was dead tired, but otherwise happily without symptoms as we took a taxi back to the *ryokan*.

David had had enough of vacationing. As he doled out my pills and observed my reactions to the smaller amounts, I concealed my bad times as best I could, although the situation didn't make for a carefree holiday. He was distracted by thoughts of the construction, too. The long conversations with Yoichi every day made clear his wish to be where the action was. He once told me if he were skillful enough he'd be working alongside the carpenters and masons.

So we returned to Tokyo and immediately went to see International Institute. Though a long way from completion, it was progressing rapidly and well. Finishing materials—hand-crafted objects, fixtures, wall coverings and carpeting—had been ordered.

Yoichi told us about a furnished apartment in a building next to where he and his wife, Hisako, lived. We went right over there and rented it, and I spent the next two months in Tokyo.

It was not the idyllic life I had anticipated. Beyond any doubt David cared deeply for me. But now, as our affair became a continuing experience, I sensed a distancing in his treatment of me. Perhaps when I was a child and growing up he was, by necessity, more actively concerned for my welfare. Had he now receded into a passivity that was closer to his true character? Then again I thought he might simply be acting out a parental desire for me to develop an independence from him. That did not exist. Nor was it what I wanted.

A few days after we moved into the apartment, Yoichi's wife came over to visit me. I liked her at once. In some ways Hisako fit the pattern of a traditional Japanese woman. Small and pretty, she had straight black hair with bangs that covered her forehead, and when she was at home she wore a *yukata*. Being a Buddhist, she had a small *butsudan*, a miniature copy of the elaborate altars in temples. It stood in one corner of the living room, yet it dominated the room. It held photographs of ancestors and offerings of fruit and rice cakes and fresh flowers. Once I observed Hisako praying silently at the altar, and the scent of incense filled the room. This was a contradiction to her secular side, for she enjoyed Western pursuits. Her English was good, and we were able to communicate, but the Saitos had two little girls who kept her busy, and there was not much time in which we could be alone together.

Left to myself, I concentrated on mastering the skills of domesticity. At first, my efforts were satisfactory. Cooking was my downfall. Hisako was a great cook and often invited us to eat with her family. Like everything else Japanese, David enjoyed the food, so I tried to follow my friend's recipes, only to find them tediously long and complicated. My attempts at short-cutting were disasters. Still I persevered.

Then came the day when even a simple *tempura* threw me. The oil was too hot and the batter too thick, resulting in an unsightly batch of overdone greasy globs. And the kitchen was a mess. To cover my ineptitude I rushed out and bought some restaurant food. David laughed at my attempted subterfuge and I cried in frustration.

"I want so much to please you. I can't make anything that's edible," I said.

"Caroline, it's not important!" he kept saying. "Stop trying so hard. You can't become an accomplished Japanese chef in a few months."

The truth was I had no real interest in doing so. After that, I stuck to American dishes I knew how to make and when we ate out, David satisfied his Japanese taste. I continued to go through a monotonous daily routine, though my heart wasn't in it and I was bored, utterly bored.

David, on the other hand, was thoroughly occupied with what he was doing and happy. The commission to build in Virginia was still open for him, and in the evenings he often pored over the plans he had originally made for that institution. I envied him, realizing that I missed academia and wanted to be in the midst of it.

The only pleasure left to me now was my love life, which endured, never waning. No longer dependent on drugs, I told David I was going to stop taking birth control pills. He was reluctant, but when I reminded him of his promise, he agreed.

Seeking ways to fill my idle hours I became a dilettante, dabbling in the traditional arts, first a class in tea ceremony and then *ikebana*, flower arranging, the latter of more interest to me, and I stuck with it longer. The school I attended was famous, directed by Hiroshi Teshagahara, who is also a film director.

"How do you like the class, Caroline?" David asked me one day.

It was hard to answer, so I told him the gist of what I remembered from a passage in a book called *Japanese Things* by Basil Hall Chamberlain. "'Have we not cause to be perplexed at the spectacle of a nation's intellect going off on such devious tracks as tea ceremonies, bouquets arranged philosophically, gardens representing the cardinal virtues? Strict rules, grave faces, so much ado about nothing!' I'm beginning to wonder, too, David."

"That was Chamberlain at the turn of the century. Japan is a far different place than it was then. I think it's those esoteric preoccupations by relatively few people now that lend charm to the country's present-day modernity. If they don't make sense to you, what would, Caroline? What would you like to do?"

I did know. I ached to be back in school preparing for a professional career. But I didn't tell him. I didn't want him to turn parental on me and try to send me off to school in America or England. I didn't want to leave him and was silent.

I chastised myself for not trying harder to become proficient at Japanese. That would have helped as bookstores, films and theaters were cut off from me because of my lack of the language. To compensate, I began hanging out in American tourist-style hotels, where the bookshops had English-language publications and comfortable lobbies where I sat and read. I liked the New Otoni best. It was immense, a community in itself, and I made a habit of spending every afternoon there, sitting in the lounge that overlooked a pretty garden and enjoying the hotel's atmosphere.

But that was not filling my needs, and in the midst of the bustling activity going on about me, I felt lonely and sought a new diversion. I found it—at one of the hotel bars. The conversation was always cheerful and expectedly, men came on to me. I liked the attention, but let it go no further, elated at my virtuousness. At first that was enjoyable, though I was developing a new concern, drinking, and many days I came home in a state bordering on drunkenness. I had found a new drug to replace the old one.

I could tell how distraught David was, seeing me stagger about, unable to maintain any kind of conversation. He would help me into bed and sit for hours watching over me. Then, on one of those nights, he left and didn't return until the next morning. I panicked. Mayumi. I was driving him back to her, and from then on, I carefully limited the amount of liquor I drank and came home sober.

"I'm off drugs, Andy." I told him in one of our phone conversations.

"You don't sound triumphant."

"I'm not sure I don't still have the craving. At first those little pills made me forget my unhappiness. Can't I ever be satisfied? I used to think if I could be with David all the time I'd be home safe. I'm not. His work supersedes everything else in his life. I don't know what to do with myself most of the time. The people who work at the New Otoni are getting to know me—I spend so much time there. I'll bet they think I'm a prostitute looking for business."

"You can change that."

His response irritated me. "Oh? Well, tell me this: David never mentions his divorce. Why isn't it important to him?"

"You've changed the subject, but I'll give you an answer. I think it *is* important to him because he knows it's something you want him to do. He did file for the divorce, but he had to leave before the decree was granted. His attorney in Monterey might be able to finalize it. What he wants to do is go to California and end his relationship with Martha in an amicable way. Do you know why you want the divorce so much?"

"I sure do!" I said. "Martha made my life miserable when I was young and I had to live with her even when he didn't. I know he couldn't get a divorce during those years, but now he can. I still feel like that little kid. David shouldn't make me keep sharing himself with her."

He laughed. "That's irrational. You're not sharing him with anybody. He belongs to you. He'll get the divorce. Then what?"

"I don't know what I want anymore. I'm legally adopted, and I used to think I wanted to be married. I still have some girlish, romantic ideas, but the thought of David and me marrying is outrageous even to me. In our hearts, we know we are already outcasts from our tribe."

"Dave had a bad marriage with Martha. He had a beautiful love affair with Ana and now with you. So the formality of marriage is not the source of happiness for him."

"Andy, I'm depressed."

"No wonder! You have conflicting feelings that you're not resolving. You're like a crook fearful his cover will be blown. It wears you out. 'The truth shall make you free.' That's not a cliché, Caroline."

"Please don't start on that again. I'm convinced David is my biological parent. Confirming it won't change anything."

"It worries me when you tell me your life feels pointless and empty. You don't have to settle for a tragic view of life. You can find the magic in it and be hopeful for the future. Right now you're as dependent on Dave for everything—for his love and attention—as when you were little and truly dependent on him. You'll be happier with him, too, if you don't live in his shadow."

I changed the subject. "Andy, would I make a good mother? I yearn to have a baby."

"You think you're switching topics, Caroline. You're not. You're still on it. But as to your question: Yes, you'll make a wonderful mother someday."

"Someday?"

"When you grow up."

"Andy!"

"You don't like to hear that, do you? That's my opinion. You're not ready for motherhood. Right now you think a baby would fill the void that exists in your life and make you happy. Having a child can be fulfilling, but it can't perform miracles."

"Well, David has agreed now that I'm off drugs."

"He can't deny you anything, even this. I think he's as immature as you are. You two haven't had a paternity test. Do it!"

"No!"

"Omigod! I feel like I'm talking to the wind."

"Andy, you're mad at me."

"Yeah, I am. I'm your dearest friend, Caroline, and I'm worried about your conduct. Your problem won't be solved having a child. It might make it worse. I'm angry at Dave, too. I feel close to him. I was a lonely only child, and knowing him has been like having a marvelous older brother. Now I feel like I'm the older brother. I don't want him hurt, either."

"I can't help my desires."

"You mean you don't want to use your fine mind to examine your desires. That wouldn't destroy them. It might even make your life better."

His reproachfulness and the harsh tone in his voice took me aback and I couldn't reply.

"Caroline?"

"Yes?"

"Forgive me. I have a problem of my own, and today I took it out on you."

"Do you want to talk about it?" I said, imitating him and laughing.

"I wish I could. By the way, that Dutch journal, *Education Today*, has an English edition now, and I read an article in the last issue that praised your course. I'll send it to you. It said you're a gifted young teacher, not just a lecturer, and you're popular. Have you given it up altogether?"

"It was lonely moving around Europe like that."

"Well, you used to talk about going back to school so you could eventually teach in a university. What about that?"

"It would be hard here. I'm not good at languages and Japanese is tough."

I kept finding flaws in all his suggestions, and he sounded provoked. "Let's stop," he said. "We're not getting anywhere."

"I love you, Andy. Don't be mad at me."

"I love you, too, Caroline. You know I can't stay mad very long."

A few days later I told David I was leaving for London the following week.

"I'll stay with Janie if that's all right with her, and I'll enroll in a London university—I don't know which one yet—and start on my doctorate."

"You're doing the right thing. As soon as you're settled I'll come for a long visit."

Leaving him frightened me. I accepted the fact that I was not free of my dread of losing him as I had once so joyfully believed. And now there was Mayumi. In time wouldn't he return to her?

Andy praised my determination. "Dave understands your need to do this. Better to be fearful and brave than to hold back and be miserable, don't you think?" he said.

We spent more time together that last week than we had previously, but we often stopped at the office to see what was happening there. One day Yoichi handed him an envelope. It held an invitation, brush-drawn in calligraphy, for a reception in his honor, followed by dinner, on the following Saturday. It was not the way I had expected to spend my last evening before leaving for England, but a very nice way.

The occasion was extraordinary. Normally, David disliked formal affairs, but that one was different. Among friends, he was relaxed and enjoyed the evening. Hasumi was there and deserved to be. Had not his temple and garden been David's source of inspiration? Walt came and was having a fine time. Every woman in the room looked stunning, many wearing lovely *kimonos*, but Hisako was most chic in her bold Western dress, short, ruffled and flashy red.

The high point of the evening came when a member of the royal family made an appearance to meet David. I was bursting with pride as I watched them bow and then speak in Japanese for several minutes. David introduced me to the prince, and I was astonished, then, that he spoke perfect English. He looked at me curiously, just as others did, and I wondered if they were puzzled by my color, so different from my father's.

Our happy mood lingered after we arrived home. I asked him if he had noticed the curiosity my color aroused.

"Your color enhances your beauty, Caroline," he said, but then he loved me.

I clung to him as we lay together that night. By morning, our long interlude together would become a memory. He would return to the temple and I thought again of Mayumi and knew she would reenter his life as his companion and lover. Was I doing the right thing? Worried and uncertain, my motive now seemed ego-centered, trivial. Why could I not "find myself" in some way here?

Wistfully, I had hoped I would have the answer in a child, but we had no success in cajoling our bodies into awareness that nothing now stood in the way of their performing the elemental function of conception.

David tried to cheer me. "This isn't goodbye to love, Caroline. That will never change. We'll miss each other, but we've been separated before, and I'll come to London to be with you on holidays. If your plans don't work out, we'll think of other ways to make your life more satisfying."

I felt soothed and reassured, and then, just as the very first time, he took me gently in his arms and the permutation—father to lover—occurred. And then, just as countless other times, I had a fleeting schizophrenic instant of the two melding in my emotional response.

With the same lustful intensity as ever before, he now made love to me and I to him. I felt the strong pulsations of his ejaculation and as I lay very still, not wanting to give up the semen that seeped from my body, I begged the gods I did not believe in to kindle the generative force within me and give me the love-child I yearned to have.

12

One day late in July my doctor informed me that I was pregnant. He laughed at my excited response. It was the middle of the night in Tokyo, but I couldn't wait another minute and ran to a public telephone to call.

There was a long pause.

"David?"

"I'm stunned, Caroline."

"Aren't you happy?"

"I know I'm not reacting the way you'd like me to, but I suddenly feel dazed. I'll come to London and we'll talk about it."

"What is there to talk about? This is what I wanted. I thought you did, too."

"We shouldn't have done it, but there's time to reconsider."

"I won't have an abortion. I want our baby with all my heart."

"Give it some thought, Caroline. We'll talk again tomorrow."

Later I called Andy. "David wants me to terminate my pregnancy. I won't."

"Dave has finally come to his senses. I know you're sick of hearing me tell you this, but now my advice is more important than ever. Determine the truth. Don't risk the consequences of having a child."

I didn't answer and he gave up.

"When's the due date?"

"Early April."

"Who's your obstetrician?"

"His name's Josh Adams."

"What's he like?"

"Well, he has all the proper credentials, and he's friendly." I laughed. "He looks like an ex-football player—a bruiser of a guy, but he's gentle and kind. I feel comfortable with him, Andy."

"Okay. Ask him to send me copies of his regular reports."

David and I talked every day and gradually, with his original panic subsiding, he accepted what he could not change and found a natural pleasure in the anticipation of his child's birth.

"Our lives are our own, Caroline. We'll do fine." he said.

A few months passed and amniocentesis indicated I was carrying a boy. I was elated. David would have a son.

At long last, my life had taken a proper turn. The dissatisfactions of the past were erased by the contentment I now felt. Only a little more than a year had passed since I left California, but when is life measured by the days of its passage? My thoughts slipped back to events that had filled that year. Teaching had been my reason for being in Europe, my first experience, and I liked it, but it corroborated my need for a further degree and a position in a university, where students would come to me, not the reverse.

My sexuality had brought some unexpected problems. Now I recognized the naiveté in my conduct—acts I would never repeat but which I didn't regret, but also the ones I did regret. Andy must have grown weary of my pestering him for answers. "You're young, Caroline. Your behavior is normal," he kept assuring me, but he always sounded different when we spoke of my love affair with my father, expressing more than simple concern. Yet for me it overshadowed everything else in my life—always, always dreaming of being with him, weeping with joy at the sight of him, then weeping in sad parting.

Happy in the belief that all of that was in the past, I lived in the present—in love's fulfillment and its confirmation in the life that was growing within me.

Yes the world is the best place of all…for making the love scene…and kissing people and making babies….

Application to pursue my studies at the university where Janie was teaching was accepted, but in a few weeks I had to stop. Even small exertions left me fatigued. I knew I was not in robust good health. My illness had left its traces, and often I felt listless. Many days I sat in Janie's big, old-fashioned rocking chair in the sitting room, reading or dozing, relaxed as Cat—although that was no longer her name—purring on my lap.

"Cat is not a name, Caroline. We'll call her Morchella," Janie said, and that was all right with Cat, who responded to either name.

One of those days the mail included a letter from Hisako. Her life was unchanged, filled with domestic activities. From time to time she visited the construction and all was going well. Sometimes David joined her and Yoichi at events, and, in fact, she said, they had reservations for a Noh play together. She remembered my fascination with the performance I had seen. She missed me, she said. I missed her, too.

I had a vivid recollection of that Noh drama. It was quixotic, replete with symbolism, and I had told Hisako I was "lost." She laughed, explaining that the Japanese have trouble with Noh, too, because the chanting is in an archaic prose. Despite my puzzlement I found it intriguing. Presented in a form of utmost grace, it is a study in abstraction. Reality does not exist. There is no plot, only a recurring theme based on sins of one kind or another, and the action is vaguely passive.

The characters, though imbued with emotional trauma and latent violence, have no personal control over their "lives" since they are dead—ghosts from the world beyond, held fast by mysterious forces. As illusionary figures, figments of the past, glued to memories never laid to rest, they remain unforgiving and unforgiven, pathetic spirits unable to become detached from the raging passions of their former lives, preventing themselves from attaining the repose of nirvana.

Sunshine warmed the room, and I moved the rocker to the window to bask in its rare appearance as autumn more and more covered London with a leaden sky. Morchella leaped back onto my lap and promptly fell asleep again. I, too, closed my eyes, and in a reverie, I contemplated the baffling experience Noh had been for me.

In a few moments my reverie dissolved in sleep where once again I took up its theme in a dream, intertwining Noh's content with my own human drama. I became an observer. Off to the left of the darkened stage stood a shadowy figure, Andy, who also awaited the action about to commence.

Standing at the entrance, I ushered my audience along the pebbled path into the theater of my slumbering mind. They came single file and in pairs, finding seats. I knew them all, their images clearly defined: friends, students, lovers. And they acknowledged me—a nod, a wave of a hand, one audaciously blowing me a kiss.

My dream stage was small, intimate, square in shape, just as its real counterpart. Projecting out into the auditorium itself, it had a three-dimensional quality, allowing the performance to be more than merely pictorial, drawing in the audience, as well. Were they not all part of my life?

A soft light focused on the rear of the stage and my musicians began to play. How strange it was, for theirs were not the instruments of Noh: the shrill pitch of the bamboo flute with its plaintive sound and drums that whispered or boomed. Mine were a bass and clarinet. In the background, unseen but faintly heard was the tinkling of a monk's hand-held bell. That was my group—incongruous on this stage, as dreams have a way of being, yet pleasing to my ear.

A lone Japanese woman now appeared. A quick nod to my musicians and she sang the blues of unrequited love, sensual and melancholy—then vanished from the scene, and as quickly the musicians, as well. Only the tiny sound of the temple bell could be heard.

That then stopped, too, and an eerie stillness filled the hall. Only a bit of light remained on my dream stage. Tense with foreboding, I looked toward the stage-wing, seeking comfort in Andy's barely visible presence. Suddenly my head reverberated with shrieks and howls, lamentations from deep in the netherworld of

Noh. Scenes of lust and hate and revenge flashed swiftly across the stage of my mind as fearsome demons cavorted, threatening hell's torment. Where were those characters who sought deliverance? Would their sins be expiated? The atmosphere was charged with emotion.

Then the footlights went on, heralding the entrance of the first of my characters. In simple priestly garb, a mask tightly enclosing his face, it was Hasumi. In one hand he held the tiny bell, ringing it with convulsive rapidity. Then I saw the gleam of metal as with his free hand, he drew a knife from the sheath held in a recess of his robe. He looked through the narrow slits of his mask and finding me, stepped forward. I cowered, but instantly he vanished and the lights dimmed once again.

Almost obscured by the dim illumination, a woman now appeared. Her mask concealed her face, yet I knew it was she—Mayumi. She stepped close to the footlights and finding me, bowed. Slowly she unpinned her hair. Then untying her *obi*, the scarlet lining of her *kimono* was exposed. Without hesitation she let the gown fall to the floor, revealing her feminine beauty.

Kneeling, she remained motionless, her head slightly inclined, her hands over her eyes. As she raised her head again, her tear-stained face shone in the faint light. At once, the stage darkened and she was gone.

If only then I could have awakened! It was not to be. Held fast in my dream state, tremulous apprehension seized me. The emptiness of the stage, its stillness and indistinct light augured ill, and I desperately hoped that what I knew was inevitable would not occur. I dreamed on. As the lights brightened he was there, my beloved, in majestic robe and mask, exalted, noble in stature. He sought me out, but unlike the others, he addressed me:

"I cannot stay, my dearest."

"David, don't leave me!"

But he was gone.

"David, stay with me!"

And he reappeared. In a gesture as abstruse as any in Noh, he put his hand to his heart and then was gone. Frantically, I kept calling him. He must not leave. I must conjure him back. But the stage remained dark and he was gone.

"Andy! I can't see you, either," I screamed. "Where are you? Don't leave me."

"I'm here, Caroline, right here."

Again I called his name, but this time, aloud, as I awakened. I jumped to my feet and Morchella fell from my lap. How long had I been asleep? Dreams can be swift in their passage. Yet I was agitated, trembling and craving the pills that once had relieved my symptoms. I had none of my own any longer, but Janie might have some, and I ran to the bathroom. Only aspirin. I stood facing my terrified reflection in the mirror. Liquor. I had drunk too much sometimes and in combination with pills, which I now knew could be lethal, but alcohol was not my addiction and I rushed to the kitchen. Janie often stocked a little beer or a bottle of wine. Nothing. She had been told. That was it. All of them—they were protecting me from myself.

Andy! Had he not been a witness with me in my dream? I called him. "Andy, I was taking a nap and had an awful dream. There was this Noh drama," and I told him its content. "We—you and I—weren't in it. We were just observers. It was so frightening."

"It was a dream, darling."

"But you've told me that so much in our lives has its essence in the unconscious. Now when my unconscious is revealed to me you minimize the truth that may be in it. This dream—it was so ominous, evil. It had a tragic inevitability."

"You have it wrong, Caroline. There is great truth in your dream, but you've misread its message. It's your fear that forecast a tragic event. If a calamity should occur it wouldn't be because your dream was a prophesy."

"It was not an idle dream, Andy."

"Do you want to examine it?"

"I don't know what to think. I'm just frightened."

"All right, listen to me. Beneath your present happiness you still feel vulnerable, threatened. Dave is in Japan. He has adapted to the culture in positive ways and wants to remain. You like Japan, but not as he does. You weren't able to adjust to a permanent life there. The thought is unsettling. You don't know what you will do when the baby is born.

"Hasumi was an evil character in your dream. Why didn't he call you when Dave was troubled? Instead he brought him a Japanese woman, didn't he? He's a villain leading Dave to abandon you for Mayumi. But Mayumi is weeping, isn't she? She knows what her position is. Hasn't she removed her *kimono* and bowed? She knows, as you do, that you will always be Dave's beloved.

"You must put this dream aside. It is not reality. All of us at one time or another fear the loss of those we love, and you created the dream out of your fears. You gave your characters their cryptic messages.

"Soon Dave will be with you. You'll see how unchanged his love is, and once the baby is born, you will make a decision with him on how you will handle your lives together so that both of you can be happy with your child.

"Now I have a suggestion: get out of the house! Surprise Janie—buy some crazy mushrooms for dinner. I'll call you tomorrow."

My friends seldom left me alone for long periods. Matt took me for drives, sometimes to soccer matches that he loved and sometimes to museums that I loved. Once we went to my favorite London museum, the Victoria and Albert. That was when I remembered Jim and called him. He lived in Mayfair, not far away, and came right over. His frank expression of disappointment that I was pregnant was refreshing.

"I don't have much luck with beautiful women. There's Liza. Whenever I'm in Morocco I go to Marrakesh just to be with her, but she's all 'business,'" he said, laughing.

Jim and I became close friends. Whenever he was in town we went out together—always in the daytime, because I craved sleep so much. Pregnancy affects many women that way, my physician said. It was inconvenient. One time we went to a matinee performance at a theater, but even at that hour, I fell asleep at what Jim said was a most dramatic point. We had lunch together often, and then we went to art institutions where he pointed out acquisitions he had made for them.

Acting typically pregnant, I told him I craved minestrone, but not just any minestrone. It had to be some I'd found at an Italian take-away called Delizioso in Regent's Park. That was far from Janie's but he went there anyway, and brought some for me.

While I greedily consumed the soup, Janie made some pasta and heaped a pile of sauteed morels over it for Jim and herself. Always eager to share her knowledge of mushrooms, she referred to them as *morchella esculenta*, and thus I learned how Cat got her new name.

A number of times when Jim and I were out together, people would stop to talk to him and I would be introduced, but I had no idea how well-known he was until one day Janie spotted a small article in a tabloid that hinted broadly of our having an affair.

"Is our own James Crawford romantically attached to the obviously pregnant daughter of David Shaw, the famous architect now in Tokyo?" it suggested, and went on about observations of frequent "sightings" of us together.

Once a cameraman spotted us, and that night we saw ourselves on television. Jim and I felt mischievous, never giving interviews and never denying the story, so the innuendoes continued. Jim was delighted. He had been married and divorced years ago and didn't care in the least if we let the rumor persist. In fact, he said, he hoped his former wife, whom he disliked, would hear about it and be jealous.

I missed Jim when he went on his trips and was happy when he returned. Feeling very fond of him, and Liza, too, I began to plot how I might get them together.

In November David came to London, planning to remain until after the first of the year. Janie insisted that we have the flat to ourselves, even though I knew it was a sacrifice for her, preferring her own place to Matt's.

David marveled at the protuberance that had already taken shape on my small body, and the infant inside me performed with lively movements, pleasing both of us. Probably like all prospective parents, we speculated about him. I had no doubt he would have the brilliance and good looks of his father, but I wondered what skin color he would have.

"I hope it's yours, Caroline," he said.

Our days and weeks passed quietly. We went out. We stayed in. Janie and Matt spent some time with us, but mostly we were alone together, never tiring of being together. How often in my life I had viewed events, good and bad, in retrospect. This was not one of them. I perceived the immediacy of my happiness and permitted myself a look into a future sweetened by our child. Still fearsome were the flashes of remembrance of my nightmarish dream, but in time I hoped I would be able to view it as Andy had said—symbolic of my fears, but not reality—"only a dream."

Late in December Andy called to tell me he would be in London the next day. I was overjoyed. Then Jim called. He was back from his current trip to Eastern Europe, and I called Liza to invite her to a New Year's weekend. She accepted. My spirits soared as I anticipated being surrounded by my friends. I was well aware of how rare such devoted friendships were. Never was there a whisper of criticism about David's and my deviant relationship. If they were concerned for us, should our baby's parentage be questioned, I knew for certain any one of those men—Andy, Jim, even Matt—would claim fatherhood.

When Andy arrived I learned the significance of his sudden trip. He himself was a physician, having interned before turning to psychiatry. He had kept in touch with Dr. Adams, whose monthly reports until now indicated only a slight anemia. In the latest, the result of a blood test showed that even with medication, I had a higher white cell count than at the start of my pregnancy.

My doctor had never mentioned any of that to me, but Andy was worried. The pathology of my condition was ambiguous, but Andy thought the severe infection and general malaise I had experienced only weeks before I became pregnant might have caused it. I had a persistent low-grade fever, as well, but Dr. Adams had been unwilling to give me more medicine until the baby was born.

The three of us went to Dr. Adams' office, where Andy recommended a blood transfusion and another unit reserved for later, if needed. My doctor agreed. Janie and Matt arrived shortly afterward and everyone was tested, but only Matt's blood type would do. Without hesitation, he offered to provide it, and after further testing a unit was transfused.

Dr. Adams had never met Andy but their communications probably led him to believe he was the baby's father. Now he met David, too, and hearing his worrisome questions, reassured him.

"Caroline will be fine, Mr. Shaw," he said. "Come back in a few months and we'll deliver a fine little grandson for you."

David didn't bat an eye, thanking him for the care he was taking of me. The rest of us sat quietly, but I don't think I was the only one startled by that remark. I was pregnant with David's son and indeed, his grandson, as well!

The medical procedure took several hours. Late in the day as we were leaving Dr. Adams' office, David suddenly stopped.

"Wait for me. I won't be long. I have another question," he said, and went back in.

But he didn't come out right away, and finally Andy went in after him. More time passed and all of us were about to reenter the office when they came out together and we left.

"What was that about, David?" I asked.

"Oh, I'm just a fussbudget, Caroline. Everything's fine."

I wondered. Was it my kind of "fine"—not really fine at all?

Liza arrived early the next day. She and Jim appeared pleased to see each other and I felt like an Old World matchmaker. Now they could relate to each other on something other than a paying basis.

I wanted everybody to stay at Janie's with us for that special weekend. It didn't work out exactly like that. Janie and Matt did come and they had one of the bedrooms. David and I had another. Liza chose to accept Jim's invitation and went off with him to his townhouse, and for a few nights Andy slept on the oversized couch in the study. Surrounded by books, he said it was the best room in the house, but on the last day of the year when I awoke early to get the paper, I saw his bag in the front hall.

"Andy!"

He came out of the study, dressed and ready to leave.

"Why are you going? Tonight's New Year's Eve! Stay till tomorrow, anyway."

"I can't, Caroline. I'll be back when your baby's due. I must go now."

Impulsively, I put my arms around him and kissed him. "Andy?"

"No questions, Caroline. I must go. We'll talk on the phone soon."

Matt appeared just then, ready to drive him to the airport. I stood for a moment bewildered at the unexpectedness of his departure. David found me later, still in my nightgown, sitting in the rocker with Morchella on my lap.

"Why did Andy leave in such a hurry?" I asked.

"He's been seeing someone in Monterey. He probably wants to spend the holiday with her."

Why hadn't I thought of that?

There was no doubt about Janie's pleasure at being back in her own digs. I urged her to stay on after the holiday since David would be leaving soon afterward. She quickly agreed to that, confiding that living with Matt was not perfect.

"What's wrong?"

"It was probably a good thing staying with him. We were planning to marry, but I'm not sure now. The sex is great, but Matt and I bicker. Then he clams up."

"Men and women are different, Janie. We want to talk things out. They want to think about them and solve them by themselves. It doesn't make communicating easy, I know."

I did know. Wasn't that what had caused David's and my problem—his inability to express his worries and needs and my inability to respond to his unspoken cry for help?

That day Janie was her usual cheerful self. Constant chatter accompanied everything she did. She brushed Morchella. She checked the plants it had been my duty to baby-sit during her absence. When David returned from shopping for snacks and drinks and brought a bouquet of flowers, she did her thing, giving them their botanical names and declaring them good specimens.

Later when Liza and Jim arrived, bringing an array of Indian food they'd picked up at Gaylord's on their way, she was delighted. She wouldn't have to cook and she loved Indian food. She once told me the food in India was the best thing about her visit with her parents.

My success in matchmaking Liza and Jim was shortlived. Liza had brought her luggage back to the house.

"What's wrong?"

"He's nice, Caroline. But not exciting."

"Then you create the excitement," I suggested.

She laughed, but no more was said and I realized I had been offering my friends unsolicited advice and that I should stop.

I watched as David and Jim made drinks for themselves and sat down to talk. Listening to them I was struck by how much alike they were. David told him that in his youth he had planned to become a sculptor, but later found architecture of greater interest; Jim had thought of becoming an architect but switched to art and had a degree in archeology, as well, from Cambridge, which he said had proved to be important in his work. They both loved Japan. At least once a year Jim saw his Japanese clients, but after his business was completed he remained for a month. He and David conversed in Japanese now and then and teased the rest of us by refusing to translate their remarks.

Suddenly I had the answer to the question I'd been mulling since I first met Jim. Why had I not realized it? Though different looking, the two could have been brothers in their similar personalities, even to their slow manner of speech and the soft expressions in their eyes.

David asked if Japan was his favorite country.

"I would say so, except that I'm drawn to Morocco. Has Caroline told you we met there? When she gets her shape back, you must ask her to belly-dance for you, Dave. Let me know if she goes to your room afterward," he said, smiling.

Everybody wanted to hear about Jim's recent trip to Eastern Europe. It involved a great deal of intrigue and risk to himself. How wrong Liza was! Jim was a very exciting man, despite his quiet exterior.

A curator of a museum of religious art had some time before, in great secrecy, contacted him. The newly formed government of his country had ordered all sacred art, some priceless in its age and beauty, to be distributed among Eastern Orthodox churches. It was a marvelous little museum, Jim told us, with every modern technique used to preserve the rare collection. Each gallery had a hydrothermographic device to measure the relative humidity and temperature.

"That's international practice, but less often used in Eastern Europe," Jim said, "And they're never found in those broken-down old churches, where the deterioration would be rapid. What, the curator asked me, would become of those things in such surroundings? Even security systems were of little use in combating the wanton ransacking of churches. The once-immense amassment of such art was being removed in wholesale quantities, and he said he felt like a parent giving up children in order to save them. He offered me three of the finest icons in the museum and a magnificent painting for permanent safekeeping in London. Selling any more than that would be too risky. The money from the sale would be used to maintain the institution that was now without funds."

Such situations created a serious dilemma for Jim. He would not take unique national treasures no matter how enticing the offers. He had also become watchful as thieves, posing as collectors, offered him ancient objects or pieces from recent digs. He spent sleepless nights troubled over whether to use his business acumen to acquire particular things for a museum or refuse to diminish another country's repository of fine art. He was a rebel in his own profession, urging the return of the Elgin Marbles to Greece, though he knew that would open the floodgates to demands by other countries for the return of their precious art. In the present situation, he made the purchase and luckily brought the objects out of the country without incident.

Matt had taken charge of the disc selections, providing a background of music for us during the evening. Now it was an album of ballads. As if to offset the previous serious topic, Jim stood up and asked which of us would dance with him. Janie was snuggled up to Matt and Liza smiled but didn't move.

"Will the fat lady do?" I asked.

"You're as good at this as the belly stuff, Caroline," he said as we danced.

"I should be! I learned as a taxi dancer one summer."

Jim knew the words to one of the numbers and sang them softly.

"You're a romantic fella, Jim."

"It depends on the woman I'm with. Hey, look!"

Liza was asking David to dance with her. We watched them for a few minutes.

"Move in close, Jim. I have something to say to her."

"He's mine, Liza," I said. "Behave yourself."

"I'm going to belly-dance for Dave," she said.

It sounded like teasing, but she was looking at Jim. Maybe she had not lost interest in him, after all. When the music stopped, I asked Jim to come to the front parlor with me.

"Listen, Jim, I don't want you going home in the middle of the night. Stop being so nice! Don't *ask* Liza if you can stay with her here; tell her you're going to. She'll like that. There's a little room at the back of the flat, but the study is nicer. You'll find everything you need. Take the back cushions off the couch. There's plenty of room for both of you."

He put his arms around me. "I could fall in love with you real easy, Caroline."

"I already love you, Jim. You and David are so much alike, it seems natural. But he and I are inseparable. You know that."

As a New Year's Eve celebration, our party had no sparkle. We talked. We laughed. It was surface cheer, each of us content in the company of the others, yet each separate, betraying an underlying distraction, and as the time drew closer to midnight, we became even less jolly, retreating into our private cubicles of contemplation.

I looked at David. He, too, appeared to move from our common space to his own, meandering in his own stream of thought. About what? The project in Tokyo? His forthcoming parenthood? Was he recalling last year's holiday with Mayumi, just as I now thought of Karl? Bitter though the memory was, had he not touched my heart?

What was wrong, I mused. Twice that day I had asked that question of others. This time I asked it of myself. My thoughts wandered off to Andy. All day, then all evening, his image kept appearing to me. His departure had been abrupt and I could not adjust to his absence. Childlike, I simply wanted him. I wanted to call him. I wanted to hear his voice. I wanted to know he was home and all was well with him. But he wouldn't be home. He was in Monterey by now and perhaps, at that very moment, making love to "someone." Why wasn't I glad for him, my best friend in all the world? Omigod, I thought, using his expression, could I be jealous? I rejected that instantly.

Feeling weary, I went off to sleep before the others. Late in the night David came quietly into the room, not turning on a light, and after undressing, he slipped into bed. But I awoke.

"Jim's staying for the night," he whispered.

"Good!"

"You've turned Janie's place into a den of fornication."

"Yes, I know. Nice, isn't it?"

We kissed goodnight and laughingly adjusted our positions. With my big belly between us, I tried to lie as close as I could.

"Caroline, stop that! It isn't easy right now."

"Why? We'll manage. We always have before."

"Okay, but remember, Janie and Matt are in the next bedroom and Liza and Jim, not far away. You have a certain exuberance. Will you be discreet?"

"What do you mean?"

"They may be making love. Notice how quiet they are? They're discreet."

"David, my whole life has been indiscreet."

"Well, try to lie quietly. I'll make it worthwhile."

He did. And I was discreet.

One week later I accompanied David to the airport for his return to Tokyo. As always, the prospect of separation set off my old fear of loss. Now coupled with the ominous content of my dream, fresh as when it had occurred, I was numb with a dread of some undefined impending evil.

"Why must you go?" I demanded. "Walt and Yoichi are excellent supervisors and care as much as we do that all should go well. Wait till after the baby is born. International Institute will be on its way to completion and we can go back together to celebrate."

"I have some new ideas I'd like to consider for another project—that museum in Virginia, Caroline. They keep running through my head, but I have no equipment to construct a model here. You know I'll be back well before the baby is born."

"It frightens me to see you leave."

"Caroline, Andy has talked to you about those feelings you have and I've tried to reassure you. They are fears, not reality. All leave-taking from those we love is tinged with sadness and everyone has the fleeting fear that it is the last time we will see those we care deeply about. I worry about you, too. Don't you know that? We must not give in to groundless fears."

"You don't understand, David. It's not the same for me."

He didn't respond and was undeterred.

"Let's not say goodbye," he said, smiling, and without another word, we kissed in farewell.

Now I was alone again. Not quite alone. Janie was living at home but fully occupied with her teaching duties and she often stayed overnight at Matt's, so I saw little of her. She must have thought I'd given up my interest in an academic career. Actually, it was still important to me. I just didn't talk about it. I had ideas for my thesis clearly in mind and there were occasional days when I went to the architectural college library to do some research. Though unable to go to school in a formal way, I studied at home, too.

Thinking I needed things to do, Janie assigned the care of Morchella to me, which I was doing anyway. She was punctual for her meals and there was no concern that she would turn the place into a feline nursery. She was spayed. Also I was once again in charge of the house plants, having been given a watering and spraying schedule. Though I did with them as I was told, my heart wasn't in it.

Feeling stronger and more energetic than throughout my pregnancy I was now frustrated by the clumsiness caused by my greatly inflated midsection. As my huge belly preceded me in those last weeks, I made my daily circuit of the flat. Once I counted the seedlings in their tiny pots, fifty-four in all, waiting for me on the table Janie had set up in the back room, and using a dropper, administered the proper number of drops of water to each one. Now and then Janie took some to school but always replaced them with others.

In every room were big pots hanging from hooks in the ceiling and I cautiously stood on a stool to reach them. But the most irksome were in the bathroom, the often steamy atmosphere best for those, Janie said. A few sat in the tub itself, so taking a bath meant bending and lifting them out and afterward, replacing them. I cursed those plants and wished they'd perish. They didn't. They flourished as I compulsively cared for them, much of the time sponging myself rather than bathing.

One day in the midst of my chores I heard from Jim. He was in Hong Kong by special invitation to a private sale of antique Chinese art, with plans to fly to Tokyo when he was through.

"It's not a long trip from here," he said. "I'll get to see Dave and the Institute and have a lot to tell you when I get back.

"Caroline?"

"What, Jim?"

"I keep thinking about what good times we have had together. I wonder if you miss me the way I miss you."

"You know I do."

His affair with Liza was over and I wondered: If I were not pregnant would I take her place? The thought was unsettling. I was drawn to him because of his likeness to David and all the fine qualities they shared. A frivolous affair without deeper meaning would be impossible. I felt guilty even speculating on such a possibility and rejected it. Ah, the virtuousness of monogamy: freedom's jailer.

It was March. One month to go. My greatly increased girth was becoming burdensome and I longed for the day when my baby would come to term. I picked up books on child care and was delighted to find a copy of the original Benjamin Spock book. It sent me back to my own childhood, remembering the well-worn paperback in my father's study.

Now and then Matt appeared unexpectedly to show me his latest drawings of furniture he planned to make for the flat. Still confident he and Janie would marry, he spent his spare time dreaming up new designs. Janie swore she'd never let him replace her "antiques."

He drove me to my appointments with Dr. Adams, and on the last visit, I was given good news. My fever was gone and my blood count normal. Best of all, the baby was doing well. That I already knew by his vigorous activity inside me.

David was planning to arrive in London in a few weeks. It was early, but he said he didn't want to take a chance missing that thrilling event in our lives. He told me about Jim's visit.

"The man's in love with you, Caroline. But then is there one who isn't?"

"David, you are the one I care about."

"I know, dear. See you soon."

13

A few days later I heard from Andy. He was on his way to London.

"Andy, Dr. Adams says I'm all right."

"Yes. You're in good health."

"Then why are you coming here?"

"I have to be in London tomorrow. I'll see you around noon."

"Andy, wait!"

"I'm in a hurry, Caroline. See you tomorrow."

"Wait!"

The phone was dead. Instantly—for how could I believe otherwise?—I sensed that something was dreadfully wrong. Unable to still my fear, it only generated more. Once again, as following my dream of Noh, I cursed myself for not keeping a reserve of pills for such moments. Again, as then, I ransacked the house. Nothing. I called Janie at school and she came home at once. Matt was with her, and they tried to calm me.

"You have a vivid imagination and now you're overstressed," Janie said. "About what? You don't know. Andy was probably in a hurry to make his plane on time. Maybe he's going to be interviewed for a job in London. He's looking for a change. You'd like that, wouldn't you?"

My friend's assurances were useless. An incomprehensible fear enveloped me. "I must call David!" I told her.

"No, you can't. It's the middle of the night in Tokyo. Come to the kitchen with me and we'll make some tea. There's nothing we can do now except wait for Andy. I'll call Dr. Adams. He'll prescribe something."

Matt picked up the medication at a chemist's and in a little while I was asleep. Early in the evening Janie had a caller. His presence had been intended for me, but mercifully, I was unaware of it. A Japanese embassy representative had delivered a formal letter of condolence from his government. David had died that day.

Everything was being done the next day to shield me from hearing the news until Andy would arrive, and he had instructed Janie to give me another pill just before noon. During the interim, constant activity was going on, much of which I was unaware. My friends lied repeatedly.

"Why are you sniffling, Janie? Do you have a cold?"

"Yeah, I'm not going to school."

"What's with the telephone today?"

"Oh, those pesky reporters," she said, and took it off the stand.

The press had, in fact, lost much of its interest in me once Jim left on his most recent trip, but now a more serious situation roused their curiosity. In addition, there were condolence calls from around the world. There was one from Martha, who, of course, had been informed.

"Tell her I'm sad for her," she told Janie.

When the doorbell began ringing time after time, Matt stayed outside, putting the bouquets and pots of flowers that were being delivered in a storage area of the garage. He disconnected the television set, complaining convincingly that we'd need to call for repairs, and Janie reported that the morning paper had not arrived. She had clipped the long laudatory obituary and discarded the rest.

None of those things did I know then, for that was how Andy wanted it. Nor did I know Andy's call had come from Tokyo, not home. Now, within a few hours he would tell me the tragic news, but it was not until the following morning that inadvertently I would learn the horrible circumstances. He had hoped to prepare me for it. Too late, he would then reveal what had transpired, and still later, precise and detailed instructions David had prepared and confided to him and Hasumi.

But that was yet to come. As she was told, Janie gave me the sedative. When I awoke, still feeling groggy, Andy was sitting beside the bed. As I reached out to him, he helped me sit up and took my hands in his.

"Andy, why are you here?"

He did not answer, and now I knew something of terrible import had occurred. No amount of shielding was to protect me any longer.

"What is it? Tell me! There are tears in your eyes. Why?"

I need not have asked. I knew. "It's David. He's sick, isn't he? His heart. I knew it! All those painful attacks he had. I knew coffee-drinking couldn't cause such illness, I must go to him, Andy!"

"Caroline, no. Listen to me. David died yesterday."

"No! You're wrong. That can't be. I spoke to him just days ago. He's going to be here for the birth of our baby. I'll prove it. I'll call him."

The phone had been restored and I did call. There was no answer and the ringing sound continued in my ear until Andy took the phone from me and walked with me back to the bedroom.

"Darling, put your face next to mine. Feel my tears and cry with me."

No! Oh, no! I will not weep. I will not acknowledge this fiendish prank. Yesterday? When yesterday? Was it when I was watering Janie's plants, feeding Morchella, daydreaming, always daydreaming about the future with our child? Was it when I was listening to music we both enjoy? Uchida playing Mozart. Was it when I slept—even in sleep wanting you close to me. Was that when....

"Andy, how can it be? I wasn't with him to hold him in my arms, to kiss his dear face one last time. He left me without even saying goodbye."

"Caroline...."

Why had fate put me here? Why was I not there with you? I would have stopped that vile act. I would have repelled death's summons. Oh, my love! Did temple bells accompany your departure? Did you drift off in a sweet dream?

Oh, how I loved you! In my childhood I loved you. Through my girlhood, dreaming only of you, until at last you took me to your heart there in the night. Was it yesterday that you lived and loved me? Was it yesterday you died? Is your life already in the past, my dearest? How cruel you were to leave me. How cruel!

"Caroline, do you hear me? Answer me!" Andy said.

I did hear him, but I couldn't respond. I had had the courage to love with all my heart, to desire a child through that forbidden love, to suffer society's outrage, if need be, but I did not have the courage to bear my loss. I would escape my pitiful state.

Where are you, my beloved? I must find you.

Andy was still holding my hands. Now he took my pulse. Without letting go, he called Janie. What was he saying? His voice became faint, far-distant. Other voices, muffled and indistinct, were silenced now, too, as I drifted in a sphere of soundlessness, in a self-hypnotic sleep.

Once when I was young, swimming beneath the sea, I felt similarly. As I slowly dove deeper and deeper into that stillness I became entranced and gave myself up to the cool, soft embrace of those dark waters and would have drowned, but my father had been there to bring me to the surface and then to shore to lie with him on the warm beach and remember life. He was there, then, rescuing me. Now—yesterday—he had forsaken me.

As the day wore on I slowly recovered, but remained in a barely conscious state, my body's functions almost ceasing. I did have an awareness of reality, but it was insignificant, and I was, in fact, angry at my returning sensibilities. If I could just have gone a bit deeper into that stillness, I thought, into that dark recess of my mind, I would surely have died, and gladly so.

Again and again I heard Andy's voice calling me. It no longer receded and I could respond but would not. Dr. Adams came to see me. First he, then Andy, examined me. They looked into my eyes, moved me about, listened with a stethoscope to my inner sounds and those of my baby swimming about in his own dark soundless sea within me. Then they abruptly left me.

In a few minutes Andy came back.

"Open your eyes, Caroline. You're going to have some broth."

"No, I'm not."

He propped me up with pillows, handed me a damp cloth and placed a napkin under my chin. Then Janie brought a cup of hot soup.

"I won't drink that. I don't like it."

"You must drink something. What would you like?" she asked.

"Give me a sedative and I'll drink some water."

"No."

"I want a reefer, Janie."

"I don't have any pot."

"You're lying. There's always some around here."

"Not now."

"Bring me a glass of beer."

They laughed.

"You haven't had a drink since you became pregnant. Are you going to start now?" Janie asked.

They walked out and closed the door, but I could hear them talking and I listened.

"What's wrong with her?" Janie asked. "Caroline can produce tears over anything. She was nuts about David. She acts—I don't know—peculiar, angry."

"She can't cry, Janie. He was alive and suddenly she's told he died. It's unreal and unacceptable, too painful to bear, so it didn't happen. She'll keep acting in this odd way until she can't deny it anymore, but it will get worse, you know. She still doesn't know how it happened."

"Oh, yes, I do!" I shouted through the closed door. "He finally did what I always knew he would. He abandoned me and my baby. Left us. Didn't want us anymore."

They were still now and in a little while they came back with mugs of frothy hot chocolate for all of us, and that I drank.

"Now go to the bathroom and clean up while I straighten this room," Janie said.

Just like her, treating me like a child, I thought sullenly, but I had to go anyway. When I came out I saw Matt bringing in the flowers.

"Get those damn things out of here! The house smells like a funeral chapel!" I knew I was being cranky, but didn't care.

"Caroline, look at them. They're lovely."

"Get rid of them! Give them away."

But when I went back to the bedroom, there was one of such exotic beauty, a pot of wild orchids, that I could not part with it.

"Who sent this?" I asked Matt.

"Here's the card. All it says is 'Jomo.'"

"How did he find me? He lives in Kenya."

"The obituary said you resided in London, nothing more."

Then I recalled our talking about London. He liked it, too, and I had told him about my friend, Janie Myers, and that I lived with her when I was here.

Jomo. For a moment, forgetting my distress, I smiled in remembrance.

Grieving as they must have been, my friends spent the evening in the room with me. I would not communicate with them, turning away and not answering when they spoke to me. I was aware of my unbalanced state but was unable to control it. They remained patient and affectionate, but finally, looking exhausted, Matt left for home and a little later, Janie went off to sleep.

"Caroline, I must get some sleep," Andy said.

"Don't leave me."

"I'll go change and be back."

When he did, he was wearing an orange-red silk robe with an embroidered dragon on the back and gold tassels on the belt. And he was carrying a blanket.

I began to laugh. "Where did you get that crazy robe?"

"A friend brought it from China for me."

"A woman friend?"

"Yes."

"Do you like her?"

"Very much, and the robe's all right. I needed a new one, anyway. Besides, she likes to see me in it. She says it's sexy."

I couldn't stop laughing.

"All right now, Caroline. That's enough making fun of my robe. I can't take it off. There's nothing underneath. I'm going to wrap up in this blanket, so you won't have to see it."

But I wasn't through.

"Do you love Red Robe?"

"No. Now turn off the light, Caroline, and let's go to sleep."

Covered with his blanket, he lay next to me. I was still for a few minutes.

"Andy, wake up!"

"What?"

"You think David died yesterday, don't you?"

"Yes."

"He didn't! I know what happened. David decided he didn't want me anymore. Mayumi's back in his life, and he wants me to know he's dead to me. He stopped loving me, Andy. That's it, isn't it?"

"No. You know that's not true. His wish would have been to live, to fulfill his dreams with you and your baby."

"Well, what did you mean then when you told Janie I didn't really know what happened? Tell me."

"Caroline, I can't talk anymore. Please, let's get some sleep."

"Andy?"

He didn't answer and instead placed his hand gently over my lips. Turning me away from him, he lay close with his arm around me, and I fell asleep.

The next morning I awoke to a quiet household. Janie had probably gone to school and the closed door of the study led me to believe Andy was there. I went to the kitchen and poured some orange juice. Then I switched on the radio, and in turning the dial to get a music station, my attention was suddenly fastened on words being spoken by a newscaster. He referred to someone as "a distinguished member of the world of architecture." The investigation, he said, had been completed. An estranged wife...ashes that would be given to his next of kin, a daughter now living in London.

A daughter living in London? I was a daughter living in London. That was David he was talking about. What investigation? Why? I stood up and would have called to Andy, but put off-balance by my ungainly body, I knocked over the chair, and then to keep from falling, I grabbed the table's edge and tipped over the glass that shattered noisily as it hit the floor. Immobilized, I simply stood there, staring down as the juice spilled and spread around me.

Andy rushed into the room as the voice droned on. A fire in Chelsea...traffic rerouted.... He understood at once, and taking my hand, led me into the study where we sat down, side by side, his hand still in mine. This had not been what he wanted, hoping for a little time to pass, especially with the imminent birth of the baby, before telling me the extent of the tragedy. It could not be avoided now and he would tell me.

"Caroline, do you remember when all of us left Dr. Adams' office, Dave went back in and when he didn't come out right away I followed him? The lab had just drawn some of your blood for testing before the transfusion, and he requested a test of his blood and yours for paternity. It was a brave act, but too long delayed. Nothing more could be done except wait for the results. The fact that Dave was doing that just then worried me. I didn't know what he had in mind, but I implored him to wait until the baby's birth before doing anything further. He agreed and planned to be with you then, no matter what the test showed. Later, he reversed himself, knowing that being with you and the baby would weaken his resolve.

"Dave and I had frequent phone conversations, but he never told me he had actually received the report and had determined what he would do. In fact, he feigned a cheerfulness that prevented me from detecting any signals of despair. If I had, maybe I could have acted earlier and more aggressively to stop him.

"Last week he called and asked me to come to Tokyo. When I arrived a priest greeted me and said Dave and Hasumi had gone off for the weekend. He explained that from time to time the two of them went away like this to a village called Hara Shizuoka, near Mt. Fuji. A temple there had been the home of an eighteenth-century master of the Rinzai school of Zen, and Hasumi was a follower of that discipline. Each time they returned the priest said Dave appeared energized by the experience and eager to pursue his work.

"The following day they returned.

" 'Andy, I had hoped to find peace of mind as I have in the past,' he said, 'but I know now no amount of meditation—nothing I do—will restore my inner peace. I must end my life.'

"He shunned efforts to help him overcome his depression. I knew he was planning suicide. I stayed with him continuously, Caroline, except to go to sleep at a hotel nearby. Again and again I told him his death was not the answer.

" 'It's the only answer. I can't live with my guilt. I'm a monster.' he said.

"I told him he was overwrought and unrealistic. I reminded him of the many conversations he and I had about this. Sex is nature's most compelling force and he had struggled hard not to give in to it, but he loved you so much, Caroline, and you loved him and wanted what he did. His was not the act of a father committing incest on an innocent child. You were twenty-one years old, not lacking in experience, and well aware of what was happening. His resistance was overcome by your love for him.

" 'Your death would bring misery to Caroline and deprive your child of a wonderful father,' I said to him.

"He looked at me as if I were out of my mind. 'I can't claim the baby as my own. That's absurd!'

" 'I'm not suggesting that,' I told him, and pointed out that the two of you might never be subjected to condemnation. The press in London had latched onto Jim as the baby's father and he would gladly accommodate it by marrying you, then later be divorced. If he couldn't do it, I would. It was no big deal.

" 'None of that is relevant now,' he said. 'I know how painful her suffering will be. Help her to understand and forgive me, Andy. I always wanted her to have a free, uncomplicated life, yet I'm the one who complicated it and destroyed her freedom. I must return it to her by releasing her from her attachment to me. This is the only way.'

"Caroline, for one terrible moment I understood his logic, and my feeling of guilt for even thinking it made me renew my efforts to dissuade him. I begged him to give himself a little more time and take a new medication for depression that I hoped might ease him away from his morbid thoughts. But I didn't trust him to do it by himself; I asked him to take the pills in my presence. His response was to laugh and refuse. Frantic near the end, I wanted to hospitalize him. He was infuriated.

"'Nothing you do will stop me, Andy,' he said. 'I know what I'm about and I'm doing the right thing. I have put all my legal affairs in order and I called you here to be aware of everything. I know how you feel. If our positions were reversed, I would try to stop you. We have had a unique friendship.'

"He stood up and embraced me. It was late in the afternoon and I asked Hasumi if he could find a place for me at the temple. He did and I left to get my things at the hotel. I shouldn't have gone. Someone else could have brought them. It took me maybe twenty minutes, no more than half an hour. I was...I was...."

Andy's voice became hesitant, quavery, as he tried to continue. "I was losing my wonderful friend and I...."

He was barely able to speak, his voice reduced to a whisper. "I didn't know how to save him. I was right there, but I didn't know how to save him."

He struggled to maintain his composure. "Caroline, I did my best. It wasn't enough."

He covered his eyes with his hands as if to shut out a sight he could not bear to see. He walked to the window, maybe hoping to replace that dreadful visualization with another—any other—sight. Then he sat down again. There were no tears, but his eyes told me as much as the words the agony he must have felt and was now experiencing again in the telling.

In a strange role reversal, it was I now who was comforting him. I held his hand in mine while remaining unemotional myself, listening dispassionately, interested in the outcome.

"Go on, Andy dear," I said. "You must tell me."

"There's not much more. When I came back to the temple, I looked for Dave. He wasn't in his room and I went in search of

Hasumi. He was gone, too. Then I looked out into the garden and saw them. Both wore *yukatas* and held knives—Dave's, a short blade and Hasumi's, really a sword. Just as I rushed out, Dave dropped to his knees in the grass, plunging the knife into himself, drawing it across his abdomen, committing *seppuku*.

"Hasumi stood back of him, slightly to his side, about to complete the ritual beheading, but he couldn't do it. His face had an expression of madness as he threw the weapon aside and grabbed the knife still held in Dave's hand. He went down on his knees and was about to kill himself. A priest had rushed out just ahead of me, and wresting the knife from Hasumi's hand, led him, sobbing loudly, back into the temple."

Andy looked at me. If he expected hysteria, revulsion at the horror of the scene he had just described, he was wrong. I sat dry-eyed, only curious, nothing more.

"Are you all right?" he asked.

"Yes."

"Are you sure?"

"I'm puzzled. David hated violence. I can't believe he would turn such violence on himself."

"An overdose, a bullet—too easy—cowardly even."

"But he was a third-generation American. That was a uniquely Japanese thing to do, probably rare even in Japan now. It's odd, Andy."

"No, it isn't. I understand it. You know how immersed Dave was in the Japanese culture. Long before he went there he steeped himself in the literature, eventually in the original language. Yukio Mishima, especially, seized his imagination, just as he had many other Western intellectuals who came under his spell through his fine writing; but there was something else about him, something deviant, because he had no connection with the real Japan. As a result he created a false image of his country for the Western world.

"On Dave's first visit to Japan years ago, he met Mishima and realized that the man was living in the past, a throw-back, who wanted to turn his country back, too. His final act of rebellion, an attempt to occupy a government office, using a small contingent of young followers, was an instant failure, a joke. Yet whatever others thought of him, his integrity was at stake. He could not give it up and it demanded *seppuku*. After that, Dave lost interest in him, but he extracted from his philosophy the *samurai* ethic. Whether historical or contemporary, Dave believed it to be an honorable way of life. So for him, *seppuku* was atonement, an expiation for what he believed was his loss of honor."

Reaching into his briefcase, Andy took out an envelope with my name on it and handed it to me. "I found this on Dave's desk, Caroline."

I opened it.

> My dearest one:
>
> To depart from you, to take leave of life in all its richness—this is not my choice. My choice would be to go on forever savoring our love for each other.
>
> My intention had been to be with you one more time and to have the joy of holding our infant son in my arms. But that moment would have destroyed any possibility of my leaving you. And I must. I must free you to live your life without the endless restraints of secrecy and pretense.
>
> How easy it was for me to give in to your desire, for it was mine, too. How without conscience—with ease, in fact—I let it go on. Love builds strength, but the passion in it prevented me from determining our true relationship. Now I know that we are flesh and blood, father and daughter, and what I did disgraced us.
>
> In *seppuku* I see a symbolic restoration of honor and I welcome the sacrifice. Always remember how deeply I have loved you to this last moment of my life.

I sat quietly looking at that familiar handwriting as Andy watched me. Once again he may have expected, even hoped for an outburst of some kind. There was none. My thoughts traveled a twisted path, seeking a destination, but finding none, no meaning, no acceptance of the event that had occurred.

I pictured the collection of David's letters secreted in the bedroom of my childhood. Read and reread through all the years, almost twenty years, each one of them had been carefully added to the particular year's packet, as treasured first by a little child, then a girl and finally, no less dear to the woman I was now. I kept looking at this final one, unseeing in a sense, because I was no longer reading it.

What had he told me here? It was imponderable. He had been about to give up his life because he loved me? He had wanted to express his *extreme* remorse, Andy had said. My love for him held no remorse, only fulfillment, pleasure. Was this not abandonment, this deliberate, calculated act, so heinous and cruel? Not grief, not despair—only anger welled up in me. What was I to do with that heroic scribbling of a disordered mind? Surely it had no place in my collection of loving correspondence, and I tore it in half.

The suddenness with which I did it startled Andy and he grabbed my arm. "Wait, Caroline! Give yourself some time."

"Isn't that the advice you gave David? What did *he* do?"

Not content with ripping it apart, I proceeded to tear it into the tiniest bits. Then, gathering them up from my lap, I went over to the wastebasket and dropped them in.

I had been betrayed, wounded beyond recovery, but now, with the letter destroyed, I felt nothing—nothing. Andy remained seated, but I didn't return to him nor even look back at him, knowing the unhappiness his face would reveal, and I went to my room.

14

I dressed hurriedly, threw a handbag over my shoulder and started out the door.

"Where are you going?" Andy asked.

"Shopping."

"What for?"

"None of your business."

"Have a little breakfast first. Come in the kitchen. We'll have some juice and toast."

"Don't tell me what to have! I don't want juice and toast."

"What do you want?"

"A doughnut and coffee."

"We'll go out later and get some doughnuts."

I wasn't interested in "later."

"Caroline, wait for me. I want to go with you."

I pretended to wait while he got a jacket, but ran out and into a taxi before he could stop me. Good thing taxis are so easy to get in London, I thought. I didn't need him tagging along with me.

It was a busy day. First I had the driver take me to a doughnut shop and I sat a long time having coffee and doughnuts. Then I took another taxi to Harrod's. The men's department had a stock of robes and I found what I knew was the most beautiful one: soft, lightweight wool, perfect for our cool California coastal nights, and blue as a spring sky after a rain. I loved it. That stupid red robe didn't even have pockets, I told myself scornfully. Pockets were important. This one had a breast pocket and two big side pockets. Despite its large size and my belly extending out in front of me, I put it on and stood looking at my reflection in a mirror, admiring the excellence of my selection. I saw a couple of clerks in the mirror observing me and smiling. I didn't care. I bought it.

The food stalls were next and I bought some morels for Janie. Then I walked out of the store and kept walking until I came to a cinema and went in. I didn't know what the film was; it didn't matter. Sleeping intermittently, I saw only parts of it, anyway. When I left I was hungry, so I found a pizza place and had pizza and beer. They were delicious and feeling pleased with myself and my day, I took a taxi home.

Everybody was there—Jim, too—just back from a trip, and I hugged him, happy to see him. Andy sat in the rocker, not saying anything, but the others, especially Janie, started fussing at me right away. Her face was flushed with anger. Now that I was safely home, she was going to let me have it.

She was yelling. "Where in hell have you been, you idiot?"

"Shut up!" I said crossly. "I'm going to bed. I have a stomachache."

"Yeah? What kind of crap did you eat today?"

I handed her the mushrooms. "Doughnuts and pizza."

"For Christ's sake, no wonder you have a bellyache! I'll make some tea."

"No!" I said and slammed the bedroom door.

I put my purchase in the closet, and after changing into a nightgown, got in bed. I was exhausted and uncomfortable and wished I could think of a ruse to get Janie to give me a pill.

Andy knocked at the door. "I want to see you," he said, and not waiting for me to protest, came in and sat down beside me on the bed.

I turned my face away from him. He turned it back. Then, putting his arms around my shoulders he lifted me from the pillow and placed my head on his chest.

"Put your arm around me. Don't reject me, Caroline."

"I'm very unhappy, Andy."

"I know, darling. I am, too."

"Andy, I had beer and coffee today. Would those hurt my baby?"

"No, not in the amounts you drank them, I'm sure."

"Could it cause him to be born early?"

"No. Are you worried about that?"

"This is not a stomachache. I'm going into labor."

"You suffered a terrible trauma. Maybe that's caused labor to start, but your baby is only a few weeks early. Are you afraid?"

"No."

"Okay. Let's start timing the contractions."

Late that night Jim drove me to the hospital. I sat in front with him, and my "family" sat in the back seat.

This is your family, too, baby dear, for there are no others. Your father deserted us, but we will care for you. You will have a happy life.

All of us were quiet but at the same time feeling the excitement of the spectacular event about to unfold. Andy stayed with me the whole time, holding my hand, kissing my forehead, checking my baby's progress with a stethoscope. The others came in from time to time to embrace me and tell me to "get on with it."

My labor was not long or hard and when I was being taken to the delivery room, Andy put on a hospital gown and went in with Dr. Adams and me. No prospective father could have been more supportive. Just before the baby was born, a nurse wanted to give me an injection, but I refused.

"I'm doing fine," I said. "Don't give me anything to dull my senses. I want to see my baby when he's born."

Then that instant came and I waited expectantly to hear his first little cry and see him, but there was only an eerie silence in the delivery room. I raised my head and saw Dr. Adams and Andy standing close together and I knew they were looking at my baby.

"Andy! Give me my baby!"

"Just a minute, darling. He's being examined."

I tried to get off the delivery table, but two nurses restrained me, and one of them quickly administered a shot of some kind.

"Andy, you're crying! Tell me, tell me! What's wrong?"

"Caroline, he was still-born. Nothing can be done."

I was becoming drowsy, but not quite asleep and Andy put the baby, wrapped in a blanket, beside me. I opened the blanket and looked at his dear little face, the fluff of hair, the tiny ears and fingers, the sweetness of his penis, the round shapeliness of his body. Perfection.

Oh, baby-mine! How I desired you, how rapturous was the moment of your conception, how impatiently I awaited your arrival. And now, before you have drawn a single breath of life, you have left me.

I buried my face in his soft little body, weeping, weeping and kissing every part I could reach, all unmoving, still. Then I turned away and closed my eyes, and Andy took him from me.

Heavily sedated, I slept until late the next morning. When I awoke, Andy was sitting at the bedside, asleep, his head resting on the bed. I lay quietly, not wanting to wake him, until an aide came in, and he sat up.

"I'm sorry you lost your baby," she said. "But he's in heaven with Jesus now."

"He's in the kiln of a crematory about now, not some mythical heaven," I told her. "If there were a god, I'd be cursing him."

My bitter remark did not affect her cheerfulness. "Oh, you don't mean that," she said. "Be back soon with your lunch."

Andy took me in his arms as he had the night before, and this time I didn't have to be told to put my head on his chest and my arm around him.

"Andy, why did my baby die?"

"He had a congenital heart defect. It may have been only coincidental with Dave's own heart problem. You guessed right about that. He was taking medication, but he wasn't in any immediate danger of dying from it."

"Why did he hide it from me?"

"He didn't want you worrying about him, hovering over him. He didn't want your intimate life together to lose its spontaneity and pleasure. I don't know if he was wrong in that or in taking his life, but in *his* mind, everything he did was based on his love for you."

"Andy, think what wondrous traits my baby must also have inherited from his father, genes that with his ashes will now vanish in the wind. Why did he have to inherit that one?"

There could be no answer, and we sat, holding each other, deep in thought at the compounding of my tragedy. I wondered how my own heart could keep beating in its rhythmic monotony as it endured one agony after another.

Yes, Mr. Ferlinghetti, the world is the best place of all for a lot of such things as making the fun scene and making the love scene and kissing people and making babies and just "living it up." Yes, but then, like you said, right in the middle of it comes the smiling mortician.

The next day we were back in Janie's flat. She was away at school or with Matt most of the time, and she urged us to stay as long as we liked. I was at an obvious impasse, but it had no significance to me. "Future" was a foreign word, and day after day I simply went through the motions of being alive, but not feeling so.

I was not suicidal in any direct way, so my friends didn't have to be vigilant that I might end my life, yet I was dying, anyway, with little effort, slowly, easily. One rare time I did try to lift my spirits by going to a head-shop in Soho, where I bought a stash of marijuana. I didn't conceal it and no one said anything. Andy knew that had never been a solitary pastime for me, always a social one, and now, each time I would light up, he asked me for a joint and smoked with me. I soon found that pot didn't work as it had when I was younger. No pleasant lift came with it and I gave it up, flushing what was left down the toilet.

After that, I refused to leave the house, remaining on the edge of things, not removing myself altogether, but not participating in anything that went on. I spent hours of every day doing nothing at all, not talking or reading or, as when Matt would be there watching television, I would sit with him, appearing to watch but totally inattentive to its content, lost in a vague reverie.

Janie took on a maternal role. I had never weighed much over a hundred pounds, but I was down to ninety now. She worried over the paucity of food I ate. There were days when I would not get out of bed at all. I would hear her, in her frustration, being angry at Andy for not "doing something." In the beginning, he had tried to talk to me and suggested I take medication he said would make me feel better. I refused.

From then on he appeared almost to disregard me. In fact, he separated himself from me in certain ways. He had stopped sleeping in my room within a few days, although he did ask me to leave the door open a little at night. He may have looked in on me sometimes, but I never asked for help. Despite that, I was sensitive to his treatment—or lack of it. Unlike the others, he never coaxed me or made suggestions about what I should do. Nor did he show displeasure or impatience or withhold affection. My unhappiness had become part of my being and I was deeply attached to it. I didn't want anyone interfering with it. He knew that and was biding his time.

He had rented a car soon after he arrived in London and twice a week he drove to Oxford where he had old friends from his years in school there. They were at work on a research project that interested him and they wanted him to join them. He had never asked me to go with him. Then one night he did.

In the evenings he often sat in the big rocker, quietly rocking and listening to music. One evening he casually asked me to come sit with him. As I sat myself down on his lap, he put his arm around me and continued rocking, not saying anything. Instantly, I regressed to my childhood, sitting on my father's lap in the armchair in his study, secure in loving arms, with no demands on my maturity or tests of my ability to cope—relaxed and contented.

As if it had already been decided, he went into "our" plans for the following day. "We'll leave early. It won't take long once we get out of London," he said, matter-of-factly, continuing to rock slowly. "You may come with me to the college. That would be all right. Or wait for me in Woodstock, a village in the Cotswolds not far away. I'll reserve rooms for us at an old coachman's inn where I've stayed before. It's nice and we'll stay a few days so we can ride around the countryside. It's something to see."

It was a masterful performance: the slow-rocking, the music, the affection, the plans for a pleasant sojourn in the country. The next morning we left. Even that was an achievement during those trying times.

It was late April, a sunny day, though cool. I wore a heavy sweat shirt but Andy was in shirt-sleeves.

"Aren't you chilly?" I asked.

"It'll warm up later in the day. Are you going to the college with me?"

"And hang out with those stuffy dons? No, thanks!"

"Not all of them are stuffy. I knew one guy who sure wasn't. I never could understand how he lived so well on his salary. He had a flat in Mayfair and always drove a new Jaguar coupe. Every time I'd see him he'd have a different beautiful woman on his arm. Well, the jig was up when a member of his stable found out she wasn't getting the same deal as the other women and created a scandal. He'd been running an elite call-girl service."

"Why did he even bother to teach?"

"He was an odd duck. Intellectual and personable. Probably missed his life at Oxford when he was thrown out."

When we arrived in Woodstock, Andy said he was hungry. "All we had this morning was juice. Let's stop for something."

"It's only ten o'clock. I'm not hungry."

"I can't help it if I'm hungry," he said.

"I'll keep you company," and we stopped at a pub.

"I know this place. They make great hamburgers. Will you share with me?"

"Hamburgers in the middle of the morning? No, thanks!"

But when the waiter brought the food, I told Andy not to put goop on my half, and I ate it all. To him, that must have been the first sign of life returning to me. Smiling, he told me to wipe my lips. Then he kissed me. I smiled, too, and so did the waiter.

Promising to be back by five, Andy left me at the inn. Woodstock has the typical charm of a small English town. I was amused by its quaintness but liked it. The activity at that hour was centered on the business street. Not a supermarket was in sight, just small stores. Many women came to shop on bicycles. They were in a hurry, dashing from one place to another, filling their wicker baskets at the butcher's or fishmonger's, the greengrocer's, picking up bouquets at the flower stall. The bakery wafted a scent far more potent than any perfume—fresh bread and sweet breakfast treats. I couldn't resist and went into a tearoom for a fresh hot scone and raspberry jam. It was as if I were rediscovering the deliciousness of food.

On the other side of the street were a few clothing stores. One was an Australian import shop with sweaters in the window. Inside were more and I found one with an aboriginal design in gorgeous muted shades. I visualized it on Andy and it pleased me to buy it, just as the robe had, but which he had not seen, still tucked away in the closet where I had left it that sorrowful night.

When I returned to the inn, I left my package in the room and went down the hall to the barroom. Part of the original coaching inn, the doorway was so low a tall man would have to bend to enter. The room even smelled old with the accumulated aromatic fragrance of the ages clinging to it. It was small with huge smoke-blackened beams on the ceiling and a stone floor that had sunk somewhat on one side. Although it was almost summer, thick walls retained a cool atmosphere and logs burned in the fireplace. I sat near it, sipping sherry. Only the barman and I were there and after a few minutes he struck up a conversation.

"This is Churchill country," he said proudly, and told me I could go over to Blenheim Palace just back of the inn to see where Churchill was born and where notabilia of his life were on display.

"He's buried in a village churchyard up in the hills near here," he said. "He could have been in Westminster, but he preferred to spend eternity in that simple country place he loved so much."

He appeared touched by his own words and did not speak for a bit. Then he remembered something else, just a few blocks away, that he thought I might like to see—a church, hundreds of years old, that was about to be restored. That did interest me, so I walked over there.

No one was around, but the gate was open and I went in. Built of the rich creamy-colored stone quarried in that part of England for centuries, its exterior had mellowed to great beauty. No bigger than a chapel, the interior was plain in the extreme, with no ornamentation except a tortured Christ figure on a cross. Here was a place you would sit up straight in your stiff-backed pew and pay attention. No grand organ or fine chorus would distract you from the lesson being taught: the difference between Good and Evil, Heaven and Hell. That was what religion was about, wasn't it?

Chilled by the musty dampness, I left quickly and walked over to the still-sunny churchyard. But the moment I set foot in the cemetery, the sky became overcast and a forbidding atmosphere enveloped me. Trees of huge girth and height, attesting to their mighty age, stretched their limbs in all directions in a dark green canopy over that ancient place. I walked among the monuments, some in a better state of preservation than others, but all darkened by time.

Then I came on one gravestone that fate had cruelly meant for me to see. A worn and mottled cherub, with wings outstretched, rested its chin on the small stone where I could read still-visible incised script: "Baby Clorissa Tanner, Born and Died July 10, 1889. Forever in our hearts."

A stone bench was nearby and I sat down, weeping and stopping and weeping more.

"I'm not crying for you, little Clorissa. Others did that long ago. My child's name was David, and he will live forever in my heart."

Then I stopped my sobbing and did not start again, but I was unable to remove myself from that place, unable to return to the living world just beyond the gate.

It was there Andy found me. He had asked the innkeeper and then the barman, who remembered me and told him where I might have gone. He looked distraught, and sitting down beside me, he put his arm around me.

"Andy, the gods are still angry at me. I have no right to feel joy in my life. David's guilt was as much mine. Didn't I entice him?

Didn't I crave his child? Was Martha right and I have yet to atone for my own sins?"

"'Sin' is not in my vocabulary. You have committed no wrong, unless being human is wrong. Through no fault of your own you've taken cruel blows, but with the passage of time, your melancholy thoughts will vanish and life will be worthwhile again."

I didn't respond, and in a few minutes, he pulled me to my feet. "It's turned cold, Caroline. Let's go back to the inn."

He went with me to my room and watched as I lay down on the bed. "I'm going to my room to clean up a little and change my clothes. You do the same, and I'll be back to get you. Then we'll have dinner."

I didn't answer. I wasn't hungry and all I wanted to do was lie quietly. He left and in a little while he was back.

"Andy, you're wearing your suit!"

He laughed. "You know me—I always wear my suit when I'm taking my girl out."

"I'm not going out."

"Yes, you are. Come on, now! Are you going to wear sweats with a well-dressed dude like me to escort you? Change your clothes."

"I'm not hungry. I don't want to go."

"I *am* hungry. Don't make me eat alone. Where is your bag? You packed a beautiful dress. Did you take shoes to go with it?"

When I didn't move, he sat me up and looked at me. "Shall I dress you?"

"Damn it, no!" I said, and angrily started to pull off my clothes.

"Omigod!" I heard him murmur. "Go to the bathroom, Caroline. Freshen up and come out smiling."

I began to cry. "Why are you doing this? Let me alone!" But I grabbed my dress and went.

When I came out, he looked me over. "You're a knock-out, Caroline. Now let's go."

"Wait! What do they serve?"

"I used to eat here a lot. The food's good. One of their chefs is a Basque. He often makes *zarzuela* and I know you like that. And the barkeep makes an excellent gin and tonic."

"What's so hard about making a gin and tonic?"

"You'll see. C'mon."

It was an elegant dining room with fresh flowers and candles on the tables. So what, I thought. The food will probably be lousy.

"Do you like your drink?" he asked.

"It's all right. I'll have another."

"No, you won't. You weigh too little to have two drinks. Gain some weight and I'll let you have two."

"Andy, if you keep treating me like this, I'll run away."

He laughed. "I won't let you out of my sight. We'll share another drink."

But when the server brought it, I took possession of it and drank it all myself. Andy thought the *zarzuela* was good, but it wasn't. I knew the real thing and declared the chef ersatz Basque.

"I'm going back to my room."

"And leave me to eat alone?"

"Well, don't dawdle."

"Let's have some ice cream for dessert."

"No."

"Will you wait while I do?"

"Hurry up!"

"Caroline, do you realize how unlike yourself you're acting?"

"You're mad at me," I said, and immediately began to cry.

"No, but you know how much your unhappiness affects me. Here's a handkerchief. Don't cry on that pretty dress."

When we were back in my room, I asked him to stay with me. "Please, Andy."

"No, I can't stay with you."

"Why?"

"It's ridiculous my sleeping on top of the covers."

"I have no interest in sex anymore."

"It will return. Meanwhile, I do have an interest and you're very attractive. It gets me crazy."

The following day we set off for London. I was neither happy nor disappointed that we weren't staying longer. What difference did it make where I was? With no independent will, I was adrift, allowing someone else to determine what happened to me.

On the trip back, Andy wore his new sweater. "It's beautiful, Caroline."

"Red Robe won't like it. If she sees the robe I got you, she won't like that, either."

"You don't even know her, but you don't like her, do you?"

"Which robe will you wear?"

"When I'm with her, I'll wear the one she gave me."

"Then I won't give you mine."

"You bought it for me. I want it."

"Will you wear it?"

"I have to see it first, don't I?"

"Stop teasing me!"

"Caroline...." He started to say something, then stopped.

"What?"

"It's nothing." And he leaned over and kissed me on the cheek.

Midway, we stopped for lunch, but once back in the car again we didn't leave right away.

"Let's talk a minute," Andy said. "I'm going to be in Oxford for the next week. I like what those guys have been doing and they want me to get the data together and write the manuscript. I can do it at home. Whatever gaps are left we can work out by e-mail. There's a good chance it'll be published.

"The Shinto dedication of the Institute will be in mid-May and a memorial service will be conducted for Dave, too. Then we'll go home."

"I don't want to go to Tokyo and I don't have a home. I want to stay at Janie's."

"You must not miss the ceremony. We'll only stay a few days, Caroline."

"I told you I don't have a home!"

"Yes, you do. Martha will make you feel welcome because it's very much your home, and I'll be just down the road as I always have been."

"Why can't I stay at Janie's?"

"Janie worries about you, but she doesn't know how to help you. Don't you think she's been exceptionally nice letting both of us stay in her flat so long? She has her own life to get on with. Also, I think you *must* go home. No place ever adheres to a person's memory of childhood like home, and your memories are more poignant than most. Recalling—feeling the pain and the joys, too—may help you put everything in its proper place in the past, where it belongs.

"Besides, I have to make some decisions for myself. I put my practice on ice. What am I going to do now?"

My answer was the usual one: tears. "Why do you tolerate me, Andy? I'll never recover. You should go back to that jazzy friend of yours in Monterey and forget about me."

"Caroline, do you remember asking me what you would do without me? What did I say?"

"You said I would never have to do without you."

"That hasn't changed, and you don't want me to leave you, do you?"

"No. But I don't understand. You are known as a brilliant psychiatrist. You help people find themselves. Why can't you help me?"

"You must want to get better and you're not ready. You're unwilling to give Dave up. How sweet your farewell was to your baby! And how much you've cried in sadness at losing him. But you've never parted from Dave. You've never shed a tear for that dearest person in your life. I think you're very angry at him for leaving you, 'abandoning' you, as you say, of his own free will. I believe you must go home because that's where you'll find him and love him as you always did. That's where you'll recover. And I'll do everything in my power to help your heart heal because I love you very much."

"Andy, I love you, too."

"All right then. That's what we're going to do."

15

Janie and Matt went with us on our trip to Tokyo and when we arrived, Liza and Jim were waiting for us there, too. I knew Jim had gone to Tangier on business, but this was a surprise. Liza always had a confidence to impart and I liked this one. When she had returned to Marrakesh after her visit in London, she was discontented and found herself thinking about how much she did like Jim. It disturbed her staying "in business," as she put it, and when Jim called her from Tangier she went there to be with him. Now they were planning to marry.

She was happy. "Your little monkey business worked, Caroline. My life was going nowhere. Jim was lonely, too, and now I'll go with him on his trips. Sometimes we'll be in Morocco so I'll get to see my relatives and old friends, and someday I'll open a belly-dancing school in London with my sinful earnings," she added, laughing.

A little later Jim asked me to have a drink with him in the hotel bar.

"I know you set Liza and me up to be together, but my heart is elsewhere. You know that. Feeling as I do, do you think I'm doing the right thing?"

"You know how fond I am of you, Jim, but it would never work out for us. I'd always see David in you. Liza and you will be fine together. You are loyal and loving people, and I think she is a very desirable woman."

"Yes, she is," he said, smiling.

"Both of you are lucky to have found each other, and our friendship will remain as close as ever."

Jim and I, along with the others, were to be together for the next few days, but he and I really said goodbye then to what might have been, as he thought, and what never could be, to me.

Both Janie and Liza offered to share a room with me so I wouldn't have to be alone that night, but I wanted them to be with the men they loved. Besides, it was Andy I wanted, and he arranged for us to have a two-bedded room. Despite the jet-lag of our long trip, I was unable to sleep, and Andy suffered, as well, because I kept waking him.

"I'm right here, Caroline. Go to sleep."

"I can't. Give me a sedative."

"I don't have any."

I was still then, but not for long. "Andy?" I whispered, but loud enough to make sure he heard me.

"You win, Caroline," he said. "Move over."

Wearing a *yukata* the hotel provided for guests, he pulled the blanket off his bed and lay on the covers of mine, and at last, with his arm around me, I quieted down.

When we arrived at the Institute the next afternoon, an assemblage of guests was seated in the forecourt, with the front row of chairs reserved for my friends and me. I recognized some of the people from the festive event David and I had attended. Several architects, famous themselves, who had come long distances to honor their friend's memory, came up to greet me, for they had known me from childhood.

Walt, who had come all the way from his current engineering project in Argentina, was there. His eyes filled with tears as he silently took me in his arms. Indeed, what *was* there to say? I asked him to sit with me, and Yoichi and Hisako, too. What appeared to be the entire contingent of Japanese who had worked on the construction was there. They stood and bowed when they saw me and I, to them.

I was about to sit down when I saw her. She was standing at the rear of the forecourt: a beautiful Japanese woman dressed in a white *kimono*. I knew at once that she was Mayumi, and we bowed in recognition. How could I not feel a closeness to her? Had she not loved David, too? I beckoned to her and led her to where my friends were sitting, and she sat beside me.

When a white-robed Shintoist priest began the ceremony, I recalled the rituals David had described in letters to me. The first one he attended was for the groundbreaking—to cleanse the land of impurities for the construction, and then later, at the framing of the building, when a symbol of the presence of *kami*, the sacred spirit of the building, was placed on a pole nearby.

The dedication was much more elaborate. Accompanied by young girls dressed in white and vermilion, their long hair hanging down their backs and tied with vermilion ribbons, the priest intoned prayers while facing the building. Purification rites—the waving of a wand made of long paper streamers and the sprinkling of salt—were followed by a folk dance performance, accompanied by musicians playing ancient instruments.

I was struck by the strangeness of the event, an enactment of rites that are centuries old, in the midst of a sophisticated irreligious society. Shintoism is still popular, still the imperial religion, if not officially so. Yet I found it understandable. A spiritual essence may or may not exist in all animate as well as inanimate things of the earth, but we are equally part of the phenomenon of nature. The faith may be exclusively Japanese, but it has a universality in striving to maintain harmony between humankind and nature. I liked it.

The ceremony was not a solemn one, as I had anticipated, and ended with prayers for an auspicious future for the Institute. Then Hasumi, as an abbot of the Buddhist religion and David's friend, stood before us holding the funerary urn. All was still as he began to speak. Though I couldn't understand the Japanese, I heard the emotional undertone in his voice. Afterward, a young priest who was standing beside him, translated:

The death of our loved one is experienced as a personal wound, and bereavement finds no comfort in philosophy. But in a greater sense, death does not exist. David will always retain a karmic link with us. This is not a commemoration of his death. His physical death is as nothing. He will return to us again and again, for those we cherish do return to us. We will feel his presence, and he will be with all of us who loved him, as now, in this beautiful place he created for us. Each time we recall him, each time we draw him back into our hearts, he will be with us, surrounding us with his goodness and his love for us.

Hasumi's words were a meaningless jumble to me. I believed none of it. Death had a finality to me and David's death remained unacceptable. But I was touched by his kindness, and when he handed me the urn, we bowed deeply to each other.

As everyone was leaving for an inaugural walk-through of the building and the serving of ceremonial food and rice wine, I told my friends I wanted to spend a little time in the garden by myself. Hasumi accompanied me to the entrance gate where a low vertical wooden structure had been erected and on it was incised in Japanese and English: The Caroline Shaw Garden. David had found great pleasure in its creation, and now I knew he had me in mind.

Carrying the urn with me, I entered the garden and stood for a moment just inside the gate. I knew it was not a big garden; David had told me it would be only a half acre. Yet such genius designed it that it appeared boundless, without end, and at the same time closely contained and warmly familiar. I looked around me. No grand views presented themselves, no exuberant floral displays shouted a greeting, and for a moment I sensed a retreat from the worldliness on the other side. I recalled the words of Mishima, who bemoaned the cacophony of our modern world where "quiet is as fleeting as a butterfly," and we seek "our lost quiet."

Here in the garden of my beloved, you would have found it, Mishima.

Before me was a grove of cedar, pine and oak, standing like old friends, close together, and here and there around them, the flowers of spring. It had been an unusually cold season in Tokyo, still chilly in May, but here they were, the earliest of spring's crop, lilies of the valley covered with drooping clusters of small white flowers intermingled with sweet young violets.

I started down a winding gravel path and at once the gate vanished and I was surrounded by a forest-like atmosphere. On all sides were creamy white and golden honeysuckle, redolent with spicy scent, and wild irises, most just beginning to bud and hint a bit of color; but a few, more favored by places in the sun, were showing off their royal purples and cool blues. Wildflowers grow in profusion in remote country places, though they are seldom seen in Tokyo, not in private gardens or the grand public ones. But here green sprouts were eagerly poking through the warming soil, promising their beauty for later show.

The trees gave greater signal that spring had arrived. It is easy to understand the affection the Japanese have for their ornamental fruit trees as, after the gloom of a long overcast winter, they magically burst forth overnight, filling the air with fragrance. The plum trees, some blossoming in purple-pink, some, white, are the first to bloom. The garden did not have very many, but the few that were there were so startling in their beauty, they tugged at my heart. Even as I watched, their fragile petals were falling and settling in feathery tinted circles around the trees.

The path I walked on branched off at one point, and curious at what I might find, I followed it. As it wandered out of sight, and I with it, it abruptly stopped, sealing off a little clearing with heavy foliage. In its center stood one small tree, a favorite of mine, a willow, whose swollen pendants had erupted into a gorgeous cloud of jade. Close by was a bench and I sat down.

A breeze, though barely perceptible, had set up an ever so slight swaying of the young tree's slender trunk and a rustling of its leaves, deep green above and silvery underneath. As the soft rays of the late afternoon sunlight penetrated the shaded alcove, they shimmered, enveloping the little tree in radiant beauty.

Oh, my dear, you planned this for me alone to find, didn't you?

How much you loved me! Then how could you bring such bitterness on me now?

Retracing my steps, I realized I had reached the heart of the garden. Here was a promontory, no taller than twice my own height, and across its face was a wall of rock, over which a wide stream of a waterfall splashed down into a pool. Wisteria had been planted on both sides of the top and that, too, cascaded in long streamers of pale purple-blue blossoms, sometimes striking the water as the breeze bestirred them.

Having become interested in early Buddhist poetry, David found one that romanticized wisteria, a flower he especially liked. He had translated it for me when we visited the Wisteria Garden of Kameido Tenjin Shrine. I remembered it now:

"I will plant wisteria as a memento for thee whom I love and soon it will blossom and will perfume the air around thee with its sweetness."

From the pool, the water fed a small stream that meandered a short distance alongside a narrow path before both curved around a bend and disappeared. Despite spring's ebullient awakening in what I thought of now as *my* garden, a dreamlike quality existed here for me, and I leaned back on a tree trunk, gazing at that pretty scene—the wisteria, the waterfall, the mysteriousness of the vanishing path. The effulgence of the atmosphere, the air, a rich amalgam of woodland scents, sensuous and beautiful—all were what I knew had been David's intention: the stirring of memories of happiness. But now they contrasted with my present heartache. I started down the path and would have followed it, if the breeze had not grown gusty and cold. Chilled and heavy of heart, I wanted to leave, but one thing remained to do. I opened the urn.

I am about to bestow a gift of greatness on you, Garden. These ashes will sift down into your soil and like the rain and the sun, will nourish you with love, and you will go on endlessly, bringing joy to those who find you.

Then I cast the ashes to the wind and watched them flutter and settle, freed from their imprisoned state, restored to the living world once again.

As if in accompaniment, I heard the faint, distant gong of the great bronze bell of the temple, a sound that Buddhists say brings all who hear it a little closer to paradise. Not a moment too soon, for I felt no repose, no peace. How, I marvelled, could I have accomplished this onerous act, this macabre farewell?

A dreadful fearfulness seized me, and holding the empty urn close to me, I rushed to escape that enchanted place. I ran all the way back to the gate, falling once and scraping my cheek on the gravel of the path. I was trembling and breathing hard when I saw Andy waiting on the other side. Sobbing with relief, I collapsed into his arms.

"Andy, what happened to me? I was doing all right. Then a cold wind started up and I became so frightened."

"It's very hard for you to acknowledge David's death, Caroline. Too painful. There in the garden you may have come close. You did a brave thing, all alone, scattering his ashes, but then combined with the harshness of the sudden cold wind you became disturbed and ran away from it. You aren't ready to face Dave's death yet. But you will."

"You and your psychology! I feel as if I'm on a couch in your office."

"Don't ask questions if you don't like my answers."

Everyone had gone; our friends, too. Andy had told them to go ahead. We walked in silence to the temple, taking the short cut through the meadow of bamboo grass and sweet-smelling purple clover. This was the path David and I had sometimes taken, and here—just here—wasn't it, where once we lay down together?

When we arrived, Hasumi looked as if he had been expecting us. I handed him the urn that I could not bear to keep and that I knew he would want. Unable to communicate with him, we bowed in respect, and started to leave.

"Before we go I'd like to walk out to the garden for a few minutes. Come with me," Andy said.

I didn't want to, but I didn't want to refuse him and we went out to a bench and sat down together.

"Why are we here?" I asked him.

"I want you to visualize what happened here and experience a little of what I did the day Dave died. What happened to him is still unreal to you. A part of you still dreams that he lives. Seeing the beautiful garden he created for you doesn't dispel that. Here in this old temple garden that he loved so much—here is where he took his life. I watched, at first in horror and then acceptance as just here he performed the ritual with grace and courage. Just here is where he ended his life, Caroline."

"Andy, David didn't want me to have our baby. In his haste to desert me, he didn't know his child would not live. Where is he, Andy? Not here. Not in those ashes I spread to the wind today. Where is he? He should be told."

Andy looked at me strangely, but not saying anymore, he stood up. Taking my arm he led me out to the street where he hailed a taxi and we returned to the hotel.

Our friends were nowhere to be found when we arrived at the hotel, so we went to the dining room by ourselves.

"Andy, if I eat a good dinner may I have two drinks?"

He looked weary. "Have as many as you want."

When I finished my gin and tonic, he asked if I wanted another.

"No, it's no fun when you aren't bossy."

"Caroline! Stop eating with your fingers."

"This is finger-food."

"No, it isn't."

"I like eating with my fingers. People in Morocco eat with their fingers."

"This isn't Morocco, and this food isn't prepared to be eaten that way."

"Andy, do you boss Red Robe around like you do me?"

"I've never seen her eat with her fingers."

"You're saying I act like a child, aren't you?"

"Caroline, I'm tired and depressed and as soon as we finish I'm going to sleep."

"Don't be mad at me."

"I'm not mad at you, darling. I understand the turmoil you are experiencing. It makes you act in erratic ways. If I sound cross, I can't help that, either. I'm not a psychiatrist twenty-four hours a day. I have personal human feelings and today was hard for me. I cared for Dave, and the thought that he will never be around anymore hurts me. I worry about you, too. I long for you to be well. I miss the woman in you I love so much. Where is she? We must find her."

He was right. I knew it and was ashamed. My behavior had become grossly inappropriate. I flew into rages over insignificant things or became petulant and sulky. From moment to moment those around me would be unable to judge whether I would be composed and cooperative or irrational.

More and more I had reverted to childlike ways. I craved being little again, cradled in the loving arms of the devoted father of my early years. Andy had shown infinite patience with me, and a few times, because of his concern, he had succumbed to playing that role. I had lost my sense of adulthood. Now I wanted it back.

That night I was awake for a long time, looking at Andy sleeping in the bed beside mine, and I yearned to have him hold me as he had before, but I didn't wake him. I wanted to go to him and lie beside him, but I didn't dare do that, either. He had told me his own feelings, but something terrible had happened to me. To ask for intimacy without sex was a torture I could no longer inflict on him.

The next morning all of us had breakfast together. My friends had come on that journey to honor David's memory, but now Jim had rented a car and was taking the others on a holiday before returning to London. They were going to spend a few days at Toba Bay, Jim said. He had been there. Andy had, too.

"It's a long drive, but beautiful," Andy told the others. "You'll pass through an area of ancient cedars and subtropical vegetation, and the bay is lovely."

"When we get to Toba Harbor we'll take a cruise that stops at some of the islands. Irukajima is my favorite," Jim said. "It's a preserve for deer and peacocks that roam all over the place. Pearl diving is becoming archaic with modern technology, but on Irukajima the *ama* still demonstrate the skill. It's fun to watch."

"Be sure to point out Futamigaura, Jim," Andy said.

All of us were curious, but Matt appeared especially so. It was his first visit to an Asian country and he was fascinated by the contrasts within the Japanese culture.

"What's Futamigaura?" he asked.

"They're the 'Wedded Rocks,'" Andy said. "When you're cruising, look to the northwest of Irukajima and you'll see them looming out of the water. The taller of the two is about thirty feet high with a small *torii* on top and both are joined together with a sacred rope of rice straw. This is the primal couple, Izanami and Izanagi, endowed with the spiritual force of *kami*. They created the whole of the Japanese world: the islands, mountains, oceans and most important, its pantheon of godly offspring. Every year a festival is held there to renew the rope. The rocks must be securely bound, because a break midyear is considered an omen of bad luck."

"Would the world unravel?" I asked.

"The Japanese are making sure it won't, Caroline," he said.

It was hard to say goodbye, and we kept having "just a little more coffee." I knew it would be a long time before we would see one another again. I already missed Janie, who had cared for me like a big sister, and I thought wryly of Martha, who would soon become my companion. I wasn't the only one shedding tears. As Andy and I watched them leave, they kept looking back and waving to us.

"We have four hours to flight time," Andy said. "Let's finish our packing and get ready to leave. Some messages were left for me at the desk and I have to return those, too."

Unwillingly, but knowing I had to do it, I made my call to Martha to let her know I was coming. "Plan to stay as long as you wish," she said.

Andy confirmed the reservations for our flight to San Francisco and the connecting flight to Monterey. Another call was to one of his Oxford colleagues. The last interested me the most. It was to "Emily," and she wanted to know if she should pick us up at the airport. Andy told her it was not necessary and that he would be in touch with her when he was home.

"Is Emily Red Robe?" I asked.

"Yes."

"What does she look like?"

"She's tall, blond and gorgeous."

"I suppose she's great in bed, too."

"Terrific. Anything else you want to know?"

"No!" I said, and lay face down on my bed.

"Caroline?"

"What?"

"Did you bring my new robe from Janie's?"

"Yes."

"I want it. Give it to me."

I did, and he put it on.

"I like it very much," he said.

"Andy, if you want me to act like a grown-up, don't treat me like a child."

"Listen, I'd be nuts not to like this beautiful robe better than that garish red thing. Now come over here."

He untied the robe and pulling me close to him, wrapped the sides of it around me, tying us together.

I couldn't help laughing.

"Feel good?" he said, laughing, too.

"I feel like Izanami, only better. Her friend's an old rock."

"Caroline, I like you much more than Emily."

"I'm not tall and gorgeous and I can't even perform in bed."

"Hey, you're right!"

"Andy!"

"Caroline, a very long time ago Dave told me he had a daughter—'a dark little beauty,' he said. Then I met her and was smitten."

"Still?"

"Still."

"Okay. Let's go have some ice cream."

Andy laughed all the way down the stairs to the coffee shop, and although I wasn't sure what I was laughing about, I did, too. It was a sound I didn't think existed in my world any longer.

16

I liked Andy's old Rover. He had bought it used when he was a student at Oxford years before. There had been some difficulty bringing it over, but it was worth it. Now, when we arrived in Monterey, he wondered if it would start after months in the airport hotel garage. It did and we were on our way home.

"'The Last Mile,'" I said.

Andy knew I wasn't joking. "It won't be easy, Caroline, and it may be painful, but this is the answer. Believe me."

It was with a sinking heart that I arrived. I would rather have been anywhere than there. But Martha greeted us with unusual graciousness for her, and after we brought in my luggage, she served us coffee and pastry. Everything looked as if not a day had passed since I left two years before. The study door was closed and I had no intention of opening it.

Andy held me in his arms for a long time, and I wished those minutes could have lasted the rest of my life. I asked him if he would give me just a couple of pills, "in case...," I said.

"In case of what? You don't need pills, Caroline. Taking them may only prevent you from facing what you must. I'll be here to see you tomorrow."

The next day Andy was back, and during my first few weeks at home he came to see me every day, but he never stayed long. Then one time he arrived carrying a long box. In it was a rolled-up, old-fashioned hammock, which he strung up between a couple of trees. It was a big challenge. We would try to lie in it together and sway back and forth, but one or the other of us kept falling out. By holding onto each other we found we could stay in better. We would be swaying nicely then, when suddenly—always a surprise—both of us would fall out together. We would lie on the grass laughing, and Andy would hold me down for a minute and kiss me. Then we would get back in and try again. It may not have been very grown-up fun, but I liked it.

At about that time Ace came into my life. Walt had described him to me when we were in Tokyo. "He's a Lab puppy and I love that little guy. You should see him. Black as the ace of spades."

Walt's wife took care of him when Walt was away. Now, having returned from the memorial service, he was in Monterey briefly to pick up his wife, who had decided to go with him to Rio. It was a job that would last a few years. What to do with Ace? He called me, but both Martha and I must have been out of the house, so he called Andy, who agreed to take Ace.

Now he was here.

"He'll belong to both of us, Caroline. He's a sweet dog."

Ace had good manners. He was polite and Martha liked that. He took his place in our household, knowing he was welcome at Andy's, as well, and trotted back and forth between his adopted homes. I did, too, now and then, but not before calling. I had a dread of finding Emily there.

When I had been home a few more weeks, two events took place on the same day. A huge box from Japan was delivered. Martha knew what the contents were.

"A letter came some time ago from a priest in the temple where David lived," she said. "He was writing on behalf of someone named Hasumi Kanna. Do you know him?"

"Yes."

"Well, he said he would be sending your father's personal effects. I suppose this is it. I have no interest in them. Do whatever you wish."

When Andy came later in the day I asked him to help me move the box to my room. For the next two months, it remained in a corner, unopened.

The other occurrence that day was a solemn task Andy had to perform for Martha and me. He brought documents David had entrusted to him in Tokyo, having made him executor of his will. Although steeped in legal language, the will was relatively simple. A trust had been set up for Martha and me, and on Martha's death I would inherit her share. It was obvious we would never be in want. David was generous in many ways. Among them he had included a large bequest to Andy and one to Hasumi, for himself and the maintenance of the temple. Another was to Langdon School of Architecture, to be used to assist deserving students.

Martha had been made aware of all of that at an earlier time, but as Andy went over it, she kept dabbing at her eyes. How maudlin, I thought. I was as dry-eyed as ever, hardly paying attention. Even before Andy was through, I called Ace and took him out to the beach with me.

We walked for a little while, then I stopped and Ace stopped, too. I stared out at the sea. At the moment the water in its sheltered cove was glassy smooth, but farther out, not even far distant, the powerful waves, dark blue-green, left no doubt that this was one of the great oceans of the world. I stood, as I had countless times in the past, entranced by its grandeur yet not misled by the serenity of its name, for I had experienced its violent nature.

I don't have your courage, David. But I could let the sea take my life from me. Do you remember when in my girlhood you saved me from its seductive grasp? You would not be here to rescue me now, and I would go down into its shadowy depths and end my ill-fated life.

I kicked off my sandals and waded out beyond the shallow water. Ace, agitated, ran back and forth on the shore, barking.

"Be still, you dumb dog!" I said in exasperation.

But he wouldn't. And then he leaped into the water and paddled out toward me.

"No! Go home!"

But he disobeyed, and in frustration, I began to laugh.

Distracted from my somber intention, I could no longer do it and didn't even want to. My clothes clung to me and I was shivering from the cold and all I wanted was a dry towel and a hot drink.

Andy and Martha had come out on the deck to see why Ace was barking just as he and I made our bedraggled way toward them. While I changed my clothes and had some tea, Andy wrapped Ace in a big towel and dried him. Then he asked me to go out to the hammock with him. With his arm around me we lay quietly. The swaying of the hammock was gentle, hardly moving at all.

"What you did today—it scared me, Caroline."

"Don't worry. I won't do that again. I was so damned uncomfortable in that icy water," I said, laughing.

But my despair was real and I wondered how else I could end my life.

We stayed in the hammock a long time, not saying anything and being careful not to fall out. Then we saw Martha come out to take her walk on the beach, and Andy stood up to leave.

"Go with her," he said as we parted, and I did.

Only two years had passed, yet the youthful look Martha had always maintained was gone. The lines, fine as they were, and the gray in her golden blond hair were making their inevitable appearance. But she still had a robust attractiveness and her lifestyle was unchanged.

It was patterned in a peculiar way after a biblical passage—the one that contained the words of the preacher, Ecclesiastes. When I was young, Martha had quoted it to me, not once, but a number of times. Applying the poetic lines to her life, every hour of her day was structured and she never veered from it. Perhaps the rigidly enforced regimen made her life bearable.

Daily she consulted the newspaper for two vital items: her astrological forecast for the day and the exact time the sun set, and unless it was overcast, she observed it. She watched from indoors, playing an operatic tape while she did so. On clear days it was indeed a glorious sight, as first the sun, immense and brilliant, descended toward the sea and then all of the western sky and the sea reflected beneath it became a spectacle of vermilion and gold. Martha had lived in the far north in her youth and was convinced that only the aurora borealis could compare with our sunsets.

The sea was one of the few things we liked in common, but for different reasons. Martha *used* the sea, swimming daily, always at ten, winter and summer, no matter how challenging the turbulent water might be, forever testing her hardiness in the Spartan program she had composed for herself. Mine was a passive pleasure, enjoying the aesthetics I found in it, never tiring of watching its changing visage, but greatly respectful of it, having almost lost my life to it. After that I swam very little, and then only when my father accompanied me.

There were times during my childhood when I would sit with him on our deck watching Martha go so far beyond the breakers that we could barely see her head bobbing in the water. If there was fog, she would disappear altogether, and then he would walk out to the beach, prepared to swim out to her. Those were my worst moments, for I feared losing him to the sea's overpowering force. My tears and trembling stopped him. Martha always laughed at our apprehensiveness and ignored my father's warnings until weary of the repetitive routine, we stopped our surveillance.

At eight every morning, Martha ran on the beach. At four, she took a walk and many afternoons, as on this one, I went with her. Only a few hours before, Ace and I had our misadventure. He was with us now, usually bounding ahead, too impatient to stay at our pace. Barefoot, we chose to walk along the water's edge where the sea had just been, and where the moist sand felt good beneath our feet.

Only the rhythmic sloshing of the surf broke the stillness all around us. The waves always approached the cove gently, but even that muted sound was enough to give us a comfortable cover for our silence. Despite Martha's gracious welcome, we remained strangers, separate. We were obeying a truce, as civilized warriors do, nothing more, and would remain so until I left again, perhaps never to return. But now I was not thinking about that future time. None existed for me. The depth of my lethargy did not permit me to consider the emptiness of my life. Robot-like, I functioned without volition.

Every day, either early or late, a wind would spring up and sweep across the beach, briefly or for many hours. Now it had died down, having, as was its wont, exhausted its daily torture of the cliffside cypresses that in their youth it had twisted into grotesque shapes and only now, as a kindly afterthought, heaped sand over their bared roots. A late afternoon fog had begun its drift into the cove, slowly floating to that same cliff wall, creeping into its crevices and settling in for the night.

I paid little heed to that natural scene. Within me, in this place, with this woman, I was seeing other things, and even though recent events had overshadowed all that had ever gone before in my life, I held fast, perversely, to the grievous memories of my childhood and maturing girlhood.

Martha, too, suffered a rancor that the years had not obliterated, and even my father's death would not change that. Long ago she and my mother had become rivals, and though Ana had lost her life in the sea, it was she who retained his love through me. But in taking her place, I became the scapegoat.

Who has not wished to erase from the mind selectively chosen memories? It is not to be. In its cleverness, the brain labors unceasingly not only to record and store but also to make connections between then and now, and worst of all, to torment with instantaneous recall. Martha and I were unwilling to expose our pain, so only cautiously singled out bits and pieces of the interim years entered our conversations, and my father was never mentioned. Mostly we discussed practical matters—what food to buy on properly observed shopping days, or what errands had to be done in Monterey. Day after day we acted out a companionship that did not exist.

Suddenly, in the midst of my brooding thoughts, we heard a sound high above us. Moving at a tremendous velocity, three huge flying objects flashed across our field of vision and in an instant were gone. They were bat-winged and black, like great prehistoric creatures. I knew what they were, for I had seen just such a sight on my way from Luxembourg to Trier: the famous stealth bombers that were being flight-tested.

Martha was impressed in an odd way. "They're an omen," she said.

"They're an abomination, not an omen," I said.

"You'll see, Caroline. Signs come in threes."

A ferocious anger boiled up in me. I could no longer tolerate Martha with her superstitions, her inflexible code of conduct, our total disconnectedness from each other. Without a word, I turned and ran to the house. Ace ran after me, but this time when I told him to stay with Martha, he obeyed—a walk on the beach preferred to lolling around the house. I looked back once and saw that she was continuing her walk without interruption. It was of no concern to her whether or not I was with her or why I had so hurriedly left.

Breathless, I rushed through that house glutted with memories of discontent and sought the refuge I had always found in my father's study. Martha had closed its door on a bitter part of her life, but it was the place I loved best in the world. With no hesitation, I flung open the door and entered.

I stood looking around the beautiful room. What had I feared? Nothing had changed. There were no distractions. The objects of my father's profession had been in his office in Monterey. This room had another purpose. Here there was tranquility, a place to read and think and seek inspiration. There was not even a phone: the one in his bedroom recorded messages for him. Centered on his desk were sheets of sketching paper and pens, charcoal and pastels. On one side were publications, a stack of them, and on the other, the disc player. Beneath it were drawers filled with discs, one for jazz and the other, classical music. I chose an album of Mozart's piano quartets, and sat down in my father's armchair. On a table beside the chair were a few books, a nearly empty bottle of *sake* and a glass.

For a little while I closed my eyes and listened and watched, as like a film projected on the screen of my mind, events of my childhood flashed in rapid succession before me, and then graduated to those times when I was grown, sitting with my father, talking, listening to music, this very music, always happy with him. I looked at the *sake*. Two years ago he had sat here enjoying his favorite drink and reading. Perhaps it was just then that he had called to me to come in. I poured what was left in the bottle into the glass and sipped it, feeling his lips on the glass with mine.

Calm and at peace, I sat in this way until I heard Martha enter the house. Quickly turning off the disc player and stealthily closing the door to my pleasurable experience, I joined her to prepare our evening meal.

Most nights I didn't sleep well, but that night I did not sleep at all. As the hours crept by, tension tightened its grip on me. I had no good thoughts to distract me. My love had abandoned me, my child had died at the moment of his birth and now I dwelled again with the person who had darkened my childhood. Was this, too, part of my unfinished retribution? What kind of future could I envision? Only a blank space appeared before me, nothing more.

As my distress increased, I felt angry at Andy. Wouldn't a sedative and a night's sleep have been better than this agony? It was three in the morning. I would not give in to weakness by calling him. A hot drink! I would make hot chocolate, and started down the dark corridor to the kitchen. No! Martha stocked sherry, only cream sherry, but it was alcoholic. I'll have a little, I told myself, and was cheered by the thought. Taking a bottle of wine and a glass, I returned to my room. Then I sat up in bed and poured some. It was tasty, easy to drink and I kept drinking. I'll sleep now, I decided, and started back down the dark hall to return the now-considerably lighter bottle.

But I was intoxicated and turned in the wrong direction. Or had that been my unconscious intention? In a few steps I found myself outside my father's study. It was the hour of our tryst. I moved close to the door.

"Father?" I had whispered then and whispered now.

"Caroline, come in!" he had called to me and called now.

And I did, closing the door behind me. Moonlight cast soft shadows on everything, but I could not see my father.

"Where are you?" I asked.

"I'm here. Come sit with me."

"In a minute," I said, putting down the wine bottle. "I'm going to make a fire. It's cold in here."

There was wood in the basket, a little paper, too, and I lit a fire in the fireplace. Then I turned on a lamp to look in the cabinet for a warm cover to wrap around myself. But the door I opened had none. Instead I found what I had never seen before. One was an open container crammed with awards, plaques, and even a statuette, all in a jumble. Designed to honor my father for his work, none had ever been hung on a wall or placed on a stand.

Next to that box was another, but it was closed. I hesitated, fearful that I might find something I would not want to see, but my curiosity won out and I opened it. What I found were cherished mementos my father had collected over the years of my life. Unlike the other box of carelessly tossed objects, here everything was neatly arranged.

A little book held a record of my childhood from infancy through my early years in school. Copious notes had been written about my emerging personality, my accomplishments and his pride in me. From scrawled pictures to sophisticated watercolors, all lay in their proper order and I remembered how I would bring them to him, waiting eagerly for his pleased expression and hug of approval. And photographs—many photographs—taken throughout those years from babyhood to the last one of me as a mature young woman, smiling at my father holding the camera. Here, too, was the correspondence—all the letters he had received from me, carefully preserved, though some were now sepia-tinged with age.

Pleasure and sadness merged as my father's devotion was revealed to me. How much it was the same as my own to him, for I, too, unbeknown to him, had saved all his letters to me and pictures I had taken of him. In my camera was the undeveloped final one taken by a stranger: father and daughter, arm in arm, smiling at each other. As the contents of the box became streaked with tears so long withheld, I closed it.

"Come sit with me." That was what he had said then and now again. I dried my eyes and sat down on the sofa, just as I had then, remembering everything, hearing our very words as we had spoken them, but now his arm was not around me and his body was not warming mine.

I went back to the cabinet and removed the futon and spread it on the floor before the fire and lay down as I had then and wrapped the quilt tightly around me in remembrance of his loving embrace.

"I want you, Father. Where are you?"

"I'm here, just beside you."

"I love you," I had said and whispered now.

"I love you, Caroline," he had said and again now.

My re-creation of the past and the pain of my loneliness and longing were more than I could bear, and my weeping began again and would not stop. Like the unstanched bleeding of a terrible wound, my heart would not cease its grieving. Martha heard me and the sight of my unhappiness frightened her. She called Andy.

Within moments he was there. Just as he had done when my baby died, he placed my head on his chest, saying not a word, waiting. I would stop, wipe my face, blow my nose, and almost at once start again. Then I got hiccups and we both laughed and Andy kissed me.

"Go to sleep now, Caroline. I won't go away."

And he didn't. In the morning we had coffee together. Then he left, promising to return later in the day.

Andy had not known how it would happen, but he did know that if ever I were to recover, it would have to begin there. And faithful to that need, I found it in the confines of the room that held the dearest memories of my life. Reality did not exist, as in my mind I reenacted the scene of my father's and my love and passion. But he was not there and would never again be there and the fantasy was over. The hard shell of my resistance to that truth was shattered.

Day after day I lay in the hammock, sometimes for hours, lazily swaying, lulled by the cradlesong of the sea, the time passing as in a dream, my thoughts always on the past. The tears no longer came in torrents, but soundlessly, filling my eyes and blurring my vision. Andy often found me asleep there and he would nudge me and lie down beside me, and sometimes I would fall asleep again, and he would hold me close, making sure we did not fall.

The passage of time—that paradoxical foe and friend—did soften my memories and heal my heart. I grew stronger, less delicate, less inclined to tears and childish behavior. My suffering did ease, remembered but no longer felt in the same terrible way. "Perfect" I would never be, for stoicism had never been part of my makeup and never would be. "You love, you hate. You're a creature of emotions," Martha had said to me in my youth and she was right.

I was unable to explain it to anyone, but I benefitted, too, from my closeness to the sea. Unlike time, here I found a timelessness that once grasped, became an uplifting force. Its vastness and power became a strength I could "lean" upon. Life, fragile and brief, might be empty of meaning and sometimes cruel, but the eternal sea would remind me to accept what I could not change and go on, daring to peer into a future that might hold more of the adventure of life.

Long ago I had put aside my journal. Now I took it up again. I sat at my father's desk, listening to music, looking out at the sea, as he must have countless times, and my words flowed as my tears had, filling the pages with reverie and recollection. Each day as I reread what I had written, I became more aware that I was coping with life without my beloved father, no longer denying his death.

Just as the objects in his collection and in my own treasured possessions drew him back to me, now, at last, I developed the picture that had lain so long in my camera and put it in a little frame to stand on my father's desk. Each such memory, sad though it was, was no longer painful as I recalled the happiness of those times. Sometimes I wore the necklace he gave me in Hakone, and all the images of that glorious day returned. Not saying anything, Andy smiled when he saw it.

But the cessation of my grieving and the acceptance of my father's death did not end my travail. I would not—I could not—forgive him. His self-inflicted death was incomprehensible to me. His final letter, though torn into bits, remained whole, engraved on my mind, a fiendish assault on my spirit.

Would not forgiveness be an admission that I, too, bore guilt? If our love was tainted, did I not share it equally with him? Should I not take my own life? But I felt no guilt. Passion had been a natural element in our love. I had desired it, been fulfilled by it and felt no shame, only happiness.

Now and then Andy joined me in my father's study and I let him read what I had written. Often he nodded as if in agreement. Then there was the day when he handed it back to me, looking at me for a long moment, a look I had come to know.

"I can't forgive him, Andy."

"Try to understand Dave's motive," he said.

"What is there to understand?"

"You don't allow yourself to think about it. You cling to your anger. If you understand, there may be nothing to forgive," he said.

I didn't answer.

"Caroline, you're jeopardizing your recovery."

"I will never forgive him."

17

When we had been back a few more weeks, Andy gave me a key to his house.

"You don't have to call before coming over here," he said. "Come any time. I like having you here."

"I don't want to find Emily."

"Don't worry about it."

So, like Ace, knowing I had an open invitation, I came often. I loved Andy's house. It wasn't big, but every room had a sliding glass door that led out to a long deck with an even more expansive view of the ocean than my own house had. His had none of the beauty of my father's architecture, but neither did it have the ghosts of my past where Martha's bitterness and my childhood distress had seeped into the very walls.

Here was an atmosphere of calm and cheerfulness. The walls were adorned with the art that reflected his catholic taste, a range that extended from blow-ups of the cave drawings of Altamira to the contemporary splashings of Pollock, Diebenkorn and Ruscha. Here and there were prints of Gauguin's Tahitian beauties and Klimt's erotic women. On the deck a couple of Calder's whimsical mobiles stirred in the sea breeze.

Everywhere were books and publications of one kind or another. Some were stored in an orderly fashion on bookshelves, but there appeared to be as many stacked on tables or simply left on the floor near his desk or wherever he might have been sitting when he was reading them.

Content to be there, I did little more than read and sleep, and if he had been away, that was how he would find me, curled up on a couch in the living room. Those were the days and weeks when I appeared to be making up for all the lost sleep of my entire life.

"That's all right, Caroline," Andy said. "It may be what you need right now. One of these days you'll have had enough and wake up refreshed."

One time I saw the manuscript on his desk and picked it up. When he came home I told him I liked the parts I'd read.

"Except your grammar is terrible."

"I'm aware of that. Would you be willing to copyread it and make corrections?"

"Does the job pay anything?"

"Not much. I'm cheap."

"Will you give me an autographed copy of the book?"

"If you do a good job."

"Andy, I used to think about writing a book."

"On architecture?"

"Yes. I even had a couple of possible titles."

"What were they?"

"*Dervishes of Deconstructivism* and the *Tao of Architecture.*"

"They sound intriguing. You could use one for your thesis."

I laughed. "You're a dreamer. All that's in the past."

"No, it isn't. I know you can do it. We're going to talk about that some more, but please go home now, Caroline. I'll see you tomorrow."

"I'll be quiet if you want to work."

"Go on now," he said and kissed me.

"Andy, do you hear yourself? You talk to me the way I talk to Ace."

"Caroline! Don't you understand?"

I didn't answer and calling Ace to me, we left.

We went out to the deck where Martha, on schedule, was setting out on her four o'clock walk. Ace watched her, too, and suddenly took off after her. He had done that before but not for long. Now he walked sedately at her side, looking up at her frequently, his tail wagging. Then, to my surprise, she stopped, bent down and patted him on the head. She picked up a piece of driftwood and threw it. He knew what to do, running ahead, leaping up to catch it and bringing it back to her. After a bit, she stopped. Down on her knees, she brushed sand from his face, and though I couldn't hear what she was saying, she was talking to him.

The next day I told Andy.

"Great!" he said. "Martha must like Ace. When we go away she'll take care of him."

That sounded like Andy had plans for us—together—but I didn't pursue it. How could our relationship ever be more than it now was with what I had come to think of as "my problem," and Emily's obviously satisfying place in his life?

I had something I liked doing now, and every day I went purposefully to his house to copyread his manuscript. When he wasn't there, I took phone messages. Callers must have thought I was a maid, but one day a call came from someone who knew I was not a maid.

"Caroline?" she said.

"Yes."

"This is Emily."

"Emily!"

She laughed. "Yes. Please tell Andy to call me. I have a troubling case I want to ask his help on."

"Sure, Emily," I said.

A troubling case? What was she talking about?

"Your girlfriend called," I said when he came home.

"Yeah? What did she want?"

I told him and he called her.

"I'll see you a little later. Is eight okay?" he asked.

It seemed to be, and he hung up.

"Andy, why don't you tell me about Emily? She knows who I am."

"Yes, she does."

"Tell me!"

"Well, Emily is a psychologist at the Bay Center Clinic. I met her at a conference last year, and we became friends. Once in a while I tell her my thoughts on how to work with her patients. She's divorced and has no interest in another marriage, but we're compatible, so we spend some time together. I like Emily, Caroline. You would, too. She's a warm, good person."

I gave him what I hoped was a withering look, but my heart wasn't in it. I walked away from him and sat down on the couch. Ace jumped up next to me and I hugged him.

"It's my turn, Ace," Andy said, and took his place, putting his arm around me.

"You're jealous, aren't you, Caroline?"

"No!"

"Yes, you are. Now stop being grumpy," he said. "Do you want me to tell you what I think the problem is?"

"I know what the problem is. I lack a very important part of love. I can't give you that."

"No, that's not it. That's just a symptom."

"I want to show you how much I love you."

"You already do in other ways. You must stop concentrating on sex as the culprit, even if it is closely tied to what happened to you. I have a couple of ideas. Do you want to hear them?"

"Yes."

"Well, sexual dysfunction is common, but everybody is different and the causes are different, too. At first, it would appear to be pretty straightforward. You don't think you have any guilty feelings, but maybe deep down you do. You may feel responsible for Dave's death because you didn't resist your feelings for him. But then, he didn't resist his own for you, did he? Maybe you feel you caused his death by your desire to have a child by him. He could have refused to impregnate you, couldn't he? Dave was as romantic as you, Caroline. Whatever immorality others read into it, your love for each other did have a uniqueness. No one was hurt by it, except, so unjustly, both of you."

"Andy, David said my passionate nature led Karl to commit suicide. Maybe you're lucky I've lost my sexual drive."

"You haven't lost anything, Caroline. And I'm not afraid of you. I won't let you kill me off," he said, laughing.

"You don't take me seriously."

"You bet I do! But you know Karl was irrational and you know David was wrong. He was disturbed himself those days. You know that, too.

"But those are recent events—traumatic, of course, but we can talk about them. What's buried deeper is much harder to deal with, even though you're aware of that, too. You told me you understood Karl because of the similarity of your childhood backgrounds of 'abandonment.' What you don't understand is how it's connected to everything in your life.

"What occurred in your earliest years still plagues you. When we're children, our minds operate on a primitive level and every goodbye has a finality. We've talked about it before. Look at the reinforcement! Again and again Dave left you. Terrifying in childhood, the fear even in maturity has clung to you.

"Then just at the height of your happiness, expecting Dave to arrive for the birth of the baby, tragedy of the worst kind destroyed everything. He did what you always feared he would. It was deliberate, cruelly removing himself from you forever. How could he do that to you? And why did he need to commit *seppuku*? Would not a less dramatic death be sufficient? No, he twisted the knife in your heart, as well, in what to us was a most heinous act.

"How hard it is for us to appreciate his mindset, his immersion in the Japanese culture! Yet he found virtue in what he did, *especially* in the way he did it. And now, for you, accepting his death has been only the beginning of your recovery. You're still embittered. It saps your energy, your sexual energy, too. Tenuous scars, not yet toughened to bear the brunt of further wounding, make you wary, fearful of letting go, taking chances, as you always did.

"How I remember your zestfulness when you were still a teenage girl—going off on adventures with Janie; always loving and kind, as you were with June/Jasmine in that dreary dance hall; curious about everything, so much fun to be with. I was mad for you, always thinking of you as 'my girl.' But I knew what was happening. Your attachment to Dave was so strong. No one could have lured you away from him, and I cared too much for him, as well as for you, to even try. Then Dave died and I shamefully admit I had pangs of terrible guilt. Ah, now, I thought, you would be mine, as I had always wistfully dreamed."

"Andy, you don't believe David did the right thing by killing himself, do you?"

"No, it isn't that he did the right thing. He believed it was right. He meditated for a long time over his decision. He told me his desire was to set you free. It reminds me of part of an anonymous poem I once read: 'Freedom doesn't come like the rain in spring,/ Like a bird on the wing./ Freedom is a hard-won thing.' That was what he wanted for you, and when it happens it will be wonderful. For me, too, because I have been waiting in the wings—just where you placed me in your Noh dream, and where you anxiously kept making sure I was there. Do you remember? Here I am, darling, right beside you."

Neither of us spoke anymore. A warmth suffused me, and succumbing to a long-repressed sensation, I snuggled into Andy's tender embrace. It lasted but a moment as suddenly, becoming agitated, I stood up.

"I'm going home now," I said.

"Why?"

"I don't want to be here if Emily walks in."

"No, that's not why."

"Emily does come here."

"Sometimes, but she never drops in. Only you have a key to my house. She's just your excuse. She *is* another issue, though, and I wish you could stop worrying about her."

"Worry about Emily? I couldn't care less about Emily."

"Oh?" he said, laughing. "When she was still Red Robe, you hated her. I'm sorry you found out about Emily, but it was inevitable. Now you worry because she can be with me in a way you can't and you view her as a rival.

"You know there's nothing wrong in my seeing Emily once in a while. When Dave was in Tokyo and you couldn't be with him for a long time, other men didn't replace him, did they? You craved sex, that's all. That was all right, wasn't it? That's all this is. Emily knows that and it's all right with her. It doesn't change my feelings for you.

"Just think about what's happening. No matter how often I tell you how I feel and show it, you're not sure of me. I may abandon you. You love me, all right, but you're afraid to expose your feelings to the light of day, afraid to surrender to them and to me. Something bad may happen again, your heart tells you, and you hold back."

"Andy, I miss David very much."

"I know you do."

"If he had loved me enough, he wouldn't have left me."

"Caroline, have you heard anything I've said this afternoon?"

I looked at him. The tone of his voice was weary and he looked so, too. "Andy, I become distracted when you talk about what's happened to me. My mind seems to wander off. Forgive me."

"No, you must forgive me. I vowed I wouldn't discuss those things with you, and I regret having said what I did today. It was impulsive. I want so much for you to be well. But you can't feel the dynamics of your situation unless they unfold from your own inner reflections and stream of consciousness. You have suffered so much, but your recovery is not complete. That's the pitiful state of things."

"What can I do?"

"Consider seeing John Golding. I've told you about him. He's a fine therapist."

"And lie on a couch for years? No thanks!"

"It needn't be like that."

"I'll think about it."

August. I rarely went to Andy's house, knowing his determination to complete his manuscript. Also, even though I didn't understand it, I had become nervous about being alone there with him. He didn't question me about it, probably understanding it better than I. We did continue to go out together as we had before. What pleased me most were our rides along the ocean to Big Sur with its endearing remembrances of my childhood. Now it was Andy who walked with me in that magnificent primeval forest, Ace always leading the way, anointing every tree for future reference. The pleasure in being there had an underlying sadness that I did my best to conceal, but it was visible to Andy, I knew, as sometimes he would simply stop along a path and take me in his arms, not saying anything.

My outlook for change appeared bleak. Introspection only increased my depression, yet I kept putting off making an appointment with Dr. Golding. Inured to Martha's way of life, I largely ignored her, as she did me. I remembered my father's remark: "We dwell together, Martha and I. That's all." That was what I was doing now, day after endless day, for as oppressive as it was, I was unable to break away. I had lost the momentum of my being, slowing almost to a halt, going nowhere and doing nothing. I was reverting to my behavior in London.

Now I am free, David. To do what? I feel lost, aimless. You were wrong to leave me.

One day as I sat in my father's study, staring down at a blank page of my journal, my mind equally blank, Martha called to me. I went to the living room where she was in the midst of preparing for her sunset ritual, pouring a glass of sherry for herself. A recording was already playing: Maria Callas as Aida, lamenting in glorious tones her dolorous fate.

She handed me the day's mail. Riffling through it, I found a letter postmarked in Nairobi. Jomo! But he was in Mombasa. Still, who else could it be from? I didn't open it right away and instead went out to the hammock. A balmy breeze had sprung up, wafting the thrilling voice of the singer.

Holding the letter, I smiled to myself at the vivid images of my reminiscence. The beautiful wild orchids Jomo had sent me when David died were the last I had heard from him. How did he find me this time? At last I opened the envelope.

Caroline dear:

I asked your friend in London for your address and she sent it to me. I haven't heard from you and I should accept that, but I can't stop thinking about you. What began as an enjoyable afternoon with a beautiful woman became the most passionate experience of my life. I wonder—was it true for you, too? I also believe there was more to our relationship than that.

I have a real job now here in Nairobi and am doing very well, working with Ron Odinga. You must know him, one of Africa's leading architects. Architecture is destined to be my life work. I truly love it. Don't we have that, too, in common?

Would you come here to be with me—to see if that one magical afternoon we spent together need not last us a lifetime, as we both at first thought? I believe I love you, Caroline. Please write to me. Jomo

I visualized Jomo and recalled my strong attraction to him. His letter was appealing. Why not? Yet as distant as his country was, he, too, now seemed remote. Was he not just another remnant of my past? I lay for a long time daring myself to accept his invitation. It would be a bold move, a complete break from the passivity of my present life, and maybe, just maybe.... An hour, perhaps more, passed. The sun had set, the music had stopped, and I arrived at a decision.

I called Andy. "Are you free to have a guest tonight?" I asked.

"If you're the guest."

"I'll be right over."

Andy gave me one of his long looks when I walked in. "I'm always happy to see you, Caroline. But why are you here just now? Any special reason?"

"Do I need a special reason?"

"No, of course not. Why do you suppose it seems so to me?"

"Well, maybe it is special."

"Are you nervous?"

"When Emily visits you do you interrogate her like you do me?"

"I care more for you, Caroline. You act upset."

"Andy, do you serve Emily drinks when she is here?"

"Sometimes. Do you want a drink?"

"Do you have gin and tonic?"

"Sure. Just a minute."

Then we sat down and Andy put his arm around me. "I've missed having you here. Let's have dinner at home tonight. Okay?"

"Please make another drink for me."

"You downed that one like it was water."

"You made it like water. I'll get my own."

It was all gin with a squeeze of lime, and that went down fast, too. I wasn't nervous anymore, but I recalled a similar sensation when I was ill, mixing drugs and alcohol and not ever feeling quite myself. That was how it was now, without the drugs.

"I bought some fresh salmon in Monterey today," he said. "Come in the kitchen. We'll broil it and I'll mix up my mystery sauce. It's delicious."

"Maybe later."

The thought of food nauseated me. Unsteadily, I made my way to the bathroom.

"Caroline, tell me what's troubling you," he said when I came back.

I put my arms around him. "Andy, please make love to me."

"No, darling."

"Why not?"

"I want to, but not now."

"Andy, I don't expect celibacy from you, but it makes me angry when I think of you with Emily. I'll please you. You'll see. Maybe the intimacy will even help."

"It would only make you feel worse right now, Caroline. Look how nervous you were and frightened, too, I think, having to drink like that."

"I don't want to go on like this. We're coming apart."

"No, we're not. I believe you'll find your answers, but you can shorten the suffering by accepting some therapy."

"Shorten the suffering? I know how therapy works and I know it's beneficial, but I can't go on for years, delving into my past."

"It sounds as if you have an alternative. What is it?"

I took Jomo's letter from my handbag and gave it to him. He read it and handed it back to me.

"Well?" I asked.

"Well, what?"

"What do you think?"

"Of the letter? It's a nicely written love letter."

"That's all?"

"Omigod! You're not actually thinking about going there, are you?"

"Why not? That was an unusual experience I had with Jomo. I may regain my sexuality with him."

"Caroline, your lack of sexual desire has nothing to do with your relationships. It's within yourself. First you must recover. Then your normal sexuality will follow. In that order."

"Andy, you've been seeing Emily for a long time. You like her and you're not willing to give her up even though you know how painful it is for me. You remind me of David. He was unwilling to give up his *geisha*, wasn't he? How would David have felt if I'd had a steady lover who pleased me? Or how would you feel? Jomo and I have a lot going for us. He is different from other men I've known, and I feel a particular closeness to him racially. It may work out and you'll be happy—you'll have Emily."

"Now listen to me, Caroline. First of all, each of the instances you give has its own aspects, totally different from what's happening here. And if you think I'm not acquainted with pain through our relationship, you're wrong.

"How strange it's been! I carefully stayed in the background of your life, yet in the most innocent way, you took me into it. Think back. You loved Dave dearly, but it was to me you opened your heart. You kept no secrets from me, except when you were ill and didn't want me to worry. All those telephone calls! You knew you could tell me anything and I wouldn't stop loving you. And you? You thought our relationship was platonic, but again and again you told me you loved me, missed me, wanted me to take holidays in Europe with you. I wanted to, Caroline, but I was afraid I'd lose control, afraid I'd awaken you to what was going on and create an even greater emotional problem than you already had. You loved Dave. You loved me, too. It happens. It happened to you.

"Try to imagine what it's been like for me all these years, caring as I have and instead having to help you and Dave get back together again—giving you advice on how to handle your little affairs. I hated thinking of you with other men. I wanted you for my very own. I wanted to possess the pretty body you exposed to me, yet I didn't dare touch you...."

"Andy, I should have known! How could I have been so dumb?"

"You weren't dumb. You were listening to another voice, darling, dreaming another dream."

"Andy?"

"What?"

"What if David had lived?"

"I don't know all the answers," he said, smiling. "But now there is something else. There was a mystique about what happened with Jomo. You were sick and on drugs. You had a lot to drink. Look at you: Two drinks and you're staggering. He was different, indeed, but talk of roots in Africa is nonsense. Dave told me about your mother's background. It's two hundred years since your ancestors came from Africa. Ana was not a black African. Dave said you look just like her, a beautiful blend of races, diluted still more by his genes. Your roots are here.

"Let's say you go to Kenya. I think you would be setting yourself up for a major disappointment. But let's say you do respond to Jomo. You think that will solve the problem; but without insight, it won't. Or let's consider that it doesn't go well between you. You're an attractive woman. Men will want you and you'll think the answer is with one or another of them. Your restlessness will only increase as you search for the 'right' one."

The right one? I know you are the right one, Andy. And I can picture what you are predicting: There I will be, sitting in a bar somewhere in the world—Nairobi, Timbuktu—my night's companion waiting until I would be sufficiently under the influence to go where he would lead me. Would I remember his name the next day? Would I even have known what it was? How he looked? Or care? In the shadows of the past, in a place where I would no longer be able to reach you, only you would remain clearly in my sight—you, whose girl I was for a little while back then in my youth.

Trapped in my fearsome reverie, he shocked me into attention. "Caroline! Listen to me! What am I to do if you leave? I won't wait forever. I'll make my compromises, and if ever you should return, I wouldn't be disloyal to someone who trusted me and shared my life with me. There would be no affair between us, no consummation of our love."

"And I would merely be your wayward neighbor, Andy?"

"Caroline! You must get to the heart of things before both our lives are destroyed. You keep skimming the surface. Isn't it clear to you how everything about you is affected, not only your sex life? You must free yourself from this misdirected search. You're aware of your depression, but much less of the seething fury just beneath the surface. It's a storm raging within you that won't subside until you truly understand Dave's death. His specter will stubbornly remain, haunting you. You hate what he did and you won't give it up. When you do, you will be free, darling. You'll regain your energy, your love of life and I dearly hope, a love life with me."

I listened, entranced, persuaded by the correctness in what he was saying when, at that moment, the phone rang.

"I can't talk now. I'll call you back later," he said.

But she persisted and he didn't hang up. "Emily, I'll call you back."

Was it anger? Desperation? I couldn't identify my emotion, yet it obliterated every word he had said. All I knew was that another woman possessed Andy as I never had and I could do nothing about it. What did I know about her? She was in an allied profession and consulted him. They were lovers, if only, as he said, "sometimes." How many of those "consultations" are held in bed, I wondered, glumly. He and I—what did we have together? Talk of love, that was all. There could be no greater bond between a man and a woman than existed between David and me. I was about to have his child.

Yet he left me, didn't he? There was nothing that held Andy and me together. He would, in time, desert me, too.

I was risking nothing by going to Kenya. In fact, I thought cheerfully, it would be the first positive thing I had done in a long time. I put the letter back in my bag and took out the key to his house. Dropping it on the table, I left while he was still holding the phone, listening to her.

My own phone was ringing as I walked in the door. Andy started talking as if we had merely paused in our conversation.

"Caroline, have you ever eaten at the Highlands Inn?"

"No."

"Well, let me pick you up in a few minutes and we'll have dinner there. The food's good. Besides I want you to see the inn."

"Why?"

"If you like it, we'll plan on having our honeymoon and conceive our first child there."

"You're outrageous!" I said, laughing.

"No, I'm not. I'm serious."

"Andy, be sensible. You know I'm not ready for that."

"You will be, and I'm willing to wait. Why aren't you?"

Andy asked me to postpone my decision and I said I would, but I refused to take his key back. Ace wasn't having emotional problems so he spent as much time at Andy's as before, but I didn't go to his house anymore.

Time was standing still for me. What had been a firm decision was not firm any more, and I lay awake for hours each night deciding "for sure" and then, in the morning, reversing myself. I composed letters to Jomo. Depending on my mood, sometimes beguiled by memories of his attractiveness, I penned notes of acceptance of his invitation. At other times I wrote about the circumstances of my life and my inability to make a commitment. The wastebasket grew fuller but I came to no conclusion.

Sensual pleasure—the memory of it—was still too sharp, too demanding to wait endlessly for its spontaneous return, and none of Andy's protestations about his relationship with Emily assuaged that frustration. I compared my jealousy of her to that of a child craving another youngster's delightful object of play. Only this that I craved was not an "object" that I could take from another. I had to find it for myself.

Despite my lack of desire, it was obvious Andy evoked a strong emotion in me—a tender sense of "belonging" to him. As a feminist, I had resented David's use of that word, but I had misunderstood him. He was not referring to me as his possession, but as our being bonded by a deep and intimate love.

As to Andy, I might have dismissed those unsisterly feelings that were aroused in me when he had made his sudden departure from London, but soon afterward the mere sight of Emily's red silk robe on him had brought the truth into the open. If I were to leave him now, even temporarily, wouldn't I be surrendering even that which I had to Emily?

One morning, very early, just as the first light of day was appearing, I stepped out onto the beach. A gentle wind was rippling the water near the shore, and as the sun, rising over the peaks of the Santa Lucias to the east, broke through the fog surrounding the cove, a million tiny diamonds of golden light shimmered on the little waves.

The earliest of the morning's gulls, skimming the water's surface, began plopping down onto the sand. Squawking raucously, they stood or padded about on their pink webbed feet. It was not an aimless presence. They were awaiting Martha's appearance, not mine, and they kept their distance from me. I was not their beneficent provider. These were Martha's gulls—Martha's, because she had trained them for years to make the daily stop for a breakfast of stale bread and leftovers from dinner the night before.

"Nourishing whole-wheat," she had said once, smiling. She did have a smattering of humor. These scavengers would eat anything, whether it was good or bad for them. After years of handouts, they were tame. They would surround her, fluttering their black tail feathers, gathering close enough to allow her to touch their soft white bodies and look into their eyes as they chomped ravenously at the food. In a few minutes the feasting would be over, but tomorrow they would be back again.

I watched, as on that particular day, Martha came out and the flock of birds padded rapidly off to greet her, making their hoarse, undoubtedly happy, cries. How many times over the years I had observed the enactment of that scene. It epitomized her life, filled with such serene moments, unvarying from day to day. How envious I was of the simple, untroubled life she led. Returning to the house, I released Ace, who was never allowed out when the gulls were on the beach, and I went back to bed. But "trying" to sleep is never successful; it must come naturally. Perhaps, I thought, the same is true for my dilemma.

From time to time I still walked on the beach with Martha and Ace. On one of those days, he stopped a short distance ahead of us to paw at a large black object. A little closer, we realized it was a stranded sea turtle, rare in our waters, for the species never migrated farther north than Baja. Martha paused only long enough to glance down, then walk away.

I was curious and for no apparent reason thought of the hapless creature as female. At our approach she had retracted her head into her shell. Wet sand adhered to it, and I wondered how long she might have been there. As Ace continued to harass her, she suddenly emitted a loud sound. To me, it sounded like a cry for help and I came to her rescue. Ace might have tired of worrying her, but I wasn't going to wait to see.

I clamped the leash onto his collar and dragged him away, feeling an alliance with the turtle. Stranded myself, in a sense, hadn't I crept into my own shell, closing off the action of any brain cells that might yet be operating under my dense carapace? As I watched the turtle from a little way off, I was cheered to see her finally make her move. Jerkily working her foreflippers, she inched her way back into the surf. Acting on instinct she had saved her life; on the sand she would surely have died. Now I had my answer. I had to take my chances and go to Kenya.

When I released Ace he rushed off to catch up with Martha and I ran in the opposite direction, back to the house. With no hesitation now I went to the phone and made a plane reservation for the following week.

Fearful that when I left, Martha might dispose of my father's things, I collected all that I treasured most to leave with Andy for safekeeping. The last thing I did was call Jomo. He sounded excited and said he would be waiting for me when I arrived at the airport in Nairobi.

Later in the day I saw Andy and explained my decision.

"I'm at an impasse, Andy. I must do something to break it."

"Not this."

"You have work you love. You have Emily. You won't miss me."

"Don't tell me what my feelings are," he said irritably. "You don't know what you feel yourself."

After that he made no attempts to dissuade me and even helped me in my preparations to leave. I applied for a visa through the consulate in Los Angeles and it came within a few days. Andy insisted I cancel the shuttle flight from Monterey to San Francisco. He said he wanted to drive me there.

"Why? We always use the shuttle."

"This will be a very long journey. You'll be waiting in Amsterdam for hours before your take-off to Nairobi."

"I'll be all right. Schipol is a comfortable airport."

"No!"

"Andy, you'll be returning home late at night. It may be foggy."

"Don't go. Then you won't have to worry."

"Please promise me you'll pull off the road if it gets bad."

"I will."

18

One evening, only a few days before my departure, I knew I could no longer avoid looking at the contents of the box that had stood for so long unopened in a corner of my bedroom. It had become merely another fixture in the room, and I disregarded it, perhaps out of fear of the emotional response it would arouse in me. I accepted that possibility now and went to the kitchen for a knife. Cutting loose the cord and tape, I opened it.

In layers were various kinds of objects, all wrapped meticulously in Japanese style. The first layer held only a watch, a wallet and a small leather case. The watch displayed the correct Tokyo time, its tiny electronic heart not having missed a beat despite its owner's demise. The wallet held a little money and a few identification cards. I unzipped the case. On one side were some pens and a pad of paper; on the other, a picture of me and a letter—a love letter—I had written my father when I was in Europe.

Beneath those was his portfolio. I opened it. Architectural material I had never seen lay on top of others I was familiar with. Among the newer ones were preliminary sketches, some construction plans, one exquisitely detailed drawing of a building, probably a museum, but there were no notations for my attention.

David had set aside his Post-Modernist work to build International Institute. These were a return to the highly imaginative designs he enjoyed most and which he had shared with me even when I was young. Just as other children derive pleasure from being shown pretty pictures, my delight as a child had been in seeing those blueprints and building plans he would take from his great leather case. The day he brought home my own first small portfolio my serious interest in the art began. I wondered now if he had deliberately put these new papers where I would be sure to see them, hoping to stimulate a renewed interest and a resumption of my own studies in the field. I put them aside to examine more carefully later.

Wearing apparel, including *yukatas*, filled the next portion. There was not much, for he had little interest in clothes. I closed my eyes for a moment, visualizing him, always looking handsome—just right, I thought lovingly.

Sad of heart, I looked at that small collection of my father's things. The upheaval I had feared did not materialize. It was not stoicism. It was acceptance.

The last layer of the box held books. Eight in all, five were in Japanese. Only one of the latter was comprehensible to me. It dealt with famous Japanese architecture, a beautifully illustrated book, and I recognized the designs of Kenzo Tange, Kisho Kurokawa and Arata Isozaki, builders whom David and I admired.

Of the English language books, one, a paperback, was of immediate interest to me. Old, twenty years old, it had the fusty scent of the pulp it was printed on and the edges of the pages were turning brown. I wondered if David had found it while browsing among the stalls of used books in Jimbocho, maybe on his way to Rihaku for coffee. It must have been important to him, for as I skimmed through it, I found scribbled notes in his handwriting along the margins of some pages, but I could not understand them. They were in Japanese.

Putting the other things back in the box, I got into bed and began to read. The book's title was *The Nobility of Defeat* and the author, Ivan Morris. As soon as I began to read I was intrigued by its theme and the elegance of the writing and continued throughout the night until I finished it.

The book introduced me to an aspect of the Japanese culture I knew little about. Modern-day Japan has a strong attachment to its past, yet an essential element of that past was the uniqueness of its empathy for doomed heroes, "failures," in a sense, who refused compromise, even ignoring common sense, in their acceptance of defeat. As success-worshipping as the West today, Japanese heroes now are sometimes scoundrels. With ease, they are willing to destroy innocent lives to gain their desires. They bear up well when brought down, paying their penalties, retreating until the furor of their villainy is less well recalled, then reappear. Who among them, though in disgrace, commits *seppuku*?

For 1500 years of the country's history, the very antithesis of the modern ethos of "success at any cost" prevailed. Through all the generations there were the heroes who chose death rather than lose their honor. Courageously accepting their destiny, painfully self-administered, they willingly, even joyfully, sacrificed their lives rather than sully that honor further.

From the era of feudal warriors through the period of World War II and the *kamikaze*, the tragic heroes of Morris's book were, for the most part, famous in wars. But that complex attitude toward life and death was part of the culture as a whole, and *seppuku* has been the choice of countless Japanese over the centuries. The best known in recent times was Yukio Mishima. The high esteem he earned for the brilliance of his writing did not diminish when he died, but his radical political machinations found no approval by the Japanese. They thought him antiquated and strange. Yet in defeat he held onto his ideals. A sense of honor would not let him compromise and he committed *seppuku*.

The nineteenth-century *samurai*-philosopher, Oshio, considering such self-inflicted deaths, said: "Physical death is unimportant. Death of the spirit—that is to be dreaded. Meditation and self-discipline clean away the rust that has accumulated through false thinking. Then with purity of spirit and sincerity of motive, life becomes lighter than the feather of a bird."

As the gray light of morning filled the room I turned off the lamp. Ace sprang from the bed, ready for any action the day might bring and I let him out to find it—gulls or not. I closed the drapery; the room was dark again. Back in bed, I lay a long time contemplating what I had read. I saw my own tragic hero in those pages. He had found himself in the Japanese psyche of the past and embraced it, and at last I understood. My own false thinking had led me astray. Now I felt the burden of my bitterness lift.

"When you understand, there will be nothing to forgive," Andy had said.

Nothing! If there were need for forgiveness, it was of my own selfish, angry heart. But had that not been based on loving and longing, my way of surviving my terrible loss? And I forgave myself. At that moment, as Oshio in his wisdom had said, I, too, felt my life become lighter than the feather of a bird.

I fell asleep then and had a sweet dream. In it a man appeared at my bedside. Who he was I could not tell, for in the dark shadows of my dream-room I could only faintly discern his naked form. I knew why he was there, but he waited. Only when I removed my gown did he lie down beside me and draw the covers around us.

Without a word whispered between us, how much he pleased me! With no hesitation I responded to his lovemaking, and at the moment of my awakening I felt the pulsations of orgasm. This man—he was a figment of my unconscious, yet distinctly real, for in the peculiar way dreams have of giving clues, he had a faint scent about him that was vaguely familiar. I tried to jog my memory, but it eluded me.

The experience drew me back to a time in my childhood when I was ill with high fever. My father had sat with me and given me sips of a cool drink that had the scent of lime. How refreshing it was to my parched lips! Was that the source of my love of gin and tonic—the squeeze of fresh lime? But now, though refreshed and contented, lime was not the subtle fragrance I sought, and this man was not my father.

The end of summer. Day after day the atmosphere had been heavy with humidity. The sun never appeared with any joyfulness, often concealed in a sullen sky, as pale and overcast at sundown as it was earlier in the day, much to Martha's dismay at having to forego her sunset ritual.

But now when I stepped out on the deck seeking a breath of fresh air, I was rewarded. Was it not proper that today nature knew to applaud my mood of hopefulness and cheer? I shaded my eyes at the sight of the sun, radiant in a blue sky. It, too, had awakened from a long melancholy slumber, I mused. As I walked on the beach, Ace trotting along beside me, a cool breeze sprang up, driving out the moisture-bloated air and fanning my warm body pleasantly.

I looked out at the bay. Not as pretty as that of Palamós, I would have to admit that, but I loved it more—much more. Just now, tiny ripples danced near the shore, rapid, mincing little waves, like the Irish jig Brian had taught me in what now seemed a thousand years ago. All was harmony here in my special place in the world and I felt very much a part of it. How could I ever have thought differently?

Suddenly I stopped, and with no one to hear me but Ace, I began to laugh. "How beautiful the world appears to me today, doggie," I told him. "But I'd be happy right now if it were pouring down rain. Let's go in the house. I have an important call to make."

"Andy, I've changed my plans," I said. "I'm not going to Kenya. I'm going back to school. I can't put off getting my degree any longer."

I could hear him laughing. "What's funny?" I asked.

"Nothing. I'm just happy hearing you talk like this. You sound like your old self. Do you know which school you'd like to go to?"

"One that will accept me."

"There isn't one that won't accept you. Listen, let's go to Carmel for dinner tonight and we'll talk more about it. How about Chang's? We haven't been there in a long time."

During dinner Andy kept looking at me, smiling, but not saying anything.

"What, Andy?"

"What what?" he said.

"You're not telling me something."

"You're not telling *me* something," he countered.

"Just like a psychiatrist, answering a question with a question."

"What you have to say tonight is more important. Come on, tell me."

I laughed. "Andy, I think I've attained enlightenment."

"That sounds good, though a little cryptic. Tell me what happened."

"Well, I had a very busy night and when it was morning, I understood something. There was more than one reason David took his life. I know he wanted to spare me, as well as himself, the dishonor he felt he had brought on us. But there was more. In normal parent-child relations the time comes when the child, seeking adulthood, breaks away. David and I had unbreakable bonds, and as long as he remained alive I would never be able to leave him. I would forever remain under his spell. I thought it was what I wanted. David knew it was wrong. For me to find my own destiny he had to reverse our roles. He had to be the one to leave. It was not abandonment. It was love."

Andy reached across the table and took my hand. He didn't say anything, but I could see tears glistening in his eyes.

A server, appearing just then, brought our fortune cookies.

Andy read his fortune: "'Spend all your kisses,'" he said, laughing.

I read mine: "'Now is the time.'"

"Maybe it is. What do you think, Caroline?"

I didn't answer.

As we left Carmel a dense fog was moving rapidly across the narrow, curving road. The sea was just beneath us to our right. By the mile driving became more difficult, and I was reminded of Luis's description of a similar situation that was fatal to his parents.

"Más peligroso," he had said, and I was relieved when Andy decided to pull off the road.

"Let's turn on the heater," I said. "It's chilly."

"It's not working. I'll get a blanket from the trunk and we'll sit in the back seat."

Sitting close and warm, I was content to remain so until the fog lifted.

"Caroline, would you like to go to Cal Berkeley for your Ph.D.? It has a good school of architecture, you know."

"That would be fine. But why?"

"It's what I was thinking about earlier. I don't ever want to give up my house, but I thought if you went to school there we could try big city life for a change in San Francisco. Berkeley is close, you know."

"We?"

"Why not?"

"What about Emily?"

"Do you want her to live with us?"

"Andy, be serious! Aren't you forgetting something?"

"No, I'm not worried. I never have been, and I think you aren't anymore, either. Am I right, Caroline?"

I changed the subject. "You've given up your practice. The book's finished. What are you going to do?"

"I'm not exactly unknown, and I've had a few offers. I could go to Oxford on a new project. Then you could resume your studies in London where Janie teaches. Or there's a research job in the psychiatric division of a medical facility in San Francisco. It's why I asked if you would like Berkeley."

We sat for a long time in the darkness, immersed in our own thoughts. I kept thinking about my erotic dream of the previous night.

"Andy, please unbutton your shirt," I said.

He did, looking quizzical but not saying anything. How curious he must have been as I put my head on his chest, then pressed my face against him! The scent was real, unmistakable. I recalled it instantly. Wearing the infamous red robe and lying close to comfort me during those terrible nights following David's death, I had breathed that faint talc-like fragrance on him. I rebuttoned his shirt and drew his jacket back around him.

"What was that about?"

"Just making an identification."

"You're being very mysterious tonight."

I didn't explain. I didn't need Andy to interpret my dream as one of wish fulfillment. Now, sitting in that stillness, the fog swirling around us, I had an odd sensation I could *not* explain to myself. Never before had I felt quite so.

I closed my eyes and although I was not asleep, I drifted into a dreamlike state. In it, like a physical force acting on me, my past was gently slipping away from me, not vanishing, yet receding, and I lost my tenacious hold on it. No longer did it occupy my life and I let it go.

Sweet memories, someone once said, are like finding roses in winter's snow. There you will be, my loved ones, roses amid the frozen wasteland of my past. I will always feel your presence across the years of my life.

You, Mother, whom I had for such a little while: I see you, hear you as you hold me and sing lullabies to me. Am I remembering or was I told? It is true, nonetheless, and I will never stop loving my memory of you. Nor that of my own tiny babe. Yours, too, was he not, Mother? For we are, all of us, fused in love with the one who now has also become a part of my past.

Partake of life, you taught me, Father. If we cannot escape the unforeseeable future, we must seize what we have before it ceases to be. That is what we did and there are no regrets. But in fate's quirky pace, through travail and tragedy, Andy has taught me something more. The unknown need not be something to dread. It may be what we crave, too, so I must leave you now, my dearest one, and go on with my life, just as you hoped I would.

"Caroline?"

Andy's voice roused me from my reverie. "Caroline," he said again. "May I spend one of my kisses?"

"You've kissed me a thousand times."

"Not like this."

"Okay, go ahead," I said, amused, but then he took me in his arms and just as he said, it was not like ever before. Or was it I who was feeling different? One thing I knew for sure—I *was* Andy's girl.

"How was it?" he asked.

"C'est bon!" I said. "Spend another."

"Gladly. Can you tell me what you feel?"

"Yes."

"Well?"

"Desire," I said.

Andy sighed. "Omigod! At last!"

Then he began to laugh and couldn't seem to stop.

"Andy, cut it out. It's not funny."

"No, it isn't. It's wonderful. Will you answer another question? I'm not talking about careers now. Do you know what you want in your life?"

"Yes."

"C'mon!"

"Well, I'd like to start with that honeymoon you told me about."

"September is beautiful in London, Caroline."

"Okay. Andy, look! The road's clear now. Let's go home."

When we arrived, he checked his answering machine and found two messages, both from Emily.

"I'll call her in the morning. I don't know what's with her lately. She's an excellent therapist and doesn't need my help most of the time. It's become an excuse to get together. In the past it was easy for her to persuade me, but now...."

"How have you handled it?"

"Well, usually I tell her I'm busy and beg off, but sometimes she's insistent. It's unlike her. I like Emily and I don't want to hurt her feelings."

"She's in love with you."

"No, that can't be. We had a clear understanding. She knows how I feel about you."

I didn't say anymore. I wasn't going to let Emily spoil our first real night together.

Early the next morning I slipped quietly out of bed and went to the closet. Looking around, I found what I was seeking—the red robe. I put it on and tied the funny tasseled belt around me. Why did I do that, I wondered. I had hated that robe.

Andy startled me when he spoke. He was sitting up in bed, watching me and smiling. "Emily was right. It is a sexy robe. Come back here, darling."

"No, you come here."

Then, just as that day in Tokyo when he wrapped us up together, I opened the belt and tied *him* to me. Symbolic, he would probably have told me, but I wasn't asking. This was not a time for analysis and, happy with each other, we went back to bed.

When I awoke a few hours later I heard the shower running and in a little while Andy appeared, dressed and ready to leave.

"I won't be long," he said. "When I get back we'll get our marriage license. All right?"

Of course it was all right. I didn't hear the door close, but assumed Andy had gone. I got my handbag and found the number of KLM, the airline I was supposed to take the following evening. I would call to cancel my reservation.

But when I picked up the phone I heard voices. Andy was talking to someone on the phone in his study. Instantly I knew who it was. Her voice was hysterical, and I was impelled to listen. Andy was trying to calm her, which only agitated her more.

"We mean so much to each other. How can you do this to me?" she said.

"Do what to you, Emily? Your friendship means a great deal to me; I value it. But we're not in love with each other, and our affair must end right now. You've known from the day we met that I was committed to Caroline. You must accept that reality and go on with your life. At the moment you're upset, and your perception of things is distorted."

At that she became rancorous.

"Shut up and listen to me!" she said. "Don't tell *me* about distortion. What about you? How can you be so goddamned blind? You're a psychiatrist with a great reputation, but you're unable to see beneath the surface of your own life.

"Wasn't I in your house when she called a couple of times?

Once you talked to her for over an hour. How many calls were like that? I knew what was going on, but you have absolutely no objectivity. Aren't you aware of her innocent seductiveness, her neurotic pattern?"

"Emily, tell me. What's normal?"

"Don't change the subject!"

"You don't know anything about Caroline. If you did, you would never talk like this."

"You don't have to tell me about her. It's obvious what's been happening, and I'd bet this is a repeat performance. Now that she's lost her father, she'll have you. You stepped right into his shoes. For Christ's sake, she's had you jumping on planes to rescue her time and time again. Then you settled down and stayed with her for months, her resident psychiatrist, neglecting your practice and finally having to give it up. Is that the kind of life you want? Don't you see you'll become a lifetime caretaker with her always dependent on you and you always at her beck and call. She won't be your wife. She'll be your patient, Andy...."

"Emily, stop! You're being irrational and insulting. I'm not going to keep listening to you discuss Caroline. She's the love of my life—the most important part of it. You're not privy to that. You must stop blaming her for your problem.

"I'm leaving the house now. If you're going to be home around noon, I'll stop by. I don't want our friendship to end in such bitterness."

They stopped talking then and immediately afterward I heard the door close.

Numb with shock, I continued to sit at the edge of the bed until a loud pulsing signal indicated the line was still open, and I put the phone back on its base. But I remained there, my mind trying to sort out what I had overheard. For the first time, I had heard someone's candid appraisal of me, and though I knew Emily was in an emotional state, I heard the simple truth in what she had said, despite her exaggeration.

When Ace appeared, barking to be let in, I dressed and we went home together. He followed me out to the hammock where I lay down, and he, having tried unsuccessfully numerous times in the past to stay in after leaping onto it, stretched out underneath.

Time passed unnoticed as I heard over and over in my head what Emily had said and found evidence in my life of her intuitive characterization. It did not change my belief that Andy and I were in love with each other, but now I felt that if he married me he would indeed have a child-wife, not the mature woman he deserved.

I did not discount my having overcome the tragedies that had befallen me, but the battle to become a strong person, independent and capable, had never been waged. Always protected—from childhood to adulthood—I had never had to face life's struggles on my very own, and never gained true maturity. Always, always, even in my short stint as a taxi-dancer, I had a safety net, unlike those unfortunate women I'd come to know. I gained in empathy from the experience, but nothing personally. When I returned to college, it was to a comfortable, secure lifestyle I never questioned.

The gentle swaying of the hammock had its usual tranquilizing effect on me and I fell asleep. Once I awoke when I heard Ace bark. He was running after Martha who was starting her afternoon walk on the beach. Four o'clock. I felt light-headed and weak, and in a few minutes dozed off again. It must have been soon after that that I felt Andy nudge me, and I moved so he could lie beside me. Neither of us spoke and I lay listlessly in his embrace.

"When did you eat last, Caroline?"

"We had dinner at Chang's. Don't you remember?"

"Don't get up," he said. "I'll be right back."

In a few minutes he returned with a glass of orange juice.

Wasn't that just what Emily was talking about? Tears welled up in my eyes and began to spill down my cheeks.

"What is it, darling? Tell me."

"Andy, I overheard your conversation with Emily this morning."

"She's in the hospital. That's why I'm so late. When I arrived at her apartment, she didn't answer the doorbell. I couldn't understand it. She knew I was coming. I called her office on a public phone and was told she hadn't come to work. Then I was really worried and got the manager of the building to unlock the door. We found her lying on a couch, unconscious. There was the sedative bottle—empty. An ambulance came right away and she'll recover. But I'm not sure she won't try again. I asked John to look in on her. If she accepts some therapy she'll be all right."

I didn't think so, but I said nothing. I saw myself in a Tokyo hotel room, knocked out by drugs and David anxiously bent over me, calling my name, begging me to respond. But my intention had not been suicide, only succor from illness and unhappiness and the result had been a dangerous addiction. Being loved and cared for, I had recovered. And now, I thought sadly, Emily's recovery may only come with Andy at her side.

"Caroline, come home with me," he said. "I have a pizza in the freezer and some beer. That's a combination you like. Besides, I did a little shopping this morning before I went to Emily's, and I want you to see what I bought."

"Another robe?" I said, mustering a smile.

"No, my lady friends provide me with those."

"Give me a hint."

"No, I'll show you after dinner."

19

"Don't you like the pizza?"

"Sure, it's fine. I'm just not hungry. Please give me some more beer."

"Caroline, what is it?"

"Nothing. Give me some beer."

No more was said and after he refilled my glass we went out to the living room and sat on the couch. As countless times before, he pulled me to him and I rested my head on his chest. But now when he tilted my chin and we kissed, I knew that as many times as we had done this—this one time, this particular time—was a moment of such pure, sweet love that never would I forget it.

Then it was over. "Don't forget to cancel your reservation," he said.

"Andy, dear. . . ." It was hard for me to tell him.

"Yes. What?"

I blurted it out. "I'm not going to cancel it."

Stunned, he stared at me in disbelief. "So that's it! It has something to do with Emily, doesn't it? How can I assure you of her insignificance in my life?"

"I believe you."

"Then what is it? Tell me."

"I want to, but I can't seem to get the words out."

"All right, let me talk to you. Then I want you to answer me. From the heart—not something you think I would like to hear."

"Okay."

"One time early in your relationship with Dave, he confided to me the experience of his love life with you. You were unlike any other woman he'd known.

"'You love each other,' I told him.

"'Yes, but there's more to it than that,' and he talked about your eagerness to please him, your spontaneity in expressing your passionate feelings for him.

"'I was jealous even of her past,' he said. 'I wondered if she was as responsive in her lovemaking with other men, but felt it was not right for me to ask her. Then one day she broached the subject herself.

"'I have always enjoyed sex, you know that, David,' she said, 'But with you it's different. If I knew my death were imminent, I would want to be in your arms during those last moments, our bodies in a final rapturous embrace.'

"Dave was not boasting. He was confiding his happiness with you. That was how it was, wasn't it?"

"Yes."

"That's a hard act to follow," he said, smiling. "There I was last night, *under* the covers with my girl! Would it be possible for her to love me as she had loved Dave? And then it was as natural and good as I had nervously hoped. But I can only judge my own feelings. Didn't I come up to your expectations? Did something go wrong? Is that why you're leaving me?"

"Oh, no! Couldn't you tell? Better in one special way. David and I were locked in a yoke of concealment, and our fear that his career would be destroyed and our lives with it was always present. Yet the intensity of my feelings made it impossible for me to break away. Now I'm free to love and be loved. I know that's what David wanted for me, too. Wouldn't he have been happy to know it is you with me?"

"Near the end of his life, I think he did know. We must not minimize his role as your devoted father, and that knowledge may have made it easier for him to take his life. He was leaving you with a close friend whom he trusted.

"Think of all we have gone through together, often with such sadness, but always loving, loving, loving. This morning we were planning to marry and spend our honeymoon in London. We thought we might stay there for a few years. But no! Now you're going to Nairobi. All right. I'll go with you. What will we do there?"

I laughed. "Andy, how did you ever get your terrific reputation as a psychiatrist? Where is that 'third ear' you're supposed to have with your patients? You heard Emily this morning. She revealed a great truth, but in your anger at her attack on me, you weren't listening to what she was saying."

"Omigod! How I wish I'd never taken up with her! If only I'd stopped seeing her long ago. She was blaming you, finding flaws in your personality, but her rage was as much directed at me. In that she was justified.

"But as to whatever ability I may have in my profession, it's reserved for my patients. You're *not* my patient. I'm reminded of Christian Zwerne. You've heard me talk about him. He's brilliant. But Chris is on his third marriage and this one's on the rocks. He compulsively analyzes his wives until they can't bear it and divorce him. I'm not your therapist, darling. I'm the man who loves you, remember?

"If there is a smattering of truth in what Emily said, it was twisted to suit her purpose. Of course I provided a transference when David died. That was not a bad thing. Bereft of Dave and without a source of comfort, I'm not sure how you would have gone on.

"So the transference was accomplished and the process for your recovery could begin. But I was too close to you to act as your analyst in helping you redirect your needs and desires and you refused to see someone else. You might have gone on endlessly, never moving beyond the hatred you felt toward Dave for leaving you. But in a rarely seen way, slowly, painfully, you did it yourself.

"Didn't you let me read your journal? Didn't I learn what you had faced that night in Dave's study? As your angry resistance weakened, you allowed the past to unfold—the sweet childhood love for Dave and all that followed. You recaptured the happiness and sadness that lay in it. You restored him to his proper place in your heart that night. But finding the meaningfulness in his death, having to accept the fate he chose was harder.

"Then, just days ago, you moved gracefully from what was a lifelong fantasy to a beautiful reality. Your sexuality was restored. You were ready to begin life anew. Now the half-truths in Emily's words have interrupted the process, but only momentarily. The gains you've made are in place. Don't go, Caroline."

"Everything you say may be true, Andy. I still believe my original decision was the right one. For the wrong reason before. I know that now. Frustration, restlessness. But now I see it as something more. I must find a stronger image for myself and I must do it alone. In this Emily was right. All my life I've been zealously cared for. David was slavish in his devotion to me. He may have been away from home more than he was there, but he never let up. I would hear Nanny reply to him again and again on the phone, promising to do this and that, and a few days later he'd have a new list of instructions that she'd have to write down and read back to him. You can say I was a child then, but he didn't stop when I was grown, not until he developed problems of his own—some through me, too.

"Isn't it true that even before David died, you became my caretaker? You closed your mind to a neurotic need in me because you loved me. Emily perceived that at once. Whatever else she said that was wrong, in that she was right."

"Are you going to take her authority over mine? Loving you hasn't destroyed my rationality. I've known you since your girlhood years and I know the problems that were foisted on you, problems you had no control over."

"Those problems instilled that very trait of dependency I want to overcome. It can't hurt to be separated awhile, can it? When I'm away, you'll have a chance to work things out with Emily. It will be easier if I'm out of the picture. And I will work things out for myself. I don't want people always treating me so delicately. Not just you and David—everyone acts that way with me. Look at Janie, like a mother hen, and Jim and Matt. Even a few of those guys I was sleeping with! It was crazy, but I just accepted it. Andy, I was more mature when I was a kid than I am now."

"No, Caroline! You talk about caring as if it's a bad thing. It's an integral component of love. Those who love you suffer when you do and want you to be happy, as you deserve to be."

We sat quietly now, but our conversation was not over. I knew that. Andy would try to dissuade me and I would try to make him understand, putting up the brave front I didn't feel. He got up once and brought us bowls of ice cream.

"You're messy," he said, and wiped my chin.

"Maybe I'll learn some manners in Africa."

"Hey, this trip may be worthwhile!"

"Let me tell you my plans. I won't stay in Nairobi long. It just happens to be the place where I know someone nice. I'm curious about Africa—Black Africa. All we in the West hear about it is the savagery of tribal warfare. It's a lot more than that. Great civilizations have existed there and monuments from the distant past still stand. Everybody knows about Egypt, but what about a country like Mali? Its historical riches are fast disappearing and I want to see them before they're gone. But mostly I want to see what today's African builders are doing. My dissertation may change and I'll write about some aspect of their architecture."

"Take your journal with you, Caroline."

I laughed. "You haven't seen it lately. I'm at the last blank page. But I have a brand-new one. I'll use it, Andy. I may even have some good things to put in it. A small part of my heritage is somewhere on that continent. I may find a trace of it and that will put to rest my search for roots."

"Go to Jamaica. You're likely to find plenty about your background there."

"Andy, if I were anywhere in the western hemisphere, we'd get together. It's what I'd want, too. But then I'd never find out if I can free myself from this clinging dependency, would I?"

"Do you think distance would stop me if you wanted me to come to Africa?"

I didn't answer.

"What about Jomo?" he asked.

"I'll see what kind of architect my star student has become."

"Both of you were intensely attracted to each other. I'm afraid I'll lose you."

"That's a gamble we have to take, isn't it? If we're going to spend the rest of our lives together, I must find out. A lingering deep inside me for someone other than you would be wrong, wouldn't it? I'll deal with it realistically now. I won't be on drugs or alcohol. I won't be in the midst of a traumatic situation. I'll find out.

"Don't you know the fears I have, too? What will you do during the long interval when we're apart? Emily is in love with you. You'll be lonely. Maybe you'll start seeing her again. But more important than anything else, Andy, the next time we're together, will I be that girl you fell in love with? You may not want the new version."

"That's beyond the scope of my imagination," he said. "Now don't move. I want to show you the purchase I made today."

He went to his desk and when he came back he had a little box in his hand. Inside were two gold wedding bands. Taking out the smaller one, he put it on my finger. Tears blurred my vision as I gave the ring back to him.

"Keep them, Andy. The last few years have taught us how unpredictable life can be. But no matter what vagaries have beset us, we have never wavered in our love for each other. Why should it suddenly stop now? My leaving is a risk worth taking."

"Last night was our first together, darling. Tonight may be...."

He could not say it and I didn't want him to.

Just as in my wishful dream of him, we did not speak. There was no need for words. It was as if we had been mated all the years we had known each other. Long after he was asleep, I pondered the changing circumstances of my life. There was a time when what I craved were the sultry, fun-filled nights in my Irishman's garret or a venturesome journey on the Costa Brava with my Spanish friend and his armed bodyguards. No longer. This was what I wanted now, what I had struggled hard to reach, this safe haven in Andy's love. Yet just as I had left the others, now I was leaving him. The thought frightened me. Would my sexuality, now restored to me, be manifest again as it was in Europe? Centered on my love for Andy as it had been on David, would I not have the same longing, the same loneliness, far from all that was dear to me; and again, as then, be cast into meaningless, even dangerous liaisons with strangers? But if fear of that possibility prevented me from leaving, it would confirm my weakness. I *had* to overcome it or, like a dormant virus, it would lie ever within me.

I drew close to him and, half-asleep, he responded, taking me in his arms, and I fell asleep. At dawn I awoke again. I looked at him as he slept. How beautiful he appeared to me with his fair skin and dark beard; his hair, released from the hair-band he wore daytimes, spread softly around his face. Relaxed in sleep, he had a look of youth, hardly that of someone approaching his fortieth birthday—and, somehow, vulnerable. In my leaving, was I not the one who, though loving him, was about to wound him?

At the foot of the bed lay the red robe where I had left it the night before. I had wrapped Andy and me in it, it is true, but it was Emily's robe, wasn't it? Did I have my symbols confused?

Weary of my dismal ruminations, I dressed and went home.

I thought I had used up all my tears in mourning for my father, but it was not so. I had accumulated another deluge for this occasion. I tried to stop myself, but it was impossible. From the minute we arrived at the airport, I began to weep.

"Caroline, why are you crying?"

"I'm leaving you, Andy, and I don't want to."

"How do you think I feel? I have spent the day weeping too, not like you, but internally, and selfishly, probably, plotting how to stop you. It had seemed to me that you were gaining the insights that would lead you to a satisfying life. Now Emily's unfair and painful words disrupted that.

"I thought today how different you are from her. You could have been furious with her, blaming her for trying to take me from you. But that is not your nature. I remember your telling me about Dave's admonition to maintain a truce with Martha and not blame her, for she was tormented with a misery of her own. Even though you were a heartsick child, you did as he told you.

"He, himself, whom you loved so dearly, turned on you like a fool and hurt you deeply that time in Tokyo. I wondered why you didn't set him straight. But you understood his own suffering and, unwilling to hurt him as he had hurt you, said nothing, only hoping he would recover. How much I love this same sweet woman who has given herself to me. She is the treasure of my life.

"And then, after all my reflections, I surprised myself. I stopped torturing myself about the correctness of your decision, and you must do the same. In truth, it doesn't matter. That's not to say I'm taking it lightly. How much I will miss you and want you! But you think this is important. Do it! Remember, you can't get a guarantee that everything will turn out exactly as you hope. It may actually turn out better than you expect. Enjoy what you're about to do. I'm envious and wish you were ready to let me come along."

I listened and didn't listen. The emotional turmoil within me was unrelenting. My state of weeping turned on and off. People were staring at me and I was embarrassed. I bent my head and squeezed my eyes shut, trying to stem the tide of tears that coursed down my cheeks. It was futile. When my small packets of tissues were exhausted, Andy went off to buy more.

Just then a tall, white-haired man, wearing enormous, black-rimmed glasses, sat down nearby. About to open his briefcase, he observed my obvious distress and came over to me.

"I'm a physician," he said. "Is there anything I can do to help you?"

His accent was British and he seemed genuinely concerned. I thanked him. "I'm unhappy, not ill," I said. "No one can help me."

"Ah, but you are wrong, my dear," he said, and was about to say more when Andy returned.

In immediate recognition of each other, they shook hands, and I, interested in the situation, stopped crying.

"Caroline," Andy said, "This is Harry Burton. He spoke at the Paris conference. Very good talk, too."

"Excellent meetings. Quite inspiring," Dr. Burton said.

"Caroline was in Paris with her father, David Shaw, during our conference."

"Ah! David Shaw. Dreadful tragedy."

They were sitting on either side of me and Andy put his arm around me, regretful perhaps that he had mentioned David and fearful I would have another attack of sobbing.

"Where are you going tonight?" Dr. Burton asked.

"I'm seeing Caroline off. She's leaving for Kenya."

"Ah, yes, Kenya. I have been there. Most interesting country."

He smiled as he looked at us, sitting close. "I hope you will return quickly, Ms. Shaw. I think Andrew will miss you greatly."

"Where are *you* going?" I asked.

"Back to London. My practice is there. Do you ever get to London?"

"Yes, we have friends there. Andy's just finished writing a book based on his findings and those of his Oxford colleagues. I've read the manuscript and it's very good."

He grinned with pleasure. "You're proud of him, aren't you?" he said. "Quite rightly! He's a gifted psychiatrist, analyst as well. He's destined to be famous one day.

"By the way, Andrew, I understand a new research project is being organized there."

"Yes, I'll be working on it."

"Wonderful! Now remember, when you two are in London you must call me. You will meet my charming wife and have a good visit with us."

Dr. Burton's flight was called and we stood up to say goodbye. I had brightened considerably during our conversation, but now, to my dismay, his friendly invitation triggered a reaction he could hardly have expected. Despite all that had happened in the recent past, I had a sudden flash of recall—memories of great times with Janie and our friends. I loved London and once told David I could live there contentedly the rest of my life. But Dr. Burton's kindness had served only to unleash another attack of sobbing. He put down his briefcase and took me affectionately in his arms. For a fleeting moment I was in the arms of my father, and how good that did feel.

"Oh, my dear!" he said. "How fortunate you are to be able to weep. I urge my patients to do so. Some are unable to and that is far worse. Whatever your secret sorrow is, the tears will wash over your heart and help it heal."

At that, Andy took me gently from him. "Caroline, come to me," he said, smiling at both of us. "Harry isn't used to having his shirt soaked with tears."

In a few minutes Dr. Burton left. Feeling hot and uncomfortable and hoping to compose myself, I went to the women's room. I approached the basin and was about to rinse my face with cool water when I saw shards of glass in it. Then I looked up. They were pieces from the mirror above, smashed in some way, fractured into a maze of uneven slices. Grotesquely reflected in them was my face, equally fractured and disfigured.

I grasped the sides of the basin and stared hypnotically at my distorted image. Then I let go and to my own amazement, simply moved to the next sink and undamaged mirror. I'm not that mess, I thought, my eyes puffy and red, but I'm still in one piece. Hold that thought, I said miserably to myself.

It was late in the evening, an hour before my plane would take off. The coffee shop was nearby so we went over there and ordered tea and scones, but hardly touched them. There were things I had to tell Andy. He had some he wanted to tell me, and we both were in a rush to get them out.

"Remember, you promised if there's fog you'll pull off the road."

"I will. Caroline, you took so little luggage. You didn't even take your backpack."

"No, It's not my style anymore, Andy. It belongs to another person—someone I don't recognize anymore. She belongs in another time of my life."

"Yes, she does, but someday you'll appreciate her more. Didn't I fall in love with her?"

"Are you going to take the Rover to Oxford?"

"Maybe."

"Well, get the heater fixed. The weather's often damp and cold there. And wear warm clothes."

"I'll have the wool sweater you gave me. Caroline, did you take anti-malaria pills with you? If not, get some when you arrive. You may be in mosquito country."

"Do I have anti-malaria pills?" I said, laughing. "What kind of pill don't I have? I'm scared of diseases. My bag is bulging with vitamins, antibiotics, antihistamines. I'm prepared for a plague, Andy."

Then he remembered something more.

"I've read it's good to wear light-colored clothing, especially at night when the mosquitoes come out. Oh! And spray the net over your bed at night."

"I'll be fine, Andy."

"Caroline, how will I know where you are?"

"You'll always know. I'll be corresponding with Janie, too. Please go into London sometimes. I want her to see you."

"I understand," he said, smiling. "I'll want to see her. I'll get together with Harry on a regular basis, too. I may need a little help myself. But mostly, I'll be hard at work. I'm intrigued by the new ideas in this project."

Back and forth. We didn't want to forget anything. Then the call to board came over the loudspeaker. My heart sank. This was it. I remembered what David had once said to me about partings. "It's a little like dying," he had said. "You think you'll never see your loved one again!"

You think you'll never see your loved one again. But wasn't that what happened the last time he and I parted? That was how I felt now. Panic seized me. Why was I doing this? I could no longer remember. Was I making a grievous error? This was a diabolical plot Andy and Emily and I had cooked up and I was carrying it out. Andy was watching me. I had never seen such anguish on his face. Was he, too, thinking this parting might be the last time we would see each other? I could not bear it and began to cry again. But as the tears took their familiar path down my cheeks, my hysteria subsided and a semblance of rationality returned to me.

Arm in arm we walked to the barrier through which he could not pass. There we stood together, not speaking, holding each other and Andy kissing me again and again on my forehead, my eyes and cheeks and lips. My face was drenched with tears, but he did not stop, and I kissed him, too, not wanting to let go.

Then people began to jostle us, and I had to move on. Swept along among them, I managed to turn slightly, hoping to see him one more time. I thought I did for an instant, but I was wrong. He was gone. Suddenly then, while reaching into my shoulder bag to get some tissues, a man collided with me. The bag fell to the floor.

"Oh, I'm sorry!" he said.

Both of us bent down to pick it up.

"Please let me carry it for you."

"It's all right. Thank you, anyway," I said, looking up at him.

Young, handsome, black, maybe African. Then I saw his eyes—a startling blue—and I caught my breath. As we hurried along together toward the jetway, he kept looking at me and smiling.

"Is Amsterdam your destination?" he asked.

"No. Nairobi."

"Mine, too," he said.

His smile broadened and I smiled, too, feeling an instinctive response.

I arrived at my seat first and he stood waiting while I fastened the seat belt.

"Goodbye for now," he said.

"Goodbye."

He started to leave, then stopped. "Can we get together in Nairobi?" he asked.

I hesitated, but only slightly. "No, I don't think so," I said, and placing my journal on my lap, began to write.